Auberon Herbert

A Politician in Trouble About his Soul

Auberon Herbert

A Politician in Trouble About his Soul

ISBN/EAN: 9783337072711

Printed in Europe, USA, Canada, Australia, Japan

Cover: Foto ©Andreas Hilbeck / pixelio.de

More available books at **www.hansebooks.com**

INTRODUCTORY NOTICE.

I WISH to call attention to two points. First, as regards the employment of the word "force" in the last chapter of this work. I wish it to be understood that the sense in which the word is used is that of physical coercion of one man by another. Thus if a man ties my hands, or by means of legal penalties directs me what I am to do or not to do, he is employing force against me. In these matters I am left without choice on my part. I am not a free mental agent. I must simply and absolutely obey the force that is superior to me, if those who possess it choose to exert it to the full. But it should be noticed that the word, as I have employed it, does not include that indirect and conditional coercion which all men by the mere act of living must exert upon each other. An employer says to a workman, "You must do such and such things, *if* you are to receive the wages I offer;" and a workman says to an employer, "You must pay such and such wages, *if* you are to obtain my services;" and both workman and employer are conditionally and indirectly compelled. Or, again, if one employer is willing to hire at a certain rate all the men who live in a parish to work for him, another employer is indirectly compelled to offer the same or a higher rate of wages to obtain such labour as he requires. It is moreover not only in the relations of labour and capital, but in all the relations of life, that we apply in some form or another this indirect or conditional coercion to each other. We may, according to our character, apply it kindly or harshly, scrupulously or unscrupulously; but from it there is no escape, any more than from the atmosphere that surrounds us, both as regards compelling and being compelled. All life is subject to it. No man dies and no child is born without in some way affecting the mass of indirect or conditional compulsion which weighs upon each of us individually.

Secondly, I would point out that wherever Socialism is referred to in the same chapter it is State—or Force-Socialism that is meant. I have not expressed any opinion as regards those forms of voluntary Socialism, the adherents of which do not propose to start on their career by the forcible expropriation of others, and to maintain themselves in existence by compelling the rest of the human race to live as Socialists. On the subject of voluntary Socialism a great deal has to be written; but I cannot enter into the discussion here. I only wish now to point out that it is of the highest importance to recognise that Force-Socialism and Voluntary Socialism are quite distinct from each other. Voluntary Socialism could only exist in a free world, if it were in itself, as a system, sufficiently adapted to the interests of men to win and to keep its place. But for Force-Socialism, just as for the Roman Catholicism of a former time or Imperialism, or any other of the world-plagues that have been imposed on men by force, there is no guarantee of fitness, but rather of great unfitness; since it is only the unfit things which require force for their establishment and maintenance.

A POLITICIAN IN TROUBLE ABOUT HIS SOUL.

CHAPTER I.

THE session of 1881 was drawing to its close. The Irish Land Bill had just passed through Committee in the House of Commons, and members were pouring out of the House, much in the fashion and temper of schoolboys released from school.

"Breakfast to-morrow with Angus," said Geoffrey Lewin to a group of three or four other men, who, having secured their coats, were lighting cigars and exchanging a few words before they dispersed homewards. Geoffrey Lewin was a young member belonging to the advanced Radicals. He had lived a good deal abroad; was well informed and well read; had worked hard and systematically at different subjects; was dry, clear, and positive in his views, and perhaps rather more aware than was always pleasant to his friends of the state of ignorance in which the rest of the world lived. He was a fairly regular supporter of the Government, of which he approved less for what it was in itself than for those enlargements of the same policy, and those bolder Governments, which he believed it would render possible in the future. He had sympathies of an intellectually cultivated kind with the mass of the people, " grown in thin soil with plenty of manure," as one of his friends said ; he believed in the dogma of a supreme Government ; looked forward, in his own words, to the establishment of collectivity ; and frankly avowed that he should belong to the socialist party in England, had the nation known enough of its own wants and beliefs to form such a party. The friends to whom he spoke were Angus Bramston, Walter Pennell, Lord Holmshill, and John Danby. Angus Bramston was a young member sitting with Geoffrey Lewin below the gangway, not very constant in his support of the Government, or settled in his political opinions, but much occupied by doubts and inquiries about all things in general and the Liberal party in particular. Danby had sat and grumbled uninterruptedly for many years on the benches somewhere behind the Government, gave them a vote on all the more important divisions, but was not supposed by those who knew him well to do it from any excess of loving-kindness towards them. Lord Holmshill had been returned at the elections of 1874, a Whig by birth and training, eldest son and heir to large estates, but not overmuch wedded to the good things which had fallen to his share ; looking with rather hopeless eyes on the present situation, and as much wanting in active desire to preserve the old order and avert changes, as in enthusiasm for the new things which were coming to their birth. Walter Pennell sat on the other side of the House, but thought and acted in a borderland between the two parties, occasionally voting with the Liberals, and well known by his friends as hoping for the formation of a third moderate party, which should be the remedy of all political evils. They were all intimate friends, bound by ties of different kinds to each other; none of them very strict party men, but possessed of sufficient philosophy of spirit to discuss with great plainness of speech their own opinions and the questions of the day. Of them all, Geoffrey Lewin was the one who saw his own way the most distinctly, and knew, or professed to know, exactly what he wanted. Angus Bramston's mental attitude was in strong contrast to that of Lewin. He was unsettled and tentative in his opinions, but was being constantly spurred on by the perception that there were great problems to solve, which could not be left without some definite attempt at their solution. He had entertained no idea of entering Parliament for some years, but an unexpected vacancy, arising from the death of a member, had led to his being pressed to sit for a borough, where he was well known personally. And now being transferred from a life of watching others and comparing opinions to a life of constant action from hour to hour, he was becoming uncomfortably aware of the mental difficulties which surrounded him. He had formed a clear opinion on the special controversy which occupied the constituencies in the 1880 election, and had been able without difficulty to give an answer in his own mind to the questions that then loomed so large before the nation: "Shall England view with favour or with jealousy the rising nationalities of the East? Shall she pursue an aggressive or non-aggressive policy abroad?" But he now found himself face to face with subjects of a different order, which, involving social reconstruction, could not fail to be full of perplexities and enigmas for philosophers, like himself, still looking about for their mental foundations, and were not made easier by the way—as it seemed to him—in which Mr. Gladstone and the party assumed that such a matter as an Irish Land Bill only required a well-balanced arrangement of details, and care that all the parts of the new mechanism should work without excessive friction.

It was but a few hours after the House had broken up that the friends met each other again.

Breakfast was finished, chairs were pushed back from the table, and cigars lighted.

" Have you been supporting the Government lately in most of their divisions ? " asked Walter Pennell of Danby, who by right of uncontested prescription was occupying the most comfortable arm-chair in the room.

" Yes, whenever I voted."

" And yet you do not like the Bill ? "

" No, I don't like the Bill ; who does ? It has almost every fault crowded into it that a Bill could have ; but I have voted for it, and I suppose I shall support the Government, if the Lords insist on having a trial of strength over it."

" That is the true Liberal way of going on ! You hate the Bill, and yet you support it. How can you defend such flagrant treachery to your own opinions ?" retorted Pennell.

" Wait a moment," said Angus. " Before he clears his character, let him first tell us why he does not like the Bill."

" Why should you make me tell you ?" answered Danby. " Pennell's friends have been telling you over and over again during the last few weeks, and most of the things they have said are substantially true. Except Argyll and Lansdowne, nobody could have said truer things about it than Gibson did. The Bill is not a straightforward measure. It is ashamed to stand in its own shoes and to look you in the face. It is a mass of ingenious complications, just because Gladstone does not like it to be said that he is giving the three F's, after having denounced them so vigorously in old days ; and therefore he wants both to do the thing and not to do it ;—in which difficult performance he can always succeed better than most of us. Moreover, it is tainted with that hypocrisy which grows so rank just at present in the dear Liberal party. It sanctimoniously pronounces it a crime in the landlord to sell what he has got at the best price he can get for it—a crime, be it understood meanwhile, which every trader and every workman, every person, rich or poor, Radical or Conservative, is committing every day to the best of his ability. Of course the first object has been to sweeten for our magnanimous selves the unpleasant task of enforcing law and order. If we are to do this dirty work of putting those, whose votes we want, into prison, you may be quite sure that we shall find a landlord or some other convenient person out of whom a little political compensation for such unpleasant proceedings can be extracted. You don't suppose that we, the party of the people, are content to fill the gaols and not do our poor friends some service in return? If we did, what difference would there be, I should like to know, between us and any brutal Conservative? You may safely trust us to make it an opportunity for exercising that most valuable political virtue of generosity; and Gladstone can always say that if unfortunately he did put a man in prison, he paid him handsomely for going there. That is our improved method. Both Gladstone and 'A. P. Robinson, he,' have an equal right to say, 'They didn't know everything down in Judee.' And next, I suppose, our object has been to buy the tenants over from the Nationalists, making them love the English Liberal party in return for these very judicious concessions, that represent a considerable money value ; so that the whole machinery of these interminable clauses is little more than a piece of decorative work to hide what a very moral and pious Government, that would not for the whole world rob anybody—unless, indeed, he were unfortunate enough to have few or no friends amongst the voters—cannot quite afford to put into plain words."

"At your old trade again, of daubing on the black paint," interposed Angus Bramston.

"My dear Angus, you are still in the age of innocency. Don't you think," went on Danby, "it would have been a simpler way of doing business, if the Bill had only one clause in it, to say that the Irish tenant, or whoever he liked to put in his place, should pay for the next fifteen years to his landlord twenty or five-and-twenty per cent. less rent., or whatever figure Gladstone chose to fix upon ? Some forty words would have arranged the whole matter, one vote in the House could have been taken, and we might then have been spared courts, commissioners, sub-commissioners, and all the other expensive fig leaves ! Dear me, what time, trouble, and temper have gone for nothing ! Think, Pennell, what a number of headaches my little Bill with its one clause would have saved some worthy men on your side, who have been trying all the session to no purpose to put together this wonderful Gladstone puzzle of landlord and tenant ! Our men were wiser ;

they never troubled themselves to understand any part of it. It is quite touching to see their faith in Gladstone when he is operating on an Irish landlord. But I suppose a Bill of something less than fifty words would have had a brutal look about it, and would have shocked our dear respectable nation ; and perhaps Gladstone, for the sake of his own feelings, likes a multitude of conventional wrappings. The Bill without any clothing would have been called indecent, and even in the case of an Irish landlord it is best to save appearances."

" Have you more to say ?" asked Pennell.

" Yes, of course I have. There is no adjective expressing mental or moral stupidity which does not apply to some part of the Bill. It has been bespattered all over by the praise of the Gladstone worshippers, but it is easy to see that in messing over details and entangling himself in contrivances to check this dodge of the landlord and that dodge of the tenant, Gladstone has never really faced the great underlying difficulty of the question. Everybody who keeps his common-sense in the matter asks, 'If there was over-competition for land in the past, will there not be over-competition in the future ? If the tenant was reckless about engaging to pay rent to the landlord, will he suddenly, to suit Mr. Gladstone's political reputation, become moderate and prudent in buying the tenant's interest from his brother tenant ?' No attempt is made to answer this question. It is left to answer itself; and Gladstone simply buys off the Irish difficulty for a few years with the landlord's purse. Of course some day the same difficulty will return on his successor in an aggravated form. It is likely enough, when good seasons again exist, that under the stimulated competition for land the tenant's interest will become simply a millstone about the neck of the farmers, enormous sums having been recklessly spent in buying, and only a small part of the real value received. In fact the true verdict on the Bill will never be pronounced until some unfortunate successor of Gladstone has the whole mess to deal with again in another period of depression like the present, and then perhaps the nation will begin to learn what an expensive process it is apt to be when party leaders have a genius for constructive legislation, and a fancy for putting feathers in their cap. If with these political gifts you could only, in Macbeth's words, 'trammel up the consequence,' but you can't; they are 'instructions which, being taught, return to plague the inventor.' In any case, however, you may take it for granted that it will end in a third slice being cut out of the landlord."

"But what would you have done?" asked Holmshill.

"I can tell you what I would not have done," answered Danby. "I would not have placed, as this Bill does, a high artificial premium on tenancy as against ownership. This Bill says to Pat, 'Don't wish, don't try to become an owner. As an owner you will be under every sort of disqualification and restriction.

Be content to remain a tenant, and all the sweets of ownership shall come to you as they do in the fairy stories, by merely wishing for them.' That is not going to reform Pat. If Pat is ever to be made a complete man, it must be by ownership, it must be by having to win his own way to ownership,—not getting there as the result of political transformations. And when he is once owner, he must be a complete owner, not a one-armed, one-legged sort of a being, that has to interpret sixty clauses of an Act of Parliament, before he knows what he may do or what he may not do with his own property. So what have you gained, I keep asking, by your session's work of wrangling and mystification? Why simply to put a bonus into the pocket of these present men—which probably will do them as much good as the French milliards have done the Germans—but which, even if it does help them for the moment, will leave their successors face to face with all the old difficulties unchanged. The next man must pay a competition price for the holding, though he will have to pay more to the outgoing tenant and less to the landlord. As regards that terrible main question of making his farm pay its expenses, he will not have cause to say ' thank you ' for this Bill. Your attempt to get away from a competition price has been almost as successful as that of the wise men who hoped to discover a place behind the north wind. Of course in saying this I don't deny that the half-permanency would be a benefit to the tenant, if it were only honestly come by, and if it were not a bribe to him to remain tenant without trying to become owner."

"But what would you have done?" persisted Holmshill.

"I am not chief constructor to Her Majesty's Government," replied Danby, "and don't profess to draw up social schemes for them. I merely sit on the dyke, as the Scotch proverb says, and therefore can hurl admirably. But if you press such a question, I should say that the clearest and best sense I have seen written on the matter was by a workman called Markham in some Manchester paper. He recalled Mill's warnings in old years that you ought to remove every artificial impediment to the sale of land in Ireland, every legal difficulty that hinders the owner from transferring his rights to the tenant. 'You are like a sick man,' said Markham, 'who has tied a band round a principal artery, and then presently cries out for the surgeon to come and perform an operation to give him relief. You are like those who have bound their feet year after year with Chinese bandages, and then wonder that the bones have grown in the wrong fashion, and that they cannot walk. Before you do anything else, away with every bandage and impediment.' As far as I remember, he advised that nothing more should be done than to give instant and complete freedom to the owner to sell. The question would then solve itself healthily and naturally, without the application of violent and sensational remedies. Land companies would be formed to help the transfer, and many owners, glad of their liberty, would be willing to sell. But if you must hasten the process, he said, if you have not patience to take off the old bandages before you begin inventing new ones, still at least keep your head, and don't pass Acts of Parliament in a panic. Avoid all fanciful creations. If you believe that there is a conflict of existing rights between owner and tenant, give facilities to either side to buy out at their full value the rights of the other. Do not be led into that hopeless and bottomless chasm of creating or transferring rights. To act in such a fashion is to treat those fundamental questions of property as open, which it is in the interest of every man, poor or rich, to treat as closed. When once the subject of property is thrown into the political melting-pot, a nation simply destroys itself in fighting over it. In presence of that bitter, all-absorbing, all-destructive controversy, and of the constructions and reconstructions that follow each other, all real progress becomes impossible. Property, full complete property, whether of the rich or of the poor, must be absolutely recognised, if only for the one reason—there are other and stronger reasons—of preventing the fatal conflicts that arise over it. A nation for ever disputing about property wastes miserably those energies that are all wanted to work out its happiness. That was the substance of what he said. It impressed me at the time, because I noticed that, oddly enough, he himself, writing almost fanatically in favour of leaving property alone, was a workman."

" And do you agree ?" asked Holmshill.

" Well, I think his proposal a good one," said Danby, "as it is a case of disputed rights, that the tenant should be allowed to buy up those rights which you consider most necessary to him, as, for example, the ownership of all improvements.   You could not do Pat, especially when you remember his nationality, a worse turn than simply transferring to him rights by Act of Parliament.   For the next twenty years he will believe that it is both more profitable and more amusing to be a politician than to follow his own dull trade of butter and cattle growing."

" What I am half puzzled and half angered about," said Bramston, " is why we have been legislating for so many months about the tenant and have done nothing for the labourer.   I dare say we are wrong in all we have been doing, but if we are to help anybody, the labourer ought to have the best claim.   He is certainly the most down in the Irish world."

" I fear you will always remain the freshest of young men up from the country, Angus," said Danby. " What has the labourer to give Gladstone ?   He has not got a vote ; he is not organized ; he has not even learnt how to shoot at the tenant ; our newspapers and the English public are scarcely aware of his existence ; and at present he has not been quoted, and is quite without value in the political market.   Rightly or wrongly, Heaven only knows, the Government calculate that if the tenants can once be detached from the National party, they will keep the labourers in order.   So the labourer may be left for the present to stew in his own juice.   Had you watched Gladstone as long as I have done, you would know that he never buys stock except in a rising market.   When once he buys, then he buys boldly. He is always a little slow at first, but he seldom lets the market slip.   You may be quite sure, if ever the Irish labourer is worth looking after, that our political leaders will take him in hand."

"But as the labourer is at present," said Walter Pennell, "it was like wringing blood from a stone to get anything from the Government for him.   When we pressed for something to be done for him the other night, the Government almost had a relapse of political economy."

"Ah! I remember that your party was in a very philanthropic mood that night," remarked Danby. "They always are whenever the Government is in diffi-culties.   If Gladstone succeeds in nothing else, he will have succeeded in teaching your party some very sound views. If ever the party will let me write his epitaph, I will duly record the amount of your debts to him. You have already learnt to believe in freedom of contract and to love the Irish labourer.   My own belief is that

Gladstone has done more for your mental development in a twelvemonth than Dizzy did in a lifetime."

" I can't flatter your party by saying they have learnt from anybody," said Pennell.   " They show more aptitude for unlearning than learning just at present.   But have you other faults to find with the Bill ? "

" Other faults ? " said Danby.   " Why the whole thing is made up of faults.   Gladstone has gone out of his way to give the Conservatives the best of the argument throughout the whole session, and has left the Liberal party and himself nothing but the dirty end of the stick.   And after all we have gone through, we are not going to succeed. Of course the Irishmen will take all that they can get out of the Bill, and for some few years there may be a lull, if Mr. Gladstone keeps his temper and does not put Parnell too often in prison. And, of course, during that lull all the mere bill-worshippers will be buzzing in our ears, ' Did we not tell you that our Gladstone plasters and our Gladstone drugs would work miracles ? '   But the lull won't last. Every sick man in a fever has his quiet moments whilst he is getting up steam for another outburst. In Ireland it is just the same ; first a lull, then an outburst, then a spasmodic remedy ; always the same series in the same order.   If I cared three straws for the fortunes of the Liberal party, I should say that we had some right to complain of our party-managers.   As they were determined to go in for national bribery, they might as well have managed their delightful and self-chosen business successfully. But I see no sign that the Irish are less inclined to spit in our faces after the bill than before it ; and as they can see exactly how much our generosity —at the landlords' expense—has cost us, I think their want of gratitude to the Liberal party does credit to their intelligence. But why should I give you a second-reading speech ? You know all the moral and econo-mical lies we have been telling this session, and so does everybody else, and so would Gladstone himself, if he were not stung with a gadfly about each new matter that he takes in hand, to the utter exclusion of all other considerations, and their banishment to some remote planet."

" We will forgive you the second-reading speech," said Bramston, "if you will now make your own confessions and tell us why you have supported the Bill."

" Well, that wants very little answer," said Danby. " Put out of consideration the outsiders with views like Markham, and I don't see anybody offering anything else. Everybody wants something done, but nobody on one side or the other tries to see distinctly what should be done, or if he sees it, has the courage to put it into words. We all blame Gladstone, but we all have a sneaking belief that we have got to swallow Parnell in some form or another, and I suppose the Gladstone sauce will do as well as any other. If we were not all of us given over, body and soul, to quackery and the medicine-men, if we were not always being driven, like a gang of slaves, by our political necessities along the road which we like the world to think that we choose of our own free-will and choice ; and if—greatest of all ifs—there were a party that spoke the truth, served the truth, and tried to save its own soul, why then, perhaps, I should not have voted as I have done. But I suppose I am philosopher enough to see that political parties are about as anxious to know and follow what is true as the churches are ; and I suppose I have been in the House long enough to see that when our leaders are in the higher regions of their eloquence, and are working up our feelings on the subjects of justice and generosity and all the other virtues, they are only doing their best to win the odd trick for the party. There may be some shades of difference between parties ; but a politician of any party nowadays would make the same wry face as Thomas the Rhymer did, were he offered the gift of ' the tongue that can never lee,'—to cheat himself about his own motives is his first necessity, if he is to succeed ; and so you see, in the absence of better things, I support the Government. What other choice is there ? As for all the eloquent speeches we have heard from Pennell's friends lately, they are true enough, but I want to know how long those who make them will care for us to remember them ? What greater reality is there in the eloquence of one side than the other ? Who ever heard of Pennell's party believing in free contract, or free trade, or peasant proprietorship, or any other sensible sort of a thing, unless it were to buy off something from the hands of the enemy that they are afraid of losing ? Their political virtue, of whatever kind it is, is always the child of necessity, and never outlives the special moment which called it into existence. How much political economy shall we hear, do you think, from Gibson, when Pennell's friends return in two or three years to power, and Chaplin, as the new Minister of Agriculture, wants to dish Mr. James Howard, as Gladstone has dished Parnell ? "

"I admit something of what you say," replied Pennell, " about our side. As we are at present, we are ceasing to be the stupid party only to be the dodgey party. The absurd thing about the whole of the present matter is, that a mere chance would have reversed the parts that we have each played this session. Had Dizzy lived, and had he remained in power, it is likely enough that our party would have been dealing with the Irish question, and that all the moral, and economical, and common-sense speeches would have come from your benches. What a picture Gladstone would have given us of the tenant called away from his sober industry by the political bribes flaunted in his face ; what tempests of denunciation he would have poured on our heads for offering him a new and royal road to property ; how our claim to be generous would have withered under his scorn ! ' Generous ! ' I can hear him exclaim.

'Such generosity, when you take pains that it should cost neither you nor the nation a single penny-piece! When it is measured and bounded and fulfilled by the easy process of sitting in this House and transferring rent from the landlord to the tenant!' Ah! how much better he would have done it than any of our men! But that is your luck. As for ourselves, I am often tempted to give the thing up in despair. Our misfortunes seem to do us no good; they give us no steadiness of purpose; we show none of the better qualities which are so often to be found in minorities; we are as much without *morale* as a man who has been again and again scandalously bankrupt; our highest aim seems to be to make a damaging speech against Gladstone—and how can you damage a man whose supporters are all caucussed?—or at best to invent some new combination for the moment, some flank movement, some clever sleight-of-hand. Our leaders are always ready at a few hours' notice to pour out any quantity of criticism, as if they were engaged to do it by the yard, and Salisbury is occasionally good enough to throw in a certain number of epigrams for us without charge; but even the epigrams, when we get them, only leave us in the same unimproving condition of mental health after as before. Of any distinct leading, of any attempt to rally the party to definite opinions, to touch our reason and redeem us with a faith—of these things there is no sign to be seen in our dark-

ness. All that happens abroad or at home is mei
material for party criticism, and nothing more. An
yet low in the world as we are, I still hope more froi
our men than from yours. There is an incurabl
'Sand-the-sugar and come-to-prayers' snuffle abou
your Government, which they share with the grocer (
pious and practical habits. I suppose you can't hel
it ; and perhaps some day, when you are all repul
licans and atheists, and are no longer half-ashamed (
your own opinions, and are not trimming between tw
or three sets of supporters, you will get rid of it. Bu
I want to know what Lewin has been doing. Have yo
supported the Government in the last divisions, Lewiu
and are you content that the Bill is so far safe ? "

"Yes," replied Lewin, " I have voted steadily for th
Bill. I don't say that I like its shape, but it goes i
the right direction. Of course the Bill is a bit of cum
bersome machinery, which was to be expected, consider
ing the ecclesiastical-metaphysical machine-yards fron
which it has come ; and I don't expect it to last even ha]
of the time that the much-praised and little-performin;
machine of 1870 lasted. However, you may throw a]
the hard names at it you like, and most of them ma;
be just enough—I don't know, and I don't care—stil
depend upon it, long after the checks and counter
checks, dodges and counter-dodges cease to meai
anything, and have been sold off as old iron, th
principle that is in it will remain and bear its frui

—I mean the acknowledgment that Government is a bigger thing than the landords, and can remodel all havings and belongings, all rights of property and all social arrangements, as it thinks best. We have got to come to that, and we have taken one right good step at least towards it. The Bill is probably all you say, but perhaps you forget that the metaphysics in it are not only the necessary product of an age of confused intelligence, but are admirably adapted for spreading a useful mist round the changes that are taking place, and for preventing our seeing too clearly what we are doing; they are therefore by no means to be looked on as useless. The great function of a Liberal leader at the present moment is to lead us just as we are going, without making us aware, or even if possible without being aware himself, of the true readings of the compass. The present is essentially a transition moment, requiring very delicate adaptations, and in Gladstone we have probably found the exactly suitable instrument, just as other times have produced other leaders exactly fitted to their special circumstances. Everybody can see that three hundred years of Protestantism have been a preparation to help us to pass from a superstitious state to a rational state of mind, and Gladstone, like Protestantism, is making the same transition easy for us in social politics. We wanted at that time a race of theologians sufficiently irreverent-minded and sufficiently enterprising to break up the

old authority, but not so logical, or consistent, o
thorough-going in their views as to be tempted to trave
in a single day's journey to the end of the new roa(
that was opened before them. Men of greater menta
hardihood, who would not have overleapt one formul;
simply to stop in front of the next, would have spoil
the slow preparation that was wanted ; perhaps woul(
have ended in refixing the old fetters upon us. It i
the same in social politics now. We want a transitioi
leader who can reconcile us gently to the inconsisten
cies of thought and action that are involved in th(
changes that we are making, and that would startl
the world if the passage from the old to the new wer(
abruptly made. Were I given the task to describe th
kind of leader most suited to the present moment,
should say that he must be modest in language, bu
confident, up to the point of presumption, in his owi
constructive enterprises, committed to a policy of satis
fying wants and difficulties as they arise, imbued witl
the English habit of mind of not looking beyond th(
twenty-four hours as regards the further consequence;
of an action, and with a reputation that he canno
afford to lose for being the people's friend. He shoul(
have a dash of the political spendthrift about him ; h(
should be fluid in character but powerful in impulse
and whilst ready to devote superabundant powers witl
enthusiasm to the movements which the people forc(
upon him, always abiding by Frederic Harrison's pre

cept of using the old terms to which we are accustomed, so that we may get as few joltings as possible in our passage from the old to the new beliefs. I have a perfect faith in natural selection producing for us in politics as in everything else the instrument which is wanted ; and whenever I listen to Gladstone lubricating for the English middle-class the process of stripping the Irish landlord, I feel the same thrill of delight that watching the apparatus of an insect-eating plant or any other bit of beautifully adapted machinery gives me. The co-ordinations in the political world are fully as perfect and admirable as those in the plant and animal world."

"You fairly puzzle me, Lewin," said Angus. "I don't know whether to envy you, or to believe that you also are among those who know nothing about their own direction.   You are always satisfied and contented with whatever happens ; you always see yourself one step nearer the end which you desire ; you tell us quite plainly what that end is, but still I cannot help asking myself whether your plain words really make you see any plainer than the rest of us.   When Government has passed its last Land Bill and performed its last operation on the landlords, when what you call collectivity is fairly established, and when we are all under its direction, is not that only the beginning rather than the end of things ?   How do you know what form the will and pleasure of the collective agency will take ?

Have you the least idea on what principles, by what methods it will act ?   Have you even distinct wishes as to what it should be ?   If you have not, are you not as much obeying forces as Gladstone is ?—perhaps deceiving yourself a little more than he does, since you set up a claim to know clearly what you mean, and Gladstone, as Danby says, has never yet had time, with so many speeches to make and so many bills to pass, even to consider the question whether he does know or does not know what he means.   I cannot see that it helps us much to know that we are being carried nearer the collective agency, unless we are told what kind of a thing the collective agency is to be."

" Your challenge is fair enough," said Lewin, " but I don't intend to attempt to reply to it.   To answer such questions as you propose would require that I should be master of the secrets of evolution.   The little mar-supial of a few inches long that lived at the time of the Purbeck beds near Swanage might have told you what he thought was best for himself, but he could not have told you what would be best for the great race of mammals who were to tread so closely in his diminutive footsteps.   I can only say that to me the collective agency is the best instrument for general happiness ;. that it is better that people should agree by a majority as to what they want, and then proceed to carry it out, than that every man should be ceaselessly labouring to fashion his own muck-heap after his own special fancy, or to make it a little broader and longer than his neighbour's. That is all I can tell you. Collective agency seems to me better than individual action ; and the work of modern politics is to accustom the mind of all classes to the idea. Without agreeing in all details with Karl Marx, I agree far more with him than with Gladstone. But I should greatly prefer Gladstone as Prime Minister under our special circumstances. Marx would do us infinite harm by raising countless antagonisms. Gladstone does as much good by involving all that we are doing in general indistinctness. He is always the last man to be convinced of the step which he is taking ; and when convinced, the most fervent in expounding the necessity under which he is acting. There is no finer method for sapping settled convictions. His regrets and hesitations, his funeral orations over the principles he is overthrowing, his skilful handling of the old familiar phrases, and his perorations in which democratic sentiment, religion, communism, and Conservatism are all mixed up together, are a work of art, which none of you sufficiently understand to admire as you ought. But even Gladstone, I think, would fail in disguising what wants disguising, if it had not been for the sort of theology on which the nation has been fed for so long a period. An ordinary Englishman cannot think except with a certain amount of fog hanging about his brain. There is no shrewder or more capable class than our well-to-do English Dissenters—they are the money-makers of the nation—but in politics you can do almost what you like with them, if you only tickle their ears with the right sort of words to which they are accustomed in their chapels."

"Here is Bramston asking you for bread," said Danby, "and you only give the poor fellow a stone. Is this wretched pittance of information all you have to offer us ? Have you no picture to give of the life we are all to live and the happiness we are all to enjoy when you have established the collective agency ? We want to hear some practical details ; we want to know, now that we have started with Government inspectors to direct us in all that we do, and Irish Land Bills for giving the tenants the sunny side of the hedge, if we are to arrive in due course at State ownership of all land and of all capital, and at State employment for everybody. Please to tell us if any of us are to be allowed to exist in independence of the Government ; if everybody is to receive an official salary for what he does, or perhaps I should say, in the case of such idle and unprofitable people as myself, for what he does not do ? Are we still to live, each man under his own fig-tree, or are we all to club together under one family roof ;—may I suggest corrugated iron to the collective agency as a cheap and expeditious way of roofing us all in ? Are we still to be allowed to marry when we like, or are we only to become happy fathers of families when we can get a certificate of collective agency permission ? You are a very uncommunicative prophet of the new faith. Please do something for our conversion by telling us a little more of your new kingdom-come; and especially of the methods by which you propose to extract a week's work—in return for the payment you are so generously going to give, I believe—from five such ornamental, if not very useful, members of society as have just been breakfasting together in this room."

"All such questions are simply idle," said Lewin. "Were I to try to answer them, I should only use words and cheat myself as much as our present leaders cheat themselves. There is no man living who can tell you what the collective agency will do. It will probably, as everybody can see, be protective in its nature at first; but when society has once been remodelled, and a new start given to every one, what form of protection it will develop afterwards, or whether it will be protective at all, can only be answered by guess-work. All that I can affirm is, that it is best for men to act as an organized body; for them to agree on what they consider happiness, and then to carry it out by organized means. It is the natural tendency of human nature to make use of the collective power, and therefore it is wise to recognise its use in the most complete form possible."

"But there is such a thing as voluntary association as well as State drill," interposed Pennell.

"It—the national organization,"—went on Lewin,

without noticing the interruption, "is the greatest of human forces ; and to tell men to live in its presence and yet not to use it is like telling them that the forces of steam and electricity surround them on all sides, but must not be employed in their service. But to give you a description of what men will consider happiness when they are once free to construct it, is not a task I pretend to undertake."

"Well," said Danby, "we are all of us very much disappointed. I am of opinion that we are not going to be much better off under the new than we were under the old leadership. I certainly don't pretend that our present state is heaven. When I try to interpret Mr. Gladstone, I find that there are many volumes a year to read, and I confess that what the sum total of the volumes amounts to in the matter of spiritual guidance, how much or how little it all means, lies altogether beyond my powers of discernment. I may at once say that I have not the least idea where I am to be led this year, next year, or any other year. I do not know, as I follow my leader, whether I shall remain a free-trader, or shall be developed into the brilliant discoverer of some new form of protection ; whether I am the column and support of Established Churches, or their declared enemy; whether I am going to back the Lords, or give them a sly kick as occasion serves ; whether I am going to construct a new system of State education that is to begin with the babies and end with the graduates, or whether I believe in letting people arrange their own systems of education ; whether I am going to enlarge our system of Poor-law relief, and generously offer free-living to all who wish for it, or whether I shall be rigidly virtuous and economical, and take my stand on the House and nothing but the House ; whether I am going to let Mr. Parnell take his coat off as many times as he likes in the day and welcome, or whether I am politely going to give him my best help in putting it on ; whether I am in my inner consciousness an Imperialist, or a Federalist, or a Separatist ; whether I abhor blood-guiltiness, or believe in the Empire on which the sun never sets ; whether I am the friend of the English tenant, or of the English labourer—I am quite clear for the moment that I am dead against the landlord ; whether I am going to present the public with new wines from Spain, Portugal, and some other sunny region of the world, or whether I am going to fine and imprison some thousands of my countrymen for taking a glass of beer ; whether I am going with the doctors for vaccinating and registering the people, or whether I shall throw doctors and registers overboard and support the liberty of the Briton to doctor himself ; whether I am going to preach economy and save the public money, or whether I am going to enter on a career of constructive enterprises, and spend with both hands. Last year I was the apostle of peace, and pledged to international moralities; next year I expect to be marching shoulder to shoulder with the Jingoes into the heart of Africa, annexing the Congo, and placing Bartle Frere on a black throne. I am quite humble-minded in the matter, I bear myself like a weaned child, I am quite conscious that, as an insignificant member of the great Liberal party, I have no rights of possession as regards my own opinions and actions for more than five minutes in advance of the present moment, and I have long ago given up the effort to make any mental connection between our zigzags of to-day and our zigzags of yesterday. Many years of practice and some philosophy have at last brought me to this state. But when a young prophet invites me to strike out a new road, and, with himself as my leader, says quietly, 'I know absolutely nothing of my direction,' as if that was the best way to inspire me with sufficient confidence to leap after him into all the dark holes for which he seems to have a fancy, I may be excused for doubting if I shall not be more comfortable in remaining where I am."

"Don't mind Danby," said Bramston, "he is only digesting his breakfast, which never agrees with his temper. Go on, Lewin, with what you were saying."

"There is not much more to say," said Lewin. "The rule of the majority is the principle that is being evolved at this moment of the world's history ; it is the principle of the future, by which the world's destiny is to be definitely shaped; and it is fast becoming possessed of that religious sanction which has belonged to other beliefs in their day. The majority, constantly urged by their wishes and wants, are learning to take their new place in the world. And whatever phrases the party leaders of the day may use, whatever credit they like to take to themselves for their diminutive Land Bills and half-hearted social constructions and so-called generous gifts, you may look on these little bits of ingenious statesmanship as the first blind acknowledgment of the force that is acting upon us all. All our phrases make no real difference to the fact, one way or the other, that whatever the majority thinks adds to their happiness, that henceforward they intend to have or to do. That is a fact which, if you don't yet see, you had better all of you see as quickly as you can, and then perhaps you will understand why I vote for a Bill that I don't take the trouble to defend from Danby's interminable attacks, that creaks and groans in all its cumbersome parts like a Spanish peasant's cart, and of which the one merit is, that in unsettling everything and settling nothing, it accustoms one part of the people to want and to ask, and the other part to give up the bone to their bigger brother and go quietly back to their own corner without it ; and this is conveniently done without the use of too much plain language. Perhaps you all suppose that there is a reality in the distinctions which our intelligent Liberal spokesmen like to draw between land and other kinds of property. Yes, there is a distinction ; but it is not the metaphysical one which they draw so glibly and to their own self-content. The distinction is that land is the most visible, the most easily seized, the most easily divided up, and the worst defended of all kinds of property. It is exactly fitted for the first meal, and when eaten it will leave a noble appetite for the other more difficult morsels. *Vive l'appétit!* Perhaps you all comfort yourselves sometimes by repeating what those same intelligent spokesmen are always telling us, that in England there is a stronger belief in property than in other countries. My own suspicion is that England will be the first country to try a real downright experiment in Socialism, not simply because property lies in few hands, but because our people have such an infinite faculty for covering up and disguising what they do with words. If only the words are right, and have a good sound in their ears, they are quite satisfied. Once call a thing by a popular name—no matter what it is— christen it in public as a just and generous measure, and the English people will be enthusiastic in its behalf. Do you remember Elmore's French cook, who used to say that he could turn horseflesh into woodcock if you let him make the sauce? Well, Gladstone is quite as good in his own way. I should consider him the superior of the French artist, if the English nation had not a certain natural weakness for being led by the nose. Criticism of all kinds is an unknown art in this country, and so long as there is plenty of political seasoning, our people are always satisfied. In other countries men like to taste and know what they are eating ; they would not stand the emptying of the pepper-pot into their dishes ; and if Dizzy with his turgid patriotism and Gladstone with his conventional morality have succeeded with us, they have owed no small part of their success to the fact that the English are by nature predestined to fall into the hands of the word-makers. I know no place where the faculty exists in the same perfection as it does in England, of seeing in a thing not what it is, but what it happens to be called. Without such a faculty, that special British product which we call cant, and for which I defy you to find a name in other languages, could hardly have become one of the national facts. But it plays a great part with us, and, when rightly understood, seems to be a very useful sort of thing in politics. English cant is a study in itself, and it would be worth the while of any of you to watch some of its forms, and put together an article about it for the *Fortnightly*."

" Please not to be in such a hurry to reform us," said Danby, " out of cant. Until the collective agency is established, I doubt if we can get on without it. What you call cant is only the innocent oil that eases the working of all social and political wheels. If I am asked to subscribe to a popular charity, I do not say to the individual who asks me, ' Sir, your charity exists to give its secretary an occupation, and to enlarge the importance of a certain number of unemployed persons by spending the money of the rest of the world,' but I say, ' My dear fellow, I have a great respect for your charity and the excellent work it is doing and the unselfish manner in which your committee devote their time to it, and I only regret that so many other calls upon my limited means do not allow of my subscribing.' But I suppose you would like us all, whenever we open our lips, to indulge forthwith in a stream of crude verities. Perhaps you would like the Liberal party to stand in a palace of truth at noonday and say, ' Not one of us in a thousand happen to be either Irish or English landlords, and we are therefore prepared quite cheerfully to pinch the landlord to any extent that may be convenient;' or for Gladstone to say, ' Prime ministers must live like everybody else, and if it is necessary for me to offer up my only son Isaac to the wants of the country, I shall know how to find the best reasons for doing it.' I can hardly think that would be an improvement on our present method. You say we are an inartistic, uncritical nation. I say we know how to admire a thing whenever it is thrown into the right form. When Gladstone has to explain why he is sacrificing some principle and paints the struggle of conflicting tides in his bosom, assuring us that sorrowfully, reluctantly, himself fighting against himself, he too at the eleventh hour has been added to the new opinion, both the House and the country instinctively feel the touch of the artist-orator, and exclaim, 'There! you see how unwilling he has been to act, how fairly he can look at both sides, how much conscience he brings to his work!' Well! is not that the better way of taking these transformation scenes? We have all of us to do ugly and disagreeable things in life, why should we not make them as pleasant for each other as we can? You may make anything sweet if you use enough rose-scented wash. Here is our friend Holmshill, who, if you only let him live in his dreams and give him enough speeches of Gladstone's to listen to and do not blurt out too many unpleasant truths to his face, will be not only ready to vote away that respectable Upper House, into which some day otherwise he would have to retire for his pre-prandial doze, but to make his tenant-farmers owners for life of all those fat and sunny farms over which we shot partridges last year; or perhaps—if we are sailing with new winds,—to sacrifice his farmers and vote it all in a lump to the labourers, with the Towers as an improved workhouse. Why not leave him to vote himself out of existence, without even enough pain to know that he is doing it? Why should we shock him with plain words and disagreeable explanations as to himself and his own actions? He is much happier as he is."

"That is the very thing of which I complain," said Pennell. "I don't quarrel with Geoffrey Lewin. He dreams of his collective agency, and I only hope to Heaven it will make him as uncomfortable when it comes as it will make the rest of us. But Holmshill and all his Whig friends are the very disgrace of the age. Was there ever a tail to a party so pitifully bedraggled ? Here are men with really great traditions, who once thought and acted for themselves, and led the country, and who now are hanging on to a party they dislike and dread, for the sake of the crumbs that are thrown to them. And if you ever ask them why they accept the kicks and the halfpence, they will tell you that they hope to check the Radicals and to keep an influence over Gladstone. They point to some half-dozen words in some clause or other, in some Bill or other, and say, ' See how we have drawn the sting out of this measure ;' or they appeal to this or that great Whig in the Cabinet, and ask you what danger can there be as long as he remains in the Government to represent landed interests. It would be fatal, they say, to separate ourselves from the Radicals when they might rush into any folly without us, and when we can always have a duke or two, and three or four other peers of our own in the Cabinet. They don't see that their duke or their earl or their somebody is a sort of decoy-creature which the rest of the Liberals think it worth while to keep with a special view to them. One of my friends who farms has had great trouble with his rats. He has now invented a large wire cage, in the inner part of which he always keeps two or three tame rats feeding on the things which are dearest to the soul of a rat. All the

other rats are so moved by the spectacle of their friends
enjoying themselves, that they walk without further.
question into the outer part of the cage from which,
except into the white terrier's jaws, there is unfortunately no return for them. My friend is full of practical
benevolence towards the two or three rats who are kept
in the inner sanctuary, and lets them live on the best
of food in return for the service they render him ; but
I scarcely know if he loves them for their own sake,
and will continue to feed them when there are no more
of their fellows to catch. You are an honest fellow,
Holmshill, and don't care a straw for office, but the
real truth is that the rest of the Whigs are the crumb-
eaters of the Radicals, and if they had a little honest
pride left, their meal would choke them. And as for
Danby, whatever line he may affect to take at the present moment, he knows well enough it is true. He has
said the same thing a hundred times himself."

"My dear Pennell," said Danby, "please tell us what
the Whigs are to do if they get out of the nest. We
know that you are ready to form a party with them,
but then they are ungrateful enough to hesitate about
the advantages of your offer. Don't be angry, Holmshill, if your admirer is a little unreasonable. As we all
know, he loves you Whigs better than all the rest of us
put together, and it is only disappointed affection which
makes him a little bad-tempered on occasions."

" I'll forgive him," said Holmshill ; "it is easy enough

to abuse the Whigs.   I don't say and I don't think we
are doing the best thing possible, but it is hard to say
what we ought to do.   There are few of us who believe
enough in what we have, to fight very desperately for
it.   We all feel that things are slipping.   We all know
well enough that we are not in the country what we
were twenty years ago, and we shall not be twenty
years hence what we are to-day.   We can guess like
other people that the principal service our presence in
the Government does to the party is, as Lewin says
about Gladstone's phrases, to disguise the changes that
are taking place and make everything more decent.
We know that we have been, after the fashion of
Lewin's Protestants, a useful sort of stop-gap between
the old and the new; and probably in return they
will let us keep Hartington or somebody else like him
in the Cabinet till the end of it all, to satisfy our
little vanities and pacify our little irritations.   It is not
very grand or very independent.   But I doubt if it is
wholly meanness on our part.   I doubt if there is
more clay mixed up with our patriotism than with
yours.   I don't pretend that it would be a profitable
political investment for us to set up on our own
account; though even if it could help us, there is
I think a sort of honourable shame which would prevent our doing it.   It is difficult to forget that we
took our stand in old days for better or worse on
the principle of 'all for the people by the people;'

and even when it is made to cover measures that have less regard for justice than for party convenience, we have a silent feeling that we are like so many others who have to reap what they sowed with their own hands. We can hardly begin to protest against the principle on the very first day and in the very first hour that it goes against our own interests. Remember also that we are entangled and impeded by an exceptional position. Had there been no favours and privileges in old days, I suppose that the Towers and myself would have had little enough to do with each other; and it is these favours and privileges which make it seem ungenerous to oppose demands made in the name of the people even when one thinks that they are founded on wrong principles and likely to end in disappointment. Perhaps I may see faults in a Land Bill as well as you, but I cannot come down to the House as easily as you can and criticise from a strictly economical point of view a Bill that may lessen what is paid into the family bankers by some thousands of pounds. Perhaps I ought to do it, but if so I ought to be rid of the old privileges and favours which have made me what I am. You seem to forget that a Whig is mortal like other people. You are asking for an amount of political virtue and courage in him which you will hardly find elsewhere. Besides, if you were fair to us, you would remember that we have had politics in the blood for many generations, that we are justly proud of the party we have belonged to and the fight we have shared in, that it is only strong convictions which make men break old ties—how difficult it is too to have strong convictions at the present day, when everything is slipping!—and that it would be a bitter humiliation to us to go and join the Tories in our latter days. We have fought them and beaten them too often to go back to-day and look for a camp of refuge in their ranks. It is best to stay where we are, and to cheat ourselves, if we can, into believing that we belong to the modern Liberal party. I don't think anything that we do matters very much, or will make a difference to anybody but ourselves. And as for ourselves I have but few hopes and few wishes. A very few years, and the only place where you will find a Whig will be in Macaulay's history."

"I give you up, Holmshill," said Danby. "I never will defend you again. I think you are thoroughly mean-spirited, and if you were to go on talking for another five minutes you would turn me into a Radical *pursang*. A humble-minded Whig is a *lusus naturæ*, a monster of inconceivable parts and affections, and if there are many others like you, I take it as a sign that the Whigs are pretty nearly done up, and that we must put some one else in their place who will be ready to fight when they are wanted. It's all very well throwing down your arms and saying, ' Pray, gentlemen, be so kind as to help yourselves,' but I think whether you are a Whig or not you are bound to fight for all that rightfully belongs to you. When I hear you talking in this worm-inspired manner I feel as if I should like to see a thousand peasant - proprietors planted at the Towers, each of them with three acres apiece cut out of the park land, and hear the answer they would make if some improving member of Parliament proposed to touch one blade of grass that grew on their outside border. I should like to hear a little of their unsophisticated mind upon unearned increment, or unexhausted improvements, or tenant-right—if one of them were proposing to let land to another—or for matter of that, collective agencies and principles of the future. There would be some downright English in it. But there's that gaby Holmshill goes down and meets his father's tenants and lets some talking fellow tell him that an English farmer ought to be able to sell his holding like an Irishman, and that all that the landlord has a right to is the rent, and that rent ought to have the approval of a tenant-farmer's court; and Holmshill smiles and makes some mild remark about the landlord's wish for fair play, and probably will end by putting his name on the back of a Bill if the talking fellow ever gets into Parliament, and complacently begs the House to make a little landlord of him in place of the big landlord, who, as he proposes should now resign in his favour. I don't think that will improve the breed. I think I am getting a Radical;

and if we are to give up our partridge-shooting at the Towers, I should like to see my thousand small owners planted there, and have done with revolutions for half a century. There were few better and straighter fellows in the country than the English farmer of old days. But there are too many of the present lot who will let any enterprising gentleman with views persuade them that the greatest want of an honest man is an Act of Parliament to empower him to dip his hands into his landlord's pocket and pick out what he happens to like best. They suddenly discover that it is the fairest thing in the world for the farmer to use his political influence to become buyer and seller at the same time, and to settle for the landlord as well as for himself the terms of the bargain; and Holmshill, who is trustee for the rights of everybody who owns property, who is bound to stand by these rights for the good of us all, palavers and hesitates, and says he has no heart to fight for property because he has so much of it. You would be a far better landlord if you told these men the plain truth. You and your hesitations make them think it is an honest thing not to stand upon the terms of a business contract, but to vote into their pocket, what they never dreamt of having when they made their contract, and what they would never dream of asking for now, if Gladstone had not the knack of teaching us all that rights go up when we are strong and troublesome, and go down when we are weak and unpopular. It is an

admirable lesson to teach hungry men, and we are all
of us apt to be hungry if we can feed ourselves by going
through the form of voting breakfast and dinner into
our mouths.   And meanwhile the Whigs play into
the hands of the Prime Minister.   They pretend to
watch the fold, and are always exchanging civilities with
the wolf and being talked over by him.   The truth is
that our watch-dogs are getting old and have lost their
teeth; they can neither bite nor bark, and if we are to
keep what we have, it is time to put somebody else in
their place.   Bismarck says that a nation that begins to
give up what it possesses is not worth thinking about;
and I say the same about a class.   A class that lays
down its rights, and, as they said in old days, gives its
poll for the shearing and its beard for the shaving, is
about done also.   Don't trouble about the Whigs,
Pennell, they will never do you any good.   They will
all follow Hartington, like Highland sheep caught
in a snowdrift, and come to their appointed end
together."

"Well," said Holmshill, quietly, "whether we are
sheep or sheep-dogs, get something better as soon as
you can.   I don't praise ourselves.   But, after all,
politics have their practical side, and what I want to
ask you is, what would you have us do?   Suppose we
were to break with the party, how many of us would
be elected at the next election?   What are we to go
and say to the country? Shall we go and say, 'Here

are a few of us, the remains of an old party, with nothing very new or definite to tell you, except that we think Mr. Gladstone does not exactly know his own mind, and is apt to be carried away by the strongest wind of doctrine that is blowing at the moment. The astronomers are prophesying that the comet of 1883 will go a little too near the sun and get dragged into it; and we also have misgivings that the same kind of accident may befall our Prime Minister. We are quite sure you will be much safer following us than him. We are ourselves in a very comfortable condition; there is nothing that we know of that particularly wants change; our shooting, hunting, and fishing prospects, we are glad to say, are in as good a state as we can expect after the present season, and we feel quite sure that you will agree with us, that there would be no better foundation for a party than the old families and the family estates of England.' Well, I don't know if Pennell has the courage to go and talk in that fashion. I am afraid, if I were to go and speak my own mind, I should say, 'Gentlemen, I am as fond of the good things of the world as anybody else, but I am a little puzzled to find myself in such ample and comfortable possession of them. I am the centre of an enormous machinery. I think in the paternal mansion there are fifteen house-maids, two cooks and a half, butler, under-butler, groom of the chambers, more footmen than I know of; outside, a tribe of keepers, foresters, bailiffs, estate agents, and other kinds of people, and of all these I am the special flower and product. I am obliged, gentlemen, to confess that if you propose to divide me up amongst you, that I shall be at some loss to find any arguments against the proceeding that are likely to move you very deeply ; though I must also honestly say that I don't think I shall do any of you much good, if you once begin to scramble for me. I doubt if I am quite worth all the cooks, butlers, and keepers it takes to produce and maintain me, but I am not yet confident that you will be on a better road to happiness after you have made a meal of me, than you were before. It is a matter more for your conscience than for mine. Now, gentlemen, pray do as you think fit.' "

"You are giving yourself unnecessary trouble, Holmshill," interposed Geoffrey Lewin, "about the digestion of the people. You may be quite sure that it will arrange itself. Why they will eat up the Towers at a mouthful when the time comes, and be as happy after it as Pluto was when we found him finishing the dead sheep."

" But seriously, Lewin," said Bramston, "let us take for granted for a moment, that it is better we should sacrifice Holmshill———"

"We shall have to go and shoot partridges in Morocco if we do," interposed Danby. "I hear there is some sport to be had there."

"—That it is better," continued Bramston, "that all

the large landowners should go, that our people will be
happier and better off, that property itself will be safer,
and agitation less,—more people inside the charmed ring
and fewer outside,—can we justify the doing of it?
Where do we get the power—the moral power—to do
what we like with Holmshill?"

"The people gave, and the people can take away,"
observed Lewin, with a grim smile.

"You are quite beyond hope, Angus," said Danby;
"You are incurably stupid! Have you seen and learnt
nothing all this session? Can you not understand that
if you want to divide Holmshill into little pieces, all
you have got to do is to turn on the Gladstone tap; call
it a just and generous measure, praise the people for
their forbearing spirit in the past, and declare confidently,
without going into details, that Holmshill himself will
be all the better for being submitted to the operation,
that he will shoot just as many partridges after as he
did before, and therefore it cannot possibly make any
difference to him. It is, of course, plain on the face of
it that we shall save him the expense of collecting rents
and of paying rates, taxes, and fire insurance. If you
wish it, I can at once give you a second-reading speech
on the subject to show that in Holmshill's case all
great principles must be laid aside; that under the present special and distressing circumstances they were never
intended to apply to him; that even Tory landholders
have used words which could only mean that he should

be cut up ; that whilst Holmshill unites all the many virtues we should expect and desire to find in him, yet there are some few other money-grubbing persons in his county for whom we must, unfortunately, hold him accountable ; and therefore an inexorable necessity—to which, indeed, I have only lent myself most reluctantly at the last moment—requires that we should submit him to a process which I will then proceed, with truly architectonic skill, to describe at full length to you. And lastly, I will let you off with only ten minutes about justice, as the guide of our actions."

"Please don't do any of it," said Bramston, with a groan ; "you have given us one second-reading speech already this morning, and now I want a serious answer to my question. Have we a right to cut up Holmshill ? Is there a right and wrong in the matter ? If there are such things in politics, on what do they depend ? If there is no right and wrong in the matter, what is to make us decide either one way or the other ?"

"My dear Angus," said Lewin, "you are still back in the darkness of the Middle Ages. If you want to discuss the metaphysics of these things, go and talk to Mr. Gladstone. He will spend the whole morning in explaining it to you, and then do exactly the opposite in the evening, when he comes down to the House of Commons."

"Go and inquire at Saturn," said Danby. "I know nowhere short of that where you will get an answer in the present day. But I must be off. Give me my *sacré* hat."

" No ; let him ask the Whips," said Pennell, " and I shall have the pleasure of watching Kensington's face whilst he answers."

" I think it is a very good question," said Holmshill, " and if we were not all of us *farceurs*, we should be able to answer it. Good-bye."

And they all dispersed to their various engagements, leaving Bramston to finish his cigar alone.

CHAPTER II.

When his friends had gone Angus remained intently watching the smoke of his cigar, but the rings that rose slowly upward, growing thinner and wider before they melted in the air, brought him no inspiration in his difficulties and no answer to his question. Still, in spite of the laughter of his friends, he felt that it was a question that could not be thrust out of his mind and so got rid of. To leave it unanswered was to leave a fortress untaken in his rear, and to prevent all farther advance along the road of his inquiry in confidence and security. Some answer must be found. "What is the right and the wrong of politics?" he kept asking himself. "What makes it right or wrong to pass a Land Bill? There must be some principle by which we can test a political action, something by reference to which we can say that it is just or unjust, good or bad." As he asked himself the question, all the well-worn political phrases came back to his mind. "'Carrying out the wishes of the people.' Then is the Land Bill right simply because the Irish people wanted a half ownership in the land; or because the English people

wanted Ireland to be satisfied ?   Do wants and wishes
make things right ?   If so, it is all plain sailing
enough.   The people have only to take the trouble to
wish, and we are at once rid of all our difficulties, and
have gained our clue to the knowledge of good and evil.
No wishing-cloak in the old stories ever answered its
purpose better."   Here he stopped, as if he had come
to an obstacle in his path.   There he tried to find an
opening in another direction.   " ' The happiness of the
people.'   That is of course what every politician answers
off-hand.   But then what does it mean ?   How do we
know if any measure does increase the happiness of the
people or not ?   You have two opposite opinions about
Ireland : one that the Land Bill in giving a sense of
security as regards the labour of the tenants will induce
content and pledge them to maintain the existing order
of things ; the other that by exciting passions it will
lead the people farther away from steady industry and
deeper into unscrupulous political action, will lower
both their sense of honesty and of self-reliance, and thus
in the end increase unhappiness rather than happiness.
How then does that expression help us ?   Each party
declares loudly that they are for the happiness of the
people.   The phrase is a sort of serviceable cloak that
all men throw over themselves, whatever are the clothes
that they wear underneath. It covers opinions of every
shade and dye.   But then what value is there, I want
to know, in the opinions of the men round us ?   Press

any man as to what his opinions really are, and after a halting recital of some two or three measures which his party opposes or supports, he goes off into the familiar phrases which mean nothing, which bind no finger on either hand, and tell you nothing of where he will be or what he will do this day six months. What man amongst us really makes his opinions and follows them? Are not his opinions the last thing in the world that he really troubles himself about, that he really tries to set in order? How little he knows what they are, where he got them from, whether they agree together or not, of what real value, moral or intellectual, they are, why he keeps them, or why he gives them up! And yet, here we are, Tories and Liberals, always acting in two great crowds, and ready to shout for anything in the name of our party and to march anywhere so long as we can keep together, just as if we had consciously chosen the path on which we are treading, and both desired and realised the unseen goal that lies somewhere in front of us in the untravelled country! Is Danby right after all when he laughs openly at every party? Are we merely counters, moved by what we do not see, whilst we continue to live in the happy delusion that we move ourselves? Are we all involved, without consciousness of our own, in a huge system of self-deception from which it is impossible to escape? Are we like boys who arrive at the playground and find a great game going on, and themselves swept in to take part with one side or the other; who run and struggle and fight for some few hours, and at the end of it do not know why they should have played on one side more than the other? Is our grown-up life only an imitation and repetition of their game?" He stopped again as if this path also could lead him no farther. "Shall we appeal to first principles? But who believes in first principles? What are they? who follows them? who does not laugh at the idea of being bound at any emergency by them? Each party uses them in debate to convict its opponent of inconsistencies, and each party when it has to defend its own action declares that only pedants and doctrinaires disregard the necessities of the moment to think about first principles. They are certainly excellent as missiles to throw across the floor of the house at each other, or to use for sharpening the edge of a vituperative article, but there, as everybody agrees, their usefulness comes to an end. We are too practical a nation, it is said, to impede ourselves by any system of fixed rules of action. And one must be practical, I suppose," he added with a sigh. He made a last attempt. "'The general merits of the case.' Are we then to try and balance against each other all the things that can be said on both sides by those who have most knowledge of a question? But what a multitude of excellent reasons each man and each party are always able to urge on their own behalf! Dismiss the appeal to general principles, as unsuited to politics, and then whose eye is true enough and knowledge wide enough to strike the balance justly, when all the opposed reasons are thrown into their own scale?   Besides, I doubt if men really decide and act on the merits of the case, I doubt if they really weigh the conflicting reasons, and arrive at an impartial decision; to speak the truth, in nine cases out of ten they have prejudged the measure before the first reading of it; else by what marvellous coincidence could it happen, when a Land Bill is placed before the House, that, with some few exceptions, those who are called Liberals walk into one lobby, and those called Conservatives into the other?   By what miracle have all these men, each by way of possessing a judgment of their own, weighed all the merits of this most difficult case, and come to the same conclusion?   To do so in any real sense would be to spend a part of a lifetime over this single question, not to speak of the many other equally complicated questions that we deal with in the same session."   And he stopped again.   No road offered him an escape from his difficulties.   There was the question, facing him, as it seemed, in an almost threatening manner, and demanding its answer like many another question, both in early and modern days, under penalties which could not be avoided, whilst as yet no clear and true answer, satisfying to the mind of a man, was forthcoming.

"Damn it!" at last exclaimed Angus, relieving his feelings, "what a mess and tangle the whole thing is!"

But he was not left many minutes to himself. His friends were scarcely gone when the maid Alice, the smiling possessor of willing feet and clever hands, came tripping back and showed in two other members of Parliament. Frank Manley and Lucian Standish were Liberal members for another borough in the same county with Angus, and had come to make arrangements about a banquet at which the town and county members were to be assembled in honour of the Liberal victory at the last elections. Frank Manley was an enthusiastic young Liberal, full of belief in the Liberal party, of devotion to Mr. Gladstone, of indignation against all traitors, as he summarily named those who did not always walk into the lobby suggested by the Liberal whips, and had a hearty, fighting dislike, but without any real bitterness in it, of the other side. Standish was a man of a different type. He belonged to an old north country family, some of whom still remained Catholics, and had inherited some years ago, on the death of his brother, a considerable estate ; but being a born politician, and having a shrewd perception that the drift of the Liberal party would take a direction more and more opposed to the interests of the land-owners, he had slipped out of the family estate during the good years that succeeded 1870. He had placed his money in other investments, and could now look on at any number of Land Bills with perfect complacency. " You may give as many turns to the screw as you like," he used to say, " so far as I care, provided you don't drive any of our men out of the party.   Bless them! it will only brighten their wits."   He was a member of considerable standing, had seen and known much, was rich in the learning of forms and precedents, acted and voted with a certain independence of the Government, but always refrained from joining any organized opposition to them, and preserved the attitude of a friend who, not without pain to himself, is obliged to remonstrate when things go wrong.   Having once made a deliverance of himself on the matter in question, and having given the Government the advantage of hearing some plain truths, he usually took them again under his protection, voted with them, and often helped to reduce the remaining elements of opposition within the party to insignificance.   Most men looked on him as a strong man, possessed of considerable political independence and a cool impartial judgment; all men gave him the credit of tact and skill in filling a position which obtained for him a considerable influence both inside and outside the House; a few men laughed whilst they acknowledged his success.   Danby used to call him the Government safety-expansion gear, and added, that though he often saved the Government from the immediate consequences of their mistakes, he was in reality the most dangerous man in the House, since whenever they went wrong he satisfied the discontent of the party by a series of caustic remarks, and then led the House to feel that even from the point of view of those who disapproved, the best thing to be done was to warn the Government against similar mistakes in the future, but at the same time to discourage the attack being pressed farther against them on the present occasion. A man who speaks in one way and votes in another, if only he compounds the two methods judiciously, has, as Danby would go on to remark, considerable advantages over other members. His free criticism of his own party implies an impartial mind, with the power of balancing advantages and disadvantages, it suggests that he has better and wider means of information than those with whom he generally acts, whilst at the same time his vote reassures his own friends on the important point that he is a strictly practical man who is quite aware of the importance of not disturbing the cohesion of party. It must be admitted, Danby concluded, that when Lucian Standish divided his votes and opinions between the two opposed camps, he did it so as to secure the best results.

" My dear Bramston," began Manley, after they had finished their business, " what bad company you are getting into ! I suppose all those men we met have been breakfasting with you. I have nothing to say against Holmshill, he always speaks and votes straight, and he is just the sort of man, if he had more go in him, that Mr. Gladstone likes giving office to ; but I look on Danby and Lewin as about the worst form of Liberal that we have in the House. As for Danby, he

is a sour, bad-tempered fellow with an unhealthy liver.
I should think Cockle for a twelvemonth might do
something for him ; and as for Lewin, what he likes is
the satisfaction of making himself out a better Liberal
than Mr. Gladstone and the rest of the Government
put together.   If I did not dislike him so much, I
should be glad to see him given some small berth
under Government, just to show you how tame and
domesticated he would become.   Give him an under-
secretaryship, and you could pat him the first month,
and kick him the next.   It is all very well for men like
him to have their own views, if the views of the party
are not good enough for them, but he does infinite
mischief by going about and trying to make as little as
possible of all that the Government does.   I heard him
at the Cosmopolitan the other night for a full hour
belittling the Government, and trying to make out that
Mr. Gladstone only moved when he was pushed forward
by outside forces.   Why, if there is one fault more than
another in Mr. Gladstone, it is that he is too free to
move, too ready to take work on his shoulders that
would crush other men, too ready to attack great
questions before their time has come.   It is not only
not true, but it is the very reverse of truth.   See how
splendidly and boldly he has plunged into this Irish
question, without giving a thought to difficulties that
would have kept other prime ministers shivering on
the brink.   The country has never had a really heroic
Government before."

"I'll tell Lewin and Danby what you say," said Angus, laughing, "and I hope they will profit by it. As for myself I confess to being fairly puzzled about the Government and what they do.   Of course everybody admires the matchless energy with which Gladstone throws himself into any question which he undertakes, but I can hardly believe that either he or those who act with him have not a fairly accurate perception of the distribution of forces that exists in the country. I am always asking myself the question, ' How much in him is the hero, how much is the calculator ? '   What I cannot help seeing, with, I think, perfect willingness to admire Mr. Gladstone, is that the forces which he faces look very imposing at a distance, but that they are all in reality very flimsy in their nature.   Large landowners, clubs, London society, London papers, many of them occupied with the day's interests and amusements, and half bored with the interruption of politics, what real power is there in any of them ? whilst the solid forces, the forces that Gladstone takes care to have at his back, are the enormous mass of people who are outside the good things of life, who have everything to gain from the horn of plenty which he carries in his hand, and are terribly in earnest about the matter.   To compare the two forces for him and against him is to compare steel pikes and paper breast-plates.   No man can really doubt that in any re-arrangement of property such as that we have been carrying through this session, the real forces are and must be on the side of those who are taking something from the few to give to the many ; and though Mr. Gladstone may be right in what he has been doing, I cannot help seeing that as far as political difficulties are concerned, it is a piece of down-hill, not uphill work.   Look at it in whatever way you will, whatever may be your confidence in the Government, it is a very serious thing, is it not, to enlist forces which already by their own nature strongly gravitate in the direction which we are now inviting them to take ? Grant that to-day we can find a good many reasons which appear to justify what we have been doing this session, still must we not expect as a natural conse-quence that to-morrow we shall be called upon to deal in some other place and with some other kind of property as we have just dealt with Irish land ; and will not the new claims be pressed with greater urgency than the old ones, greater pressure on the one side, and less power of resistance on the other ? ”

“ A very good thing for us if they are pressed more strongly,” interposed Manley, “ considering the way in which some of our men are always hanging back in the traces.”

“ What I feel is,” continued Angus, “ that if only Mr. Gladstone and ourselves had been engaged upon an act that imposed, for the sake of a great future good, some present sacrifice upon the mass of Irish and English electors, I should more readily be satisfied that we were right. But neither the English nor the Irish electors pay anything for the Land Bill, they only have the pleasure of watching the landlords putting their hands into their pockets. Of course, therefore, they like it, and like it only too well. It is as good to them as a free place at the play. It would be affectation not to see this. The road is too broad and smooth and the slope too pleasant in this kind of legislation for five out of every six electors not to enjoy greatly the opening of the gates which lead to it. And it is this popular satisfaction with what I heard a workman the other day call 'unbuttoning the landlords,' which does not let me feel quite sure about the heroism either of our leader or of ourselves. I should feel it if we were opposing some unjust war for which the country clamoured, if we had thought that the poor-laws were demoralising the people and had fearlessly attacked them, if we had undertaken resolutely to cut down public expenditure and to pay off part of the debt, if we had entered upon that tremendous campaign of separating Church and State, or if we had set ourselves in earnest to any of these great measures which will rather cost the Government popularity at the moment than gain it for them, which will risk place rather than secure it. But in these days, with the people on one side and only the landlords on the other, I hesitate about the word heroic."

" You forget what the Liberal party is," replied

Manley. "Their reason of existence is to work out through the people for the people what will add to their happiness. How can this be done, if some man like Gladstone, who sees more for others than for himself, does not explain to them their wants, and with his unrivalled power help them to secure what is necessary to them ? Besides, did ever a man make greater efforts to restrain the people from asking for what was beyond the line of justice ? You hear men charging him with changes of purpose and with inconsistencies. Are not one-half of these reproaches simply due to the fact that he keeps so many views before him at the same time, and that he is never led away by the advocacy of a special cause to forget any conflicting interest, whether of tenant, or labourer, or landlord, or State ? If great changes have to come, is it not everything that they should be in the hands of such a man ; and is it not the deep-rooted feeling of confidence in his moral intentions which gives him more than half of his power in the country, and makes our party, that after all represents every class and profession, so ready to follow him ? Depend upon it we have great changes to make, if we are to work out successfully the happiness of the people, and it is very fortunate for the propertied classes, who are always in a mental flutter about their interests, that it is Gladstone who has to make them for us."

"I am quite out of temper with that expression, the happiness of the people," exclaimed Angus ; "it is so utterly vague and elastic.   What do you mean by it? Each person employs it just for what he wants at the moment.   If you meet fifty Liberals, or I might even say Conservatives nowadays, they will all use the same expression, and none of them be able to tell you what they themselves mean by it.   You might as well fish for salmon in the Thames as hope to get any definite answer from them.   Forty-nine out of the fifty will tell you that it is impossible to speak exactly in the matter; that we live in a very complicated state of society and only know our own wants as they arise.   If the happiness of the people is our great object as a party, I think we ought to make an effort to find some way of translating the expression, about which we can fairly agree amongst ourselves."

"I think you are asking for too much," said Standish. "You must not expect men who are engaged in politics to be as precise as if they were grammarians at a University.   In politics all our terms are rather elastic. It would be unwise to try and be very definite in our language, for in these days things change so quickly— new wants arising, new dangers showing themselves, new forms of old difficulties constantly presenting themselves—that we cannot, except from session to session, lay down exact rules for our conduct as a party.   It is quite distinct enough for all practical purposes to say that we are placed in power to secure the happiness of the people; that is what our electors mean and what they returned us for; and except for that excellent reason they would not keep us in office for a month. Both on our side and on theirs we understand quite well enough what is meant. The people ask for a good many things, and though they don't get the whole they get a part. Our business is not to move too fast nor to give too much, but always to meet pressure by concession. This is what on the whole the Government succeeds in doing; though Gladstone's fault is that he constantly uses larger expressions than the case justifies, and therefore raises expectations of greater things than it is possible, without unduly increasing friction, to give; and this always increases the difficulty of managing the party as a whole and preventing some section or other breaking off from it. You might, if you chose, compile a small volume of infelicitous phrases into which Gladstone has stumbled, and out of which he had to pick his way afterwards with but second-rate success."

" Yes, but you forget," broke in Manley indignantly, " that he is an orator, that he does his work by oratory, that he has to rouse into movement masses of the people, touch their imaginations, raise their hopes, call them away from their everyday toil and their pleasures of a not very high kind; and that if he measured and weighed every word he used, the magician's wand which he now holds over them could scarcely work its wonders. Were we all as prudent as you, Standish, we had hardly smitten the Tories at the last election, hip and thigh, with the edge of the sword."

"It is true enough," replied Standish, "that in politics we are dealing with great masses of men, and that for work on so large a scale you must use some rough and ready methods. I know when you let loose over the country ten thousand electioneering orators, every kind of appeal will be made and rather dangerous stones set rolling; with these things as a party we always have to reckon, and fortunately a good deal of what we say at every election gets forgotten in the next interval; but still I think no leader ought to indulge in the habit of employing expressions which go beyond the necessities of the case. Every man who is not a fool can see that we must make concessions at the present day; but we can make them in a discreet instead of a prodigal and extravagant way. Besides you will be always better thanked, if you have not promised too much beforehand. I am not prepared to translate all our political expressions into exact words, as Bramston wishes us to do. Bramston is straining at gnats. We cannot, if we are to manage a party successfully, be purists or academicians, but for all that we need not throw gunpowder about as if it were sand."

"Well, even if you are right," replied Manley, "even if you can pick out here and there a phrase of Gladstone's that went too straight to the heart of the people to satisfy your caution, what does it matter? No man

who really cares for the Liberal party, who sees what it
is to have in office a Government anxious to increase
education, to improve the condition of labour, to
equalise the condition of classes, to give more voting
power to the people, to teach them to understand their
own interests, and to help them to organize themselves,—
as Mr. Gladstone so effectually did at Birmingham,—for
the purpose of securing it, and at the same time to
keep us everywhere at peace, and who sees that the
whole stock of trade of the other side is to do nothing
at home and only excite the country about foreign
politics, will throw difficulties in Mr. Gladstone's way,
or try to make the people think less of the man who is
serving them.   It is a miserable task, and only a man
who has vinegar for blood, like Danby, or who is full of
conceit and other bad gases, like Lewin, would undertake
it.   I hate these ungenerous slanders on a great work."

"You are young," said Standish, "and will pull
steadier in the traces some day.   We all know Mr.
Gladstone to be a great man ; but what you say is
what any disciple might say about any master.   As for
generosity, we have nothing to do with that in politics.
The question is whether Mr. Gladstone handles the
reins ill or well, and whether he will keep the party
together or not.   I think he will—he has a happy
knack of getting out of unprofitable ventures—but that
is no reason why Danby should think so."

"Young or not," retorted Manley, "I hope I shall

always fight for a great man when we have one amongst us. Confess now, Bramston; am I not right to quarrel with your friends ? "

" You all leave on me the sense of men fighting in a dark room with sticks, and breaking the heads that are nearest them," said Angus. " I will not say who is right or who is wrong. Of all the strange games at which men play in the world, I think politics and religion are the two strangest, only we are all so busy with our sticks that we don't find out what we are doing. A man will do anything for his church and anything for his party and ask no questions, just because some accident has pitch-forked him into his place as a member of one or the other. But whether he is right or wrong to be where he finds himself is a question that he never stops to ask."

" Don't become a philosopher," said Standish. " That is the one thing there is no room for in the House."

" And if you do, you never will be a good Liberal," said Manley. " You will be going into caves and all sorts of noisome 'places. Take my advice. Give up your friends, Lewin and Company, and come and sit on our bench behind the Government."

And the party broke up.

CHAPTER III.

At two o'clock Angus Bramston intended to be at
the Westminster Palace Hotel. There was to be a
meeting of Liberal members to consider the proposal of
inviting representatives of all the Liberal executive
committees of boroughs and counties up to London.
It was suggested that there should be a day of speeches,
and then a 'dinner'; and it was believed that a leading
member of the party intended to invite the whole
gathering to his house in the evening. It was thought
that the plan would help to keep the party united.
Liberals from the provinces would hear speeches from
some of the Ministers, who might touch upon measures
for which it was specially desired to have the support
of the country; and in addition to the political enthusiasm called out during the day's proceedings, the effect
of the social gathering at the end might be fairly
counted on to seal the services of each committee-man,
who might receive a few words of divine commu-
nication from the lips of a cabinet minister under his
own roof, and so be sent home with quite incorrupti-
ble devotion to his party. If the experiment were

found successful, it was proposed that the gathering should be established as a yearly ceremony. It was generally understood that influential persons considered it of the highest importance to bring all the working members of the Liberal party into closer connection, and thus to make the party into a more solid whole. It was perceived that the leading men in the provinces were in reality the men on whom victory depended. They had been only too much neglected in the past, but that mistake should not be repeated in the future.

"Will any of the Government be here?" asked Angus of Wolleston, the member for a Lancashire borough by whose side he found himself.

"No, I think not. I believe it is wished that the movement should be made by the party itself without any appearance of official guidance. It will look better in the country, if only we ourselves appear in it without being told what we are to do. Just watch that old fox Tyrrell, moving busily about and arranging everything. He is always the link between the seen and the unseen on these occasions. I think he is asking Standish to take the chair. Hush! our friend Lucian is going to speak."

Standish in a few neat sentences explained the object of the meeting. It was plain to them all how much organization had done for the party at the last elections. He did not say organization might not be carried too far. It was the special distinction of the Liberal party that they represented principles ; they left victories which were the result of mere organization to the other side ; but it was an advantage from every point of view that the Liberal leaders in the provinces—he would call them the non-commissioned officers—should learn to know each other, should form the habit of acting together, should, like the officers of the German army, each be at their post within twenty-four hours if a crisis arose. He also thought it would be useful for the Liberals of the provinces to have an opportunity of hearing from the lips of the leaders a statement of the policy they were pursuing ; and for the leaders in their turn to be frankly told by those who came directly from the people what they were thinking and desiring."

" I thought Standish disliked the caucus," said Angus to Wolleston.

" Yes, he does, and he opposed it for a time in a quiet way. I suppose he thinks that his own personal influence will be lessened if the House becomes more stupid and more mechanical, as some people believe it will ; but he found he could not oppose it successfully, and this is a sort of amends he is making to the Government. The caucus is flourishing,—and, like others, he must accept it. You notice, however, that he puts in a few saving words."

The discussion went on, a resolution was moved, and Bastian rose to second it. Bastian was a restlessly active member, recently elected, and fully determined to play his part in all matters. Quick-witted, with considerable coolness and address, sharp to see and to know just as much as sharpness could teach him, with the conscience of a Greek of the Lower Empire, but completely unembarrassed by his own knowledge of the fact, and not over-careful to conceal it from others, except on those occasions when the game required a special observance of the decencies. Most things in the world were food for amusement and excitement to him, including perhaps certain not very reputable episodes in his own life before he came into his money; but about which he was at times willing enough to be communicative, if the company and the circumstances were encouraging. The world had for a short time taken some interest in speculating on his past life. It was said that at one moment of his career he had raked florins under the instructions of the Government of Monaco; and his more fully informed biographers declared that he had fought a duel at a later period in which the pistol of his opponent had mysteriously refused to go off; but owing to his habit of romancing about himself in congenial smoking-rooms, it was difficult to know how much or how little truth there was in these and in other stories. There were undoubtedly incidents of a shady kind in his past life which could not by his best friends be described as "purpurei panni;" but then those who knew most of him declared on his behalf that, in his undisguised vanity, he preferred being talked of in connection with any incident rather than not being talked of at all. "He has told more lies than he has committed murders," was the blunt apology of one of his friends. It was difficult for him to count for much in the House of Commons as yet, but outside he enjoyed the sort of position which a man of quick brains may rapidly secure for himself, if he is supposed to be quite thoroughgoing in his radicalism. He had tact enough to remain neutral where he was uncertain on which side of the question the mass of the people would be, and seldom committed himself deeply except where questions of capital and labour, taxation, and enlargement of the franchise gave him a clear course. The few words which he now said were well chosen. He had picked up a vapouring, bullying manner of speaking, which he generally found effective, but as he knew that on this occasion a large part of his audience were not very favourably disposed to him, and that a good many of those present were helping to fasten fetters on themselves which they secretly disliked, he kept as well as he could on safe ground. A passing reference to the great Liberal victory at the last election ; a slight sarcasm about the crotchets and the crotchet-mongers who had not succeeded in dividing the party ; a eulogy of Mr. Gladstone and his single-handed fight during the session, with an allusion to the bow of Ulysses ; and a warm commendation of the hard work done by the non-commissioned officers of the Liberal army, as they had been so well called by the chairman, made up his speech.   Then he prepared for his ending. " It was time that they did something to mark their sense of gratitude towards those who bore the heat and the burden of the day in the service of the people, and were always at their post preparing for the battle, though themselves sharing but too little in the honour and distinctions of public life."   Here, warmed by the cheer which he got, he thought he might slip in a good popular sentence, which he could strengthen still more afterwards in the report he intended to send to the *Times* on his own account.   " And now let him say as one who only cared to speak on behalf of that great democracy, which had sent him thither, that the people were watching jealously the preparations they were making that day, that they were waiting then as ever to fight and to win the battle, but they asked that no professional blundering, no carelessness about organization, no wavering on the part of their responsible officers, and above all no lukewarm support of their great leader should render fruitless the efforts and the sacrifices they themselves were ready to make."   There was something like a laugh at the words, " on behalf of that great democracy," but he got another cheer as he sat down. The resolution was about to be put when a tall man of rather severe and impressive type of face rose, and amid a dead silence asked leave to speak.

" Damn it, of course he'll object.   When did he ever

do anything else ? " Angus could hear Manley exclaim, with an energy of speech that carried his words half across the room. "There has been a good deal said about hospitality to-day," began Maudsley Graham, "about the duty of marking our sense of the services of those who fight our battles for us ; but I think we had better be quite frank in the matter and say plainly that our special aim is to strengthen the fighting organization of the Liberal party. I know well how determined the party is to organize itself for fighting purposes, and I do not expect that any warning of mine will shake their resolve on this point ; but I shall speak plainly because I doubt if we fully measure all the future consequences of our present action. What I would ask you to bear in mind is that there are two kinds of political organization. You may have an organization to spread a particular opinion. It may place the view that is contended for before the minds of men, by calling meetings, by distributing papers and tracts, by discussions in the press, in the market-place, at the fireside, and it may carry on this propaganda until the mass of the people accept the principle that is at the bottom of the agitation, and demand its embodiment in law. For all such organizations I have not blame, but hearty ungrudging praise. We see in them the instrument of a free, of a living and thinking democracy. It was thus that the repeal of the corn laws was won ; thus that the Dissenters shook off many of the disqualifications that rested on them ; it was thus the other day that the country was led to declare emphatically in favour of a peaceful as against an aggressive policy.   I do not say that these organizations have not their faults.   They may be onesided and unfair in their advocacy, they may appeal to ignoble qualities, or to undisciplined and inconsequent emotions.   They are human ; and only as men become possessed of a far greater craving than they have at present to see justly and truly will they be purged of these faults.   But I say emphatically these organizations are good and right in themselves, because they publicly appeal to the one tribunal—the universal conscience and reason of men—where such questions should be carried ; a tribunal, before which it is open to every man to speak who has faith in his own views ; a tribunal, that would render far more justice than it does render at present, if men, without thinking of merely pleasing, learnt to speak their own thoughts openly and fearlessly before it.   But there is another kind of organization very different from that which seeks to convert the people to a definite opinion.   I mean an organization that is intended to weld men into a sort of Macedonian phalanx ; that is intended to perfect their political discipline, and to bring them under the touch and direction of their managers ; and that does this with the view of maintaining a majority for a party and power for a Government.   This is the kind of organization on which you are intent. You are addressing yourselves to-day not to the minds, but to the bodies of the people. You want to get them accustomed to the direction of their committees, just as their committees are to be accustomed to your direction. You want them in obedience to that direction to go in thousands to a meeting and pass resolutions, to go in thousands to the polling booths and record their votes. It is the bodily presence and the recorded vote that you are seeking to secure ; as for the mind of each man, it may be present with the vote, or it may not,—that is a consideration of very secondary importance to you,—for your end will be attained when the party, with or without a mind of its own, can be brought to move with the impact of one solid mass. I hear a friend interpose and say that the vote expresses the feelings and convictions that are behind it. But does it ? That is the very point. I say that it is so easy for men to act under system and under discipline, to move mechanically, to be held back, to be sent forward, to be wheeled to the right, to the left, under the impulse of those who command them—far easier than it is to act under the direction of their own-minds. Man is born a fighting animal, especially in this small island of ours, and it is this fighting part, not the thinking part of him, that you take advantage of, when you bring him under your political organizations and simply set him, with such pay as you can succeed in giving him, to defeat the party that is your rival. Well! you deny, you resent this statement! But is it not true? Answer me fairly! Do you really and in earnest want to quicken thought throughout the Liberal party, to increase discussion, and call into existence,—what must follow a real movement of thought and discussion,—differences of opinion? Would you not be shocked, dismayed, aggrieved, if at some critical moment when you wanted for the Government a solid support from the constituencies, there came up the expression of differing opinions? Would you not at once set to work to correct your machinery, to re-adjust the pulleys on your driving shaft, in order that such antagonism might cease to be? Would you not say in your resentment we have been encouraging men to think too much;—less thought and more discipline is wanted for our purpose? You know right well in your hearts what you want, though you don't put it openly into plain words. You want to secure perfect unity of movement. You talk about bringing these provincial leaders up to London, about letting them hear ministers explain their measures, about letting them join in discussion and move resolutions. Say it out frankly, — all this is the mere outside, the comparatively worthless outside of the matter. It is not a true interchange of opinion, a real discussion with frank unfettered criticism of Government measures that you want; you want only just so much of these things as shall make those who are acting the part that you have assigned to them appear to themselves to be free agents. You are willing to save their self-respect, provided that nothing interfere with your fixed intention of drawing closer the bonds between these men and the Government; of planting them as German officers, according to your own expressive phrase, everywhere at their posts; of training them to fasten their eyes upon the London Committee, so that they may consult you upon the members they elect, and be ready at any critical moment for the resolution, that will be drafted at your head quarters, and that they will pass—with perhaps some few words judiciously altered—in simultaneous support of the Government. You want them, as I think some writer has said, to roar, like the mechanical lion, at your signal, and then again to be silent at your signal; and behind them you want that, without which all the rest would be worthless, well-trained and swiftly-moving masses of supporters to follow their leaders in the same manner as their leaders are to follow you. You want party organization in the first place and in the second place and in the third place, and then you are graciously willing that individual conscience and reason should find such after place for themselves as they can. It is easy to see that your organization is not intended to leave room under it for the people to think and to act for themselves; they are to trust themselves in the hands of the Government who, in their benevolence and their wisdom, will choose such measures for them as they think appropriate. Between you and the people there is an unwritten and unspoken but well understood contract. They are to support the Government, and the Government in return undertakes to judge what is ripe and what is not ripe, according to the occasion and the opportunity. It is a compact which gives you place and power; and which pledges you in return to give such opportunist measures as shall liberally repay the votes you have received. This is the essence of caucus government; services on both sides; a people who have lost their own self-direction and their own free judgment, managed, acted upon, catered for, sometimes fed, and sometimes tricked out of their food; but if fed, then fed with measures that are prepared and digested for them, as meat is prepared for us by chewing machines when we have grown old and lost our teeth. Frankly, I don't admire the system. It is fatal to all self-respect and faith in our own views, fatal to that free and open process by which a genuine public opinion is formed, and fatal to all definitely held principles. It will corrupt you and it will corrupt the people. The one ruling principle of the party will be, " Believe in the Liberal Government and you shall be saved." On the one side you will learn to do whatever you think necessary to please at the moment; and on the other side the people will learn to forgive your mistakes and inconsistencies and desertions of principle for the sake of the advantages that they hope to get from you. And mark the result. Slowly but surely as your organization, like a huge and overgrown octopus, spreads its arms in every direction, the people will lose their habit of watchfulness and their power of free criticism. Do you not see how easily hereafter the Government will enter upon some mistaken, and it may be even fatal policy, without any warning from the best public opinion, when once the meshes of the new organization are thrown over all the active members of the Liberal party, and they have learnt to look for instructions to central offices, that are of the same flesh and blood with the Government? Do you think there is any innate quality in this or in any other Government that will make them act wisely and rightly apart from the incessant vigilance of public opinion? Governments are not born good; they are less good, having more temptations to be untrue, than the rest of the world; and if once the Liberal party, as a whole, is betrayed into unwatchfulness and dependence on those who govern, if once the interests on both sides become so closely entangled together, that neither can afford to quarrel with its partner, you will lose all guarantee that our party should be wiser or better than the party opposed to them. The good that we have done in the past has been owing to the vigour of individual minds on our side leading us to form higher conceptions of what was right. But vigorous individual minds and central organization are not things that can be made to go together. You have now as always to choose between them. And yet I know that even those who are inclined to agree with me, will answer, 'There must be some organization. What then is right to be done?' I say, in reply, popular organization for the choice of members in every constituency is right and necessary. I have nothing to urge against your two, and your four, and your six hundred ; though, valuing as I do the free judgment of each man more than any other thing in the world, I say that even such organizations, if they are to prosper, must not be built upon the ruins of individual independence. I hope most earnestly that those who differ from their town organizations on any great matter will never let themselves be deluded by those strained praises of the value of unity—which are now constantly on the lips of the organizers—so as to cease to be true to their own opinions, or to shrink from boldly and openly differing and, if needs be, acting upon that difference. As Mr. Markham—I believe his name is familiar to some present—said in a lecture that excited a good deal of public attention in Birmingham, 'Every man's first duty is to his own opinions.' I agree in that great truth, and I think we constantly forget it nowadays, when we are planning to improve our organization. He urged, as I have done after him, that the danger that inhered in the caucus is not in the existence of machinery for enabling a town to choose its

representative, but in the official tamperings and mani-
pulations, in the constant desire at head quarters to
bring all these local organizations into close connection
with the centre, and to make them a mere dependency
of the Government.   Truer words were never spoken.
It is exactly what has happened.   In the Government,
as we all know, there are men with a keen eye for party
business and an aptitude for management, and under
their influence the whole Liberal party rapidly tends to
be centralised for fighting purposes. What, then, you ask
again, is the course which we ought to take ?   I can
only reply, the very opposite of that which we are
pursuing to-day.   Lessen this vice of central management, foster local independence and local action.   Let
our effort be to loosen the ties that bind the Government and the party caucus together, rather than to draw
them closer. As any crisis arises, let the representatives of
the Liberal organization meet, at the request of a certain
number of themselves, and let them do so under their own
arrangements, and for real, honest, and open discussion.
Let those who doubt, or hesitate, or dissent have every
opportunity to say so.   Let there be no pulling of wires
behind the scenes, no stifling of differences for the mere
sake of unity, no theatrical calling together of representatives, whose only function is to go through a movement of the lips in assenting to opinions and resolutions that smell of the Government benches. Say imperatively both to my friend Mr. Chamberlain, whom I regret

not to see here to-day, and to that lesser but active luminary that revolves round him, Mr. Schnadhorst, 'Hands off'; let the nation learn to think and to speak for itself.' It is, I know, a far slower and more laborious process to build upon the free individual convictions of men instead of the mechanically obtained unity of the mass; but if your work is planned for high purposes, with nothing less should you be content. Nor will you lose in the end. There never yet was a movement, either in religion or in politics, that weakened system and management, and in doing it freed the intelligence of individual men, that did not at last add far greater forces than those it took away. In all that we do, let us remember that our effort as Liberals is to place mental independence above and before every object; not to make men think according to authority and direction, or according to their interests, or according to the fashion of thought that prevails round them, but to lead each man to exercise a fearless private judgment. Our warfare, if we rightly understand it, is less against the Tories, as Tories, than against those weaknesses of the human mind which make men in every age think in crowds and copy their justice and reason from each other. Take care that you do not bring us to the moral and intellectual level of our opponents. I have but little faith in what you christen Liberal measures. You may call anything the party happens to desire a Liberal measure. The only true foundation of Liberalism is the separate intelligence and the individual conviction of those who make up the party. Destroy or even weaken these things, turn us into an army that is merely drilled for victory, and in that very hour of victory you will have lost the real meaning of the Liberal party. It will be but a body, from which the soul has departed."   .

"That's what I call an infernally long oration," exclaimed Manley again with unabated energy from his place in the room.

"I am glad he has spoken," Angus said to Wolleston. "He has put into words for me much of what I have been thinking lately. But can we do without the caucus? Is he right in attacking it, do you think?"

"Yes and no," answered Wolleston hesitatingly. "The organization mania is strong upon us now. There is a good deal of personal ambition about the actual men who are directing it; and as for those who acquiesce in it, they have divided motives. With the larger number there is no desire to ask many questions, as long as all goes well and they find themselves sharing in a successful enterprise; they want their seats in Parliament, and the caucus gives it them by driving rivals off the ground. There are other men who look upon the caucus as a sort of buffer between them and what they dislike more. They are rather frightened at the democratic look of things, and they find comfort in the idea of any sort of centralised management. They think that they are safer under a regulated system of wire-pulling than with all the forces in the party let loose to pull against each other and to find out which is the strongest.   No professional wire-pullers are revolutionists if they can help it.   They will do, it is true, what must be done from time to time to satisfy the mass of the party ; but, like all other holders of office, they will not do more than is necessary."

"I cannot think," said Angus, "there will be much safety in the wire-pullers.   If any strain comes they will follow the line of least resistance."

"Yes, I think so," answered Wolleston ; "they are not likely to die for their opinions—if they have any. And I also doubt sometimes if the system of wire-pulling and general management does not end in more dangerous concessions than if the different classes in society openly claimed what they each believed in. Those of us who have property are not in real agreement with those who have not, however much we try in public to speak and act as if we were. We keep giving bit by bit without really facing what we are doing, or what we intend to do next.   Of course the object of the managers is before everything else to hold us together as a party ; they want to avoid or to slur over all discussions that might stir unpleasant differences—though, perhaps, a real discussion between men in earnest on both sides would be the best and healthiest thing that could happen to us ;—to put a good face on what we do ; to keep us all going by certain sets of party phrases ; to minimise each concession, that is made, to one section of the party, and to make the most of it to the other section ; whilst as to what will come of it all, what will happen the day after to-morrow, that does not come within the range of either their intelligence or their conscience. They get no official wages for thinking about the future. I am sometimes afraid we are like the half-pint men who go on sipping, and who do not find out how much they have taken until they try to walk home. Each session we take some step that means many further steps hereafter in the same direction. I daresay it is a good thing for us when a man like Graham gets up and tells us plainly that we are not moved by very high objects, but are only thinking about winning our own seats and remaining in office."

"And do you yourself think that there are real dangers in organization ? " asked Angus.

"I accept it as one does so many things in politics," answered Wolleston, "because there is not much choice in the matter. We have got arrears of work to do in this country—local government to establish, law to simplify, House of Lords to reconstruct, the Church to disestablish ; and, perhaps, organization of the constituencies is required to let us get through these necessary things. But I suppose nobody can help seeing that we are playing a dangerous game in creating a great machine, in giving the handling of it to a few ambitious men, and teaching the country to wait and expect wonders of all kinds from it. The monster that we have brought into life may go to sleep, as some men think, when we don't want him, but he may also wake by fits and starts and devour a good many things; and if he does, they may not be exactly what you and I have placed on our own programmes. It is very like having a powerful standing army in a country. Nobody not in the prophet line of business can say what it is going to do or not going to do. There is, however, so much good sense and fairness in the country that, whatever mistakes we make, I cling to the belief that we shall pull through."

"I often wonder," said Angus, "how far that un-employed fund of good sense can be trusted to get us out of our difficulties. If we are going wrong, ought not our good sense to be employed at once in making us go right? It is rather like an investment on which a man in trade depends, and which may turn out on the very day he wants it to have silently disappeared in the interval. But by-the-bye who is Markham? I am already interested in him, and want to know more of the man and his opinions."

"Oh! Graham is always talking about him," replied Wolleston. "I think he believes in nobody else. I will tell him to send you some of his pamphlets and lectures. Graham believes in them more than he does in his own."

Meanwhile the discussion went on. Graham had disturbed the even flow of the meeting, some men being inclined to agree and others to pooh-pooh what they looked on as fanciful objections. Bastian was up again on his legs, and, rendered rash by his first success, went off at score about the people being determined to sweep, like cobwebs, out of their path the timid fancies of those phrase-makers who wish to keep them for ever defenceless and unable to help themselves. " He would wish Mr. Graham to remember that they had to reckon with a people tired of trifling and not to be deluded from year to year with fine moral sentiments that fed nobody. Did Mr. Graham think that the nation would stand still, and not ask for what it wanted—aye! and take it, too—because he was good enough to have views about their moral independence ? The people knew what they were doing. They knew that all things went to the strongest, and they intended to be as strong as organization could make them." His last sentences were nearly lost in the noise, but he consoled himself by reflecting that they would read well in the report he proposed drawing up. Presently Standish rose, and applied oil to the waters. " It was well,' he said, " for them to be reminded that the Liberal weapons were not simply those of organization. As Liberals they could not remember too often that they represented the cause of principles, principles for which the party had made sacrifices, and would always make sacrifices again. They could not too faithfully follow Mr. Graham's injunction to treat the provincial leaders as men of independence who had to act and think for themselves; and, speaking in his own individual capacity, he would take no part in a scheme that could by any possibility reduce them to the position of mere wheels in a machine. But that was far from their intention. He was confident that the managing committee, in whose names the meeting would find every guarantee that they required, would act in a wise and liberal spirit; whilst at the same time he felt that Mr. Graham himself would not desire that a mass of men, brought up from all parts of the country, should be left in a disorganized condition to waste the few hours which they had at their disposal. It would be necessary for some person to issue the invitations and to throw the business into some kind of form, so as to prevent either waste of time or disorder; whilst he thought they might fully depend upon the committee acting in the spirit of Mr. Graham's thoughtful speech. He would, indeed, pledge himself that such should be the case."

"Ah! he always says the right thing," said Wolleston laughing, as Standish sat down amidst general assent. "There is no man in the whole world knows better how to oil the waves of a duck-puddle than Standish." The resolutions were passed, the meeting broke up, and Angus walked down to the House with Wolleston, meditating on what had passed. At last he said, quoting from Standish, "The party of principles, Wolleston; what should you say are our principles? What principles did Standish mean?"

"Principles—free-trade, perhaps,—no, not exactly nowadays, since we've taken to land bills;—well, re-trenchment; no, I could not say retrenchment. I believe the Tories spend less, if anything, than we do. Peace; yes, peace, perhaps. I don't think Gladstone ever had any real intention of punching the Turk's head, when he tried to be logical over 'bag and baggage;' but, hang it, in politics you need not be too particular; you can always say the happiness of the people, if anybody asks you."

"And what is the happiness of the people?" asked poor Angus, with something like a groan, as his old and irrepressible friend turned up once more.

"Oh! something of all sorts. Something to do with getting rid of worn-out old things and putting new ones in their place; with easing the shoe wherever it pinches anybody who has votes enough to make it worth while to help him; with passing a little sensational legislation now and then, so as to keep the constituencies in good-humour, and ourselves, I suppose, in office. There is good for ourselves in it, of course, as well as for the people. But it must in any case be better for them to have us than to have the Tories. There is that un-failing consolation to fall back upon if ever you have misgivings," added Wolleston philosophically.

It was still early when they reached the House, and Bramston went to the terrace for a few minutes' walk. As he paced backwards and forwards, Manley and Standish came up together and called to him to join them.   They all sat down, and the conversation glided insensibly back to the subject of their morning talk.   .

" You have always admired Gladstone," said Bramston, speaking to Manley, "have you not?   I can quite understand the charm that he exercises over you and many other men, even if I myself remain outside the charm.   Perhaps at present I am too much in the humour for speculating and questioning and criticising to indulge in unrestrained admiration for anybody. What is it that attracts you most in him ?"

" I think it is the whole type of man that attracts me," said Manley.   " I like him for his splendid working and fighting powers.   I feel for him almost as the old Greeks must have felt for their leaders.   Whenever things go against us, and our men have made but a poor fight of it, as they so often do, it is splendid to see him dash into the debate and restore the whole line of battle.   And then what man can do the work which he does ?   Every kind of possible subject, from the west coast of Ireland to South Africa, turns up in the House, and he comes down and knows all about it, though when and where and how he was able to get his knowledge passes the power of mortal imagination. His working power compared with that of other men is steam power compared with horse power.   Then I like him for the plain and simple grasp he takes of every question.   There is nothing narrow or personal in his view.   He lifts the discussion at once into a better and freer atmosphere.   Like some general whose instinct leads him to occupy the higher ground he always seizes the moral heights that surround a question.   You will hear men say that to read or listen to a speech of Gladstone is like walking on a mountain and seeing all the valleys and plains mapped out in their true position beneath them.   Then I like him also for all the subtle qualtities that are compounded together in him.   He is not a mere politician ; he has so many interests and so many sides to his character ; he lives almost as much in the past as he does in the present ; he is saturated with ideas that few men regard or understand at the present day, and yet he allows nothing to prevent the growth of his popular sympathies.   With ties of every sort that bind him to the Old World, his mind has refused no democratic idea of our generation that is true or just in itself ; and this meeting of the two tides in his mind is one reason why the men who dread and almost hate him cannot dispute his power.   If only they could think of him as they like to think of Bradlaugh—who to hear them talk you would suppose was a sort of ogre with one eye and a hundred mouths— they would feel so much more at their ease in abusing him.   But what utterly bewilders them is the knowledge that the man they hate beats them everywhere on their own ground ; cares more for and understands better than they do all the old things which give the charm to civilised life, and which they like to look on as their own special property, as intellectual mysteries of which no profane Liberal can see the real meaning. If Mr. Gladstone would only renounce Homer, Dante, and the Bible, they would feel as much relieved as savages who have deprived their enemy of some amulet of mysterious power."

"Mr. Gladstone's character must always be an interesting one; it must always claim respectful attention," said Angus. "But underneath what you say there lies a question which I am always asking myself, as I watch his leadership of the party: how do the changes of political thought, that we all see taking place in him from time to time, have their genesis in his mind? Are they the result of deliberate intellectual choice, made when Mr. Gladstone, as far as outward circumstances are concerned, is free and able to determine his own position, or when circumstances are such that, unless he takes the required step, he will weaken his position as leader and run the risk of lessening his hold upon the people? I have no fixed conviction on this point. I wish to hear all that can be said, but, to speak frankly, what strikes me, as I watch him, is that all the changes that he makes are of a kind adapted to meet the desires of those on whom he depends. How does this happen? Are the two things—the change of opinion and the increased influence with the people—only a coincidence, or are they related to each other as cause and effect? Is it only an accident that the developments of his mind result in measures that find favour with the mass of the electors, or does the coming popularity cast its shadow before and help to shape the convictions that we presently see expressed in his speeches and his measures ? "

" You can hardly suppose," said Standish, " that Mr. Gladstone thinks *in vacuo*. He is not like a mathematician calculating the forces of motion as if no atmosphere existed. Of course, when he gives up an old opinion he has the necessities of the moment strongly before him. He would be very little fit for the difficult task of leading the Liberal party if he had not."

" Yes, of course," said Manley. " Of course Mr. Gladstone neither thinks nor acts irrespective of circumstances ; but what Bramston means is, when Mr. Gladstone's conduct seems to be inconsistent with his past declarations, is it the party advantage, or is it a change in his own convictions, which has influenced him ? I say that Mr. Gladstone's whole career answers that question. You see one part of his nature continuously developing ; you see him steadily advancing in one direction, from year to year becoming more democratic, more in feeling with the masses of the people."

" Still, you do not help me," said Bramston. " We all see the democratic changes in Mr. Gladstone, but then we cannot help seeing also that it is his interest to become more democratic. Why did he and many of our other leaders only become decidedly democratic in mind after the householders became voters ?   Why do the changes coincide with such admirable results ? The real question is, do the mental changes take place in obedience to or irrespective of what is his political interest ?   If at the present moment, when public opinion is what it is, Mr. Gladstone were to declare himself for an English republic, or an Ireland separated from England, I should know—we should all know— that this was a free mental development on his part, and that he would probably lose power and place by making such a declaration.   No one would accuse him of consulting his interests—unless you supposed that he was greatly miscalculating public opinion in the country ; he would evidently do it in obedience to some strong inner conviction on the subject.   But suppose ten years hence, when perhaps public opinion will be very different from what it is now, Mr. Gladstone declares himself a Republican and in favour of the separation of Ireland, shall we not reasonably conjecture that his mind has followed the popular movement ? "

" You are making impossible suppositions," said Standish, almost vexed.   " How can Mr. Gladstone separate himself from what the nation or the party thinks ?   Do you wish an officer to gallop three hundred yards in front of his own men when he is leading an attack ?   He is not necessarily pushed on by his own men, though he may be only three yards in front of them."

"Yes," said Angus, laughing ; " but I want to know which begins to gallop first.   I seldom see our leaders galloping, until it is all downhill and the line itself has begun to gallop, and then I ask myself, can it be right for our front bench to be the last men to have opinions in the country ?   We all admired the fearless and resolute way in which Mr. Gladstone fought the battle against the war policy of the Tories—it was a really splendid thing, and deserved the admiration of the nation ; but even then, as you all remember, the nation was in a blaze before Mr. Gladstone became fairly aroused.   Lord Derby's cynical despatches, inviting the Turks to stamp out the insurrection, did not seem to move him.   He had spoken once in favour of the Christian races, but had taken no prominent part in the effort of a few men in the House to force attention to what the Government was doing; and had not the *Daily News* suddenly lifted the curtain from a Bulgarian village, perhaps neither the nation nor Mr. Gladstone himself would have awoken from their slumber. And as for the rest of our present leaders, not only at a later stage did they not gallop three yards in front, but a good clear half mile in the rear. It was only when the battle was fairly won, and public opinion fairly turned, and Gladstone by a very gallant fight had made it safe for them to reappear, that all the other right honourable gentlemen came galloping up, brandishing their swords, as if they, too, had helped to win the victory.

It is a sight like this that makes one wonder how much any men in politics have to do with their own opinions."

" Whatever the others did," exclaimed Manley, " never was there a better piece of fighting than that done by Mr. Gladstone. Amidst strong opposition and luke-warm support he led the party, which was worse than defeated, which was utterly demoralised and despairing of itself, back to victory and belief in its own fortunes."

" My praises must seem cold and ungenerous to you," replied Bramston. " I heartily admired Mr. Gladstone in many ways for that campaign against the Tories, but I want to get at the innermost truth,—what makes him or any other political leader arrive at certain convictions ? Are they really judging the right and the wrong that are involved, or are they acted upon by the movement of the mind of the people and themselves moved by it ? The question that I want answered is, how far was Mr. Gladstone's agitation made by the circumstances of the moment,—the anger of a part of the English people against oppression, their sympathy with suffering, their dislike to an adventurous policy, the mess in which it was felt that the Tories were gradually involving themselves, and much pent-up resentment at the defeat experienced at the last election ; how far was it a noble effort on his part, irrespective of all these circumstances, and simply and purely springing from a deep love of national independence and the overpowering desire to secure for every nation, small or great, the right to live its own life, free from interference outside itself ? "

" Yes, I think you are ungenerous," said Manley. " Why should you peer below the surface of a great action ? You acknowledge how splendidly Gladstone behaved, and yet you go out of your way to suggest time-serving motives. What has he ever done to justify such suspicion on your part ? "

" I am quite clear," continued Bramston, " that Mr. Gladstone sympathised with his cause, that it was congenial to him to plead for the liberty of other nations, to denounce oppression, and to batter into pieces the empty and sonorous imperialism of the Dizzy period. Of course to every man of powerful mind a great cause always commends itself, and brings out his highest powers. But then I want to learn the moral worth of his action. Was it a cause into which he would have flung himself, as he did, if the turning out of Dizzy's Government had not depended on it ? I see the way in which a great lawyer undertakes a cause. There are no moral pretensions about it ; it comes to him in the way of business and of advancement in his profession, and as a matter of business he gives the best part of himself and of his powers to it. Is it the same with all of us in politics ? Is it with us a professional matter ? Do we on the Liberal side undertake all such causes when they come to us, because they afford us a famous opportunity for drawing moral contrasts between our opponents and ourselves, and for showing how deficient they are in the noble feelings when compared with ourselves? or do we seek to move a nation with our pleading, because our opinions are an imperative part of ourselves that we must obey, whether the world is for us or against us, whether we fail or we succeed, whether we lead a party or remain in a minority of one? What you have to tell me is, whether we are enthusiasts or impostors?"

"I should say it was in the pure spirit of enthusiasm that Mr. Gladstone fought the Eastern Question," said Manley, "and, whatever you have done, the rest of the nation has recognised that there is no man in the whole country who cares so really and so deeply for national independence; no man on whom we can rely with such absolute confidence to save us from being led, either in Europe, Asia, or Africa, into acts of aggression, or from sacrificing the national aspirations of any people, however humble and weak, to our own interests. Does not all Europe feel that he is the one man who will never let England assert her own claims in a violent and high-handed manner; who will always respect and strengthen, even, if needs be, to her own disadvantage, the concert of Europe; whose hand is the one hand alone of which it may be said that, whenever and wherever liberty is claimed, it will never break the bruised reed or quench the smouldering flax? I do not think you are very happy in your suspicions. Have you no graver accusation to bring against him?"

" Well," said Bramston, " the future can be the only judge of much that you say, but I think that this very Land Bill raises the question how far Gladstone's actions are with him a matter of free choice. I do not pretend to have sufficient knowledge of character to say how far it is possible for a strong believer in free trade, and all that is implied in it, to continue to respect his own opinions, whilst he lends his hand to protective measures like this Land Bill—there must be violence done to his opinions, somewhere, I should think—but, apart from that, I do not understand the changes he has gone through in the last eleven years. In 1870 he studied this whole question, giving himself up to it with that power of absorption in a subject that adds so much to his great natural gifts, until he had made himself completely master of it. As the result he formed certain opinions, concluded that certain things were right and certain things wrong, as regards the two classes principally interested in the matter, and embodied these opinions in law. Well, a few years pass. There is no real change in the position ; there is a recurrence of some distress in Ireland, and a recurrence of agitation carried on by not very scrupulous men and with not very scrupulous weapons ; but the principles on which he acted, if good for anything in 1870, must have remained good in 1881. However, they all go for nothing ; he consents to look at the relation of landlord and tenant in a different light; what he thought fair in 1870, he thinks unfair in 1881; and what he would not give in 1870, he gives in 1881. In one sense I understand the change; I see many things pressing on him to make it; I see that perhaps he satisfies Ireland; perhaps he strengthens the Liberal party; perhaps he closes up an old wound in the empire; but speaking in a moral sense, speaking of him as a free agent, as a man dealing quite honestly and truthfully with his own mind, basing his actions upon moral reasons deliberately chosen and consistently maintained, I do not understand the change. I do not see how his own sense of what was just as between landlord and tenant can have changed in those eleven years. He had all the materials for forming a most deliberate judgment in 1870. What has happened to make him this year depart from that judgment and overthrow his own work? How in eleven years, as between landlord and tenant, has the right become wrong, and the wrong right?"

"My dear Bramston," replied Manley, "you cannot argue about what is right and wrong in politics as you do in other things. No man can do all that he wishes in politics. Even Mr. Gladstone cannot. I know that he has given a great deal of thought to what is just to the landlord. I think I may say as much as that to you. But in politics one must look to the end, and be satisfied with that, even when one does not like the means. If in a few years' time we see Ireland at peace with itself, the tenants contented and supporting the English connection, and the landlords selling their estates for even more than the old price they could have obtained, you will feel that you did not judge these things as broadly and truly as Mr. Gladstone did. There is no man who has so strong a sense of what is right and wrong as Mr. Gladstone has, but then politics are a thing by themselves, and I don't think that you can always lay down fixed rules for them."

"Ah," sighed Bramston, "there it is. There is my difficulty——"

"What is the use of this discussion?" broke in Standish rather impatiently. "You can't play a game of whist, you can't move thirty thousand men into Hyde Park and out again, by talking about right and wrong in the abstract; and how can you hope to manage a party by talking about it? You have got to think of circumstances, and very awkward and contradictory things circumstances are. I know no more complicated piece of work than leading a large party that, like our own, differs considerably in itself. There is a great mass of men in our party whose hopes you must excite, not too much so as to let them get out of hand, as Gladstone is apt to do, but enough to make them quite sure that it is better worth their while to support you than the other side; then there are other sections who have little special jobs which they expect you to do for them, and who must be both checked and encouraged with great lightness of touch. You must always give them a little, and always keep back a little. My impression is, that were we to disestablish the Church at a blow, we should lose a great many of our Dissenters. A large number of them want to be Conservatives, and will only remain with us as long as the nosebag is kept just out of their reach. A Burials Bill, an amendment to the Education Act, a Tithes Bill, a Bishops' Liberation from the House of Lords Bill, a Deceased Wife's Sister Bill, are the kind of measures we ought to keep passing from time to time. These things whet the appetite without destroying it. Then you have still more careful steering as regards some other sections of the party. There is a strong agitation beginning among the English farmers. It is only from us that they will get what they want, and after they have got it they will naturally go back to the Conservatives. I don't see how they can eventually remain with us. There will be the devil of a pull presently between them and the labourers, and I suppose we shall have to go with the labourers. If this tenants agitation continues, and if the Government manage well, they will, some time before the next election, give the farmers a decent sort of a measure, so as to put them in good humour and to get their support in case we have to go to the country on the old franchise. Presently, when household suffrage is passed, we can afford to let them betake themselves wherever they like. They will be pretty nearly lost sight of in the larger electorate, and such Tories as remain in existence will be welcome to the whole lot of them. The tenant-farmers will probably by that time be more in our way than they will be of use to us. Then there is the difficulty in the towns. There is the workman who wants capital-and-labour legislation, and the small and big trader, both of whom are sensitive on these subjects, though radical enough on all questions outside the towns. The land question, if carefully handled, will keep these men together for a time ; and it could not have been more safely and judiciously opened than by the farmers' agitation. But our difficulty will be to prevent the question growing into too large proportions, so that we should lose the moderate section of our party. Our effort must always be to carry these last men with us, and not to let the dust-blowers and noise-makers like Bastian become of too much importance in the party. They are excellent for making a row when it is wanted, but they must be kept in their place and used for their own kind of work. I am all for keeping the party as respectable as we can under the circumstances. Neither you nor I should care to have much more to do with politics, if the mere spouters by competition ever got the management of the thing. The trade and its tackle would be a trifle too coarse for me, and I suppose for you also. It would be like having to begin to fish for jack, after fishing for trout all one's life. But I don't think that this need happen. All these land-nationalisation leagues are most useful allies to us. I wish there were more of them. They make the landowners think that the devil is close behind them, and they become quite reasonable and tractable, and ready to accept any compromise that the party says must be accepted. After all, it is only paying their salvage-money, as Lord Derby tells them. But from every point of view there are plenty of difficulties in front of us, and very nice steering required ; and to talk as if you could lay down abstract principles, or as if the Ten Commandments were a complete political guide for a Prime Minister in the present day, is to argue like schoolboys who undertake to decide in their discussion-clubs whether Cromwell was right or wrong to cut off Charles's head. After you have both been in the House of Commons more than twenty years, as I have, you won't waste your time over this sort of thing. But it's nearly prayer-time. Let us go and take our places."

And Standish and Manley went towards the House.

" Well, Angus, you have got a rise out of Standish. I have not heard him so eloquent for a long time," said Danby, who had silently joined the group during the last few minutes, and had stood listening with his cigar between his teeth. " But I expect you'll presently become the terror of the House of Commons. There is generally some one of the sort about the place, from whom men fly as soon as he appears on the terrace. There's

Standish looking back over his shoulder now, as if you had taken a subscription-list out of your pocket. I think you have fairly frightened him this time."

" Standish is only a——" began Angus indignantly, but stopped short without finishing his sentence.

"That's right," said Danby ; "philosophers in search of the eternal truths should not call names. Don't go to prayers, and we will stop and have a smoke and watch the barges."

CHAPTER IV.

The session of 1883 had already made some progress. Wolleston had lately joined the little set of five friends ; otherwise to them personally time had brought but few changes. Danby had not discovered any new virtues in the human race ; Holmshill still calmly accepted the coming extinction of the Whigs ; Lewin still followed Mr. Gladstone as the most successful pioneer that could be found at present for the new views ; Pennell had nearly persuaded one young Conservative and one old Whig to declare themselves in favour of the third party; Angus Bramston was still living in a world of perplexities.

"What are you doing to-day, Angus ?" asked Danby one Sunday morning.

"I am going down to see Lady Grace. She is expecting you and some of the others to lunch," said Bramston.

"I hope to go," replied Danby ; "in the meanwhile let us have a walk."

They walked across the park, began discussing the subject of Egypt, and sat down to smoke. Whilst they were talking Bastian came towards them. "Here is a house to let," said Danby. "Any tenant, who offers the best rent, may have it from the top attic down to the basement. No references given or required. I think he means to join us."

"What treason are you two men talking?" said Bastian, as he took a seat beside them.

"I was wondering," answered Angus, "what the mass of the people are really saying about Egypt. Were they pleased or not with that little Government adventure?"

"I do not feel quite sure," answered Bastian. "There are a good many conflicting currents, and it is not easy to say which is the strongest. It is a case for that judicious word 'but.' When I addressed my electors before the opening of Parliament I zig-zagged a good deal. I went strongly against war and inter-vention and the British lion with his tail up, in a general sort of way; then I touched on our determina-tion not to stand anarchy and military pretenders on the banks of the Nile; then I went back to Gladstone's love of peace, and his enthusiasm for the liberty of subject nations; and I finished by declaring gravely that we had done it all for the good of Europe and the sake of civilisation, and intended to keep nothing for ourselves. It is all a little risky, as I think myself that we shall end by staying. But if we do stay, one can at worst fall back upon the old entanglements of the Tories, which have all through obliged us to act against our best intentions. It was really very thoughtful and considerate of the Tories establishing the control in old days, so as to save us from any responsibility for what we have been doing ; and it was very quick of Gladstone the other day to put them into the hole instead of ourselves. It will be always safe to call it their mess, if there is nothing else to say ; and at the same time we can offer up the bondholders as a ready-made sacrifice. The democracy don't like the bondholders. Unfortunately I hold a few Egyptians myself, and some fool wanted to put me on a special committee at the last meeting, so my name got into the papers. For the present, however, I recommend any one who has to speak on the subject not to go much beyond confidence in Gladstone and his moral intentions. That is very satisfying, and it leaves you free for all the eventualities ; but if the Government get into a mess with France, as I think there is a fair chance of their doing at any moment, now that Dilke has left the Foreign Office, and shilly-shally is again written up in the largest letters over the doors of that sacred edifice, I shall take a stronger line. Anyway, I shall get quit of my Egyptians at once, so as to have my hands free ; and if I find that my people have heard of my having them, I shall tell them a long and pious story about my getting rid of these last remnants of the unregenerate man, like the converted drinker at Exeter Hall, who describes his final struggle with the Evil One, as he renounced his last glass of beer. Of course it is quite on the cards that after being in Egypt a little time, the democracy may get a taste for it, and wish to stay longer; and that will make it smooth enough for all of us."

"But by hedging in this way you can only get a second place," said Danby, "whatever happens. If the clouds break up and the sun comes out and all goes well, you won't get much share of the credit; and if things go wrong and the workmen end by going against the war, Lawson will have had all the running to himself, and the rest of you Radicals will be nowhere."

"Yes, but it's better than making great mistakes and having to step back as one best can. Lawson is Lawson, and does not care whether he gets over the brook or into it, though he more often gets to the other side, than one would expect with his wild rushes. But Lawson knows nothing about playing a difficult game. If he had a handful of trumps or only a single one, he would play them in the same fashion. It is all hammer and tongs with him and his half-million of teetotallers. Whether he wins or is beaten, it does not make the slightest difference to him. He has always got his psalm-singing army behind him, and he can make just as many speeches in Exeter Hall, and hear himself just as much cheered one way as the other. It is very plain work when you have got the fanatics at your back."

"Ah! they are useful people the fanatics," said

Danby, "I doubt if you ought to neglect them. But as you say, Lawson is Lawson, and when men are given to worship pumps, it is perhaps a little difficult to calculate exactly on their movements. They say that some one saw him throwing his arms about in an odd fashion the other day in front of the drinking fountain at Hyde Park Corner. I suppose it was some part of his religious observances on the subject of water. For myself I prefer the Parsee ceremonial. I see, by-the-bye, that the French chemists have lately been tracing alcohol in different kinds of water. It was very inconsiderate, to say the least of it, on the part of Providence to put the alcohol there. What a blow it must have been to Lawson to find the principles of good and evil so perversely confounded together! 'Oh! beneficent and adorable pump, were it not for that thrice-damned drop of alcohol, that taint of original sin which is in thee also'—but under the circumstances it is hard to go on with the hymn of praise. I am really sorry for Lawson, whom quite I love at intervals. It is hard, infernally hard for him that, after all the acts of Parliament he has passed and is going to pass in favour of the pump, he will be obliged to drink alcohol to the end of his life. It was a real shame on the part of that French chemist to destroy so pretty an ideal, and to put Providence on the side of the sinners instead of the saints. Lawson must feel like the man who discovers that the kisses of his divine mistress, on which he has so long and so passionately fed, have all the while been treacherously poisoned. I hope that Canon Wilberforce, or Dawson Burns, or somebody—I think Lawson is a little weak in his theology—will make haste and vindicate Providence in the matter. I am much afraid that either Providence or the National Alliance have put their foot in it. With my own unaided intelligence I can only imagine that the alcohol got mixed with the water when Adam ate the apple. But we may leave Providence and the National Alliance to settle the matter between them as they like, only please don't think that I am recommending Lawson's conscience for imitation; I should say it was too stiff in the neck and hard in the mouth. Still there are plenty of other Radicals who understand the art of having a conscience, a kindly-tempered, adjustable sort of conscience, not a stiff-necked, star-gazing jade that will land you in the first ditch. If you take my advice you will study some of these other men. The English people like their moral politicians. It warms their hearts amazingly, when they happen to want some special thing, to be told that all the eternal moralities as well as the shillings and pence are on their side. And how can you do this unless you keep some sort of a conscience ready for the occasion ?"

" There's a good deal to be said for that view," replied Bastian ; " but things change too quickly for a conscience nowadays. You may find yourself on any side of a question at five minutes' notice. I thought the whole thing carefully over when I first went down to my people. I asked myself the question, 'Shall I go as a moral politician, in sublime raptures over the character of Mr. Gladstone, or shall I declare myself as the humble interpreter of the popular will and the delegate of my constituents?' After balancing the respective advantages of conscience and delegate, I decided for the latter. On the whole I thought there was a good democratic ring in the word delegate that the people would like, and any mistakes made would be more easy to patch up. It would only be to ask for fresh instructions. Besides, if you tell people you are their humble servant, waiting for their orders, they will generally let you do as you like."

"I think you have chosen the most difficult part. You can't be a delegate to an English constituency when they have not got opinions ; and just now they are all see-sawing. What instructions can you get about Egypt, for example ? "

" But you can't have a conscience, at least not to do the thing artistically, when they are see-sawing," replied Bastian. " Besides, nature in my case was against the experiment. She had not provided me with even a rudimentary one, so that was another difficulty in the way. And then there are so many men on our side already who have consciences. We are overdone in that direction. Why, Gladstone himself has enough for a whole party. There's more freshness nowadays about being a delegate. It opens up a new field. The very word frightens the Tories, and makes them believe that I am armed with secret instructions about dividing their property."

"Well, I shall be curious to watch how the experiment answers," said Danby. "I expect you'll come back to a conscience. You must have one for this country, at least for the present. And take care you don't hopelessly muddle the two systems. In that case you'll be forgiven neither by gods nor men."

So they went their different ways.

"That's a scoundrel," said Angus.

"That's a man who does not cheat himself," said Danby. "He's got to tell lies, and he doesn't put his lies under a bushel. There are men on our side, Angus, who are on their way to church this morning with their families, who tell worse lies than Bastian. These men lie from the moment they get up till the moment they lie down again; their whole life is a lie. They have never yet spoken the truth to themselves, and they never will. They have lied until they live believing their own lies, and have ceased to be able to know what is a lie and what is not; like a man who has not had a tub for years, and doesn't know whether he is clean or whether he is dirty."

"Say what you will," replied Angus, "it is the men like Bastian who are the real filth of politics."

"Maybe, but it is not filth covered over. I like

Bastian better than many men in our party. When I sat for Millfield there was an old man who always wanted his sovereign at election times. He was quite straightforward : he just thanked us, talked no rubbish, pocketed the gold, and stood true to his colours. I always liked that man. There was another man who also took his sovereign, but we had to take pains to put it under a box of figs or dates on his counter. He always expected his twenty minutes of moral conversation from me about Mr. Gladstone, and progress, and the education of the people, and other elevating subjects. One day I lost my temper, and told him he could not have both. I would either talk piously with him or I would pay him his sovereign, whichever he chose, but I would not do both. Well, Bastian is as much better than some of us as the old man was better than the greasy one, who wanted both the money and the piety at the same time."

"Yes, but you cannot really like Bastian," said Bramston.

" Well, by comparison," replied Danby. ." The world is so fond of sinning decently that the indecent sinners are refreshing, if only for a change."

At the gate of the park they parted. Angus often spent his mornings in a certain street near Stanhope Gate. He and Lady Grace Chatfield were cousins in some indescribable way. Lady Grace and Lady Maude Chatfield were daughters of the Earl of Mannaley, an old Whig, who for many years had been a widower. He was

the most genial of politicians and pleasantest of fathers.
Lady Grace and Angus used all the privileges of cousin-
hood; they called each other by their Christian names
and had become great friends since Angus had been in
Parliament.   Her sitting-room was, according to Angus,
a room made for philosophy.   It looked away from the
street into a large garden that belonged to another
house, and had a sense of shade and quiet and green coolness about it that was very blessed to the senses as one
stepped out of a London thoroughfare.   That morning
the church bells were still busily ringing their invitations,
and currents of church-goers, each setting towards its
own point, were meeting and crossing each other in the
streets, when Angus and Lady Grace drew their chairs
towards the large window that looked on the garden, with
the pleasant feeling that the world, or as much of it as
they cared to have, belonged to them for the next few
hours.

"In a few minutes the bells will leave us in peace,"
said Lady Grace.   "Tell me what you have been doing,
and whether Mr. Danby consents to invite me to your
next breakfast, and if you have seen anything yet of
your new acquaintance, Mr. Markham, the workman?
Mr. Graham wants me to go and hear him lecture when
he is next in town.   He says you are to be sure and go;
and he sends me an address that he has lately given,
and which you may read first, if you solemnly promise
to return it."

"Danby comes to lunch," said Angus, "and shall speak for himself. I have not yet seen Markham, but I am looking forward to meeting him. He writes that he has soon to be in London about a patent, and that he has promised both to lecture and to attend a discussion at one of the North London clubs. As one or two members representing Socialist leagues are likely to speak, he thinks the discussion may be interesting. Would there be any chance of our persuading your brother to join us, so that we could all go together? He is always wishing to improve his mind whenever cricket allows him."

"Will you ask him?" said Lady Grace. "He is always desperately hurt whenever his friends think of him as given over to cricket, and he is always pleased when you or some other member of Parliament propose something for him to do. Notwithstanding cricket he reads a good deal. There was a discussion at lunch the other day about the Crimean war, and he quite surprised his father by knowing what Mr. Gladstone said when he resigned office at that time. Now tell me what first interested you in Mr. Markham."

"I had heard both Danby and Graham speak about him, and was wishing to know more about him. Then I came upon a letter of his in reply to some person with whom he had been engaged in a controversy in one of the morning papers ; and I was much struck with the clear way in which he thought and wrote. He seems to me so outspoken and straightforward, not caring the least whom he offends, if he has anything to say ; full of hopes about the future of his own class, but neither scolding the richer classes nor whining about them, like so many men who speak to the workmen. His ideals seem to exist apart from and independently of the rich people, but he accepts the whole class quite frankly as persons who have just as much right to exist as himself. What I dislike so much in politics is the sickly and unreal way in which so many of our men speak when they find themselves on a platform, as if just for that one half-hour in their lives it had been suddenly revealed to them that it was a crime to be rich. If it is, why do we continue to have and to enjoy what we have? We could very easily get rid of it all. I went to a meeting the other night where a couple of members who sit on my bench made speeches about the better distribution of wealth, and talked to the workmen as if some law ought to be invented for putting them in a better position and ourselves in a worse ; and I could not help asking myself all the time why half their words did not stick in their throats. We had all dined to-gether, before we went, at the club—a good dinner of an ordinary kind, with a little good wine; we had all we wanted—not an extravagant dinner, but what I suppose would have cost a London workman nearly a couple of days' wages to pay for each of us. Then you know Colbert, with everything about him as good as plenty of

money, good taste, and care can make it. Not one of
the three of us could be fairly called extravagant men,
but we were just like everybody else, spending what we
wanted to spend.   Well, as I listened to Colbert being
enthusiastically cheered by the workmen as he told
them in his neat epigrammatic sentences, and in all
good faith, I suppose, of a certain kind, that the time
was come when labour should get its better reward, and
means must be found not only to produce but to distribute wealth, I kept thinking of that dinner, and that
bottle of hock, and that good cigar, and that bill at
Poole's, and wondered if one ought not first to get rid of
these things and a good many other things like them,
before one talks the political socialism that is in fashion
just now.   And then I thought of the London workman
in his turn—who had just cheered Colbert so heartily—
spending his shilling at an evening's amusement, as we
spend our pound.   Where, after all, was the difference
between us ?   We have more to spend, and he has less ;
but if he had more, would he not spend in proportion ?
Are we not speaking untruly, without real conviction,
when we invite him to forget all about himself and his
own pleasures, and to sit in judgment on all those who
are richer than himself, and who, having more, spend
more than he does ?   With some very few exceptions,
would not all men do the same, and be glad to do it ?
I am not, as you know well, defending either selfishness
or extravagance or waste—there is plenty of all three—

but I want to know what is the truest way in which we who are rich, and yet not wholly selfish, should speak about the differences of wealth that exist. I want to feel quite true in the matter. Granted that we are not to talk Socialism without meaning it, what are we to do? Shall we talk it and really live it, or shall we tell every man to accept the means of enjoyment that he has, and, in all reason and conscience, make the most of them, without troubling himself about other men having more than he has? But in this last case I am afraid Colbert's speeches will lose some of their point, and he won't get so many cheers as he does now."

"I understand well your difficulty," said Lady Grace. "If we could only live our lives more simply and un-pretendingly than we do, I suppose we could talk with easier hearts about it all. It is a sense of money spent in foolish imitation of what others do—wasted, and worse than wasted, not money spent in true enjoyment—that makes us ashamed of our own lives and unable to defend them. I feel no sting of conscience about money spent in real enjoyment. I believe in the gospel of enjoyment, and I often wish that those of you who speak to the people would more often preach to them of this gospel. I believe almost more in the spread of amusements and pleasant occupations amongst the people than in anything else, and I wish that our charitable impulses and the work we try to do among the people could more often take this form. But in real truth we rich people have ourselves nearly lost the power of enjoyment. We live imitating each other so much, that scarcely anything we do is done truly and purely for its own sake. It is wretched to think of the enormous sums wasted in doing things that we certainly should not do, if it were not for the stupid reason that others are doing them."

"But are there not people who are really magnificent in their tastes and ideas," asked Angus, "whose enjoyment scarcely begins until they have spent a thousand pounds?"

"I must leave them," said Lady Grace, "to settle the matter with their own selves. I am not going to settle it for them. All that I want to do is quietly to influence the people who spend the thousand pounds without getting any real enjoyment from it, to spend the money better, and at the same time with greater happiness to themselves. Just now Maude and I are fighting our little battle on this very point. We are trying to persuade my father to let us have only maidservants in the house as a beginning of simpler things, and to give diminutive dinner parties. And, let me tell you, you are not to have champagne any more, sir. We have discovered a light wine which is quite good enough for you all. Now don't make faces, and I promise you shall have it good."

"What does he say," asked Angus, laughing, "about the maidservants?"

"He says that we are not fashionable enough for

such bold undertakings, and that he will have to sell his family silver and buy electro-plate.   To which Maude replies that if we must have the silver plate she will sleep in the pantry with a revolver.   But I think, in reality, he likes the idea and will consent, and we shall both be infinitely happier.   I want to enjoy life and help others to enjoy life ; and the first necessity for us is not to follow the crowd in ways that one sees to be foolish and unprofitable.   And now tell me a little more what it was in Mr. Markham's way of speaking that you liked," added Lady Grace.

"He spoke to the workmen in such a different way from that in which all of us politicians, with our objects to gain, speak to them.   He seemed to have something that he cared very much to say, and only to be intent upon saying it without any after motives.   The man seemed so simple and made of such good stuff, that he could afford to be real.   I often feel a sense of sickness at the way in which the rest of us speak at our public meetings.   If we have to go to a meeting we spend some miserable hours in walking about our rooms and saying, 'What the devil am I to say?'   Then after feeling for twenty-four hours as if everybody else had already said everything that is to be said, we pick out all the things that are best fitted to flatter and please and get a cheer ; and at the end of it, as the result of saying what we do not really care to say, of just throwing together a certain number of artificial and coloured

things that are no true part of ourselves, we as often as
not leave on the mind of the people a sense that they
are wronged by everybody who is richer than themselves, and that we who speak are amongst the few
generous-minded people belonging to the richer class
who feel their wrongs.   We set a certain number of
passions going, and we leave them with a dim unsatisfied
expectation that a time is coming when some great
act of righteousness will make working classes and
richer classes change places.   I doubt if we are doing
the people much good.   I doubt if the larger part of our
political work is not done in mere selfishness and for
the sake of our own exaltation, without a thought as
to what the mental effects will be on the people."

"I remember," said Lady Grace, "hearing Mr. Peters,
who was one of the great speakers at the time of the
Anti-Corn Laws League, tell my father that he would
have given very much to recall some of the things he
said during that agitation.   He was a very powerful
speaker, and he used to yield to what he described as
the intoxication of hearing the people cheer.   My father
says of him that some of his sentences had an edge like
a knife to them, and that the people would roar like
hungry beasts for their food, when he set himself to
hash up the opinions of some old Protectionist squire,
and generally with the opinions the unfortunate squire
himself.   Last year Mr. Peters was lunching with us,
and he described how at one of their meetings he heard

a Mr. Joshua Attwell speak.   Instead of holding up the Protection party to ridicule and hatred, Mr. Attwell slowly and with great feeling described how dimly as yet the sense of justice had dawned upon any part of the world ; how each class still thought that the justest measure was that which served its own interests best ; and how some day, when a higher sense of justice came to us, no class, whether poor or rich, would force upon others a worse position for the sake of bettering itself. Then he appealed to them not simply to undo an unfair corn law that helped some by burdening others, but to renounce with it that willingness to be unjust towards each other, which still existed in every part and class of the human race.   Mr. Peters had to speak next, and had prepared one of his brilliant speeches, full of bitter points about the landowners and their demand for a public endowment to keep up their rents ; but as he listened to Mr. Attwell's appeal, which made the wrong of the landowners only part of the wider wrong that was in all their own breasts, he said a revulsion of feeling came over him, and he felt as if his own prepared sentences would have choked him.   When he rose to speak he faltered and hesitated, and at last made a clean confession of all that was passing through his mind.   He acknowledged how Mr. Attwell's view was the truer and better one, and how little he himself had helped the people to rise out of their own selves in breaking down a bad law.   He only spoke, he said, for ten minutes, but the people were almost as much moved as he was."

" I like that story of yours," said Angus. " I have at times so much faith in the English people. They are so generous and so noble-minded, and could be led, I think, to such great things, if only those who spoke to them spoke from their soul, without the desire to please and without care for their own political reputations. But tell me more of Mr. Peters. In what way did he speak at the next meetings he attended ? "

" He said it was very difficult to get out of the old manner," replied Lady Grace. " He never let himself be completely intoxicated again, but the old impulses still remained strong within him. He tried to set it as an aim before himself to lessen instead of increasing hatreds, and not to use the vague oratorical expressions which he had so often used before, and which left a sense of general indefinite wrong."

" I am afraid," said Angus, " we do a good deal of harm in politics. In religion, in art, in science, in questions of history, men seem to me to have real convictions, and to wish genuinely to persuade others as to what they believe. But in politics so much the largest part of what we do is only clever adaptation to meet opinions which are not really our own. I don't share Danby's black views. He sees in the world nothing but a devil's pit all round him, and declares that the highest art in politics is to tell lies as if they were moral truths, and, if possible, to tell them so impressively that you cheat yourself. But, whether he is right or wrong, I know that I am persistently haunted by a great sense of unreality. When I hear the Government defending this Egyptian mess, or an Arrears Bill, or a Land Bill, I feel as if I heard voices only, which had no real owners belonging to them. I watch our two great political parties, and wonder how much reality there is beneath the decorous mask that each wears. Is it true that the end and aim of both of them are,—put into plain words,—to please the people, and that to do it they will both pay whatever price is necessary? Is it true, if we go to the heart of the matter, that we are just as little moved by our own eloquence and our appeals to great motives as if we were two armies drawn up in face of each other. We know that both armies will issue their proclamations, with many references to civilisation and to their own good intentions, but this does not alter the fact that it is not civilisation any more than a change in the moon that will decide the question between them. Behind the appeals to civilisation are ranged the guns and the bayonets; and any. and every weapon will be used before they accomplish their destiny of either destroying or of being destroyed. In the same way can I doubt about the leaders of either my own party or the other party, that they are both determined to win, and to do whatever is necessary to win? And as for those of us who make up the mere rank and file, do we not lose all control and direction of our own selves, and even all volition about ourselves, as soon as we are once involved in this mysterious thing, party?"

"I agree with you in distrusting party," said Lady Grace. "I suppose it always happens when people act together in a crowd that they do things which they would not do if acting and thinking for themselves. It is just as true about London society. We are blinded about what we do because everybody else round us is doing it. People use each other, struggle to make and to keep a position, spend any time and trouble and lose any amount of self-respect to be able to swim at the top; but I still hold to the belief that even in the midst of it those who choose can keep themselves clean from these things. After all, each one of us is master of his own self, and the one contribution he can make towards the bettering of things is just to be true to that self. No person is obliged to push, to manœuvre, to like and dislike with the rest of the world; and it must be much the same, is it not, in politics? May not a man determine to be true to his own convictions and not to say one word in which he does not really believe? May he not do this in politics, or must he go with his party?"

"I cannot see how a man can be true to his convictions in politics," said Angus gloomily. "What oppresses me and makes me sometimes hate the life I am leading is the feeling that we cannot be true. We seem to be divided into two sets. One set—and they

are the unhappiest men in the House—know in their
hearts that they are not true to their own convictions,
and they are always labouring to find for themselves
such excuses as they best can. The other set persuade
themselves that they really believe in what they say
and do, and would be shocked if you told them that
their convictions and enthusiasms and party zeal are
only made for them by the circumstances of the moment ;
that it is only an accident on which side and towards
what end their energies are being employed ; and that
they are only editions on a grander scale of the simple
countryman who votes yellow or blue because that is
the colour of his party. Do you know Manley ? He
is an example, though a very favourable example of
these men. He is honest, upright, loyal, ready for any
sacrifice either of himself or of others, but, as everybody
knows and says, as much without self-direction or self-
responsibility as any Highlander who worshipped Charles
Edward. Once enlist his sympathies and his devotion,
and there is nothing which Mr. Gladstone or the Liberal
party could do, which he would not declare and believe
to be right, and in which he would not take his share.
Of course these men are the happiest. They throw
themselves without reserve into their work and give
heart and life to it ; but then one feels that they are the
men whom every priesthood and every superstitious
system has always used for its own purposes, just because
when once enlisted they may be spent as you like, and

will die without a murmur at their post.   But after all, if the truth is to be spoken, are they anything more than four-inch pipes which the pipe-layer—whoever it is— may place in any direction, and which will give their volume of water just as he lays them?   Even Danby, however, can't help liking Manley, and has a kinder word for him than for the rest of us.   It is not often, as you know, that Danby spares any of us."

"I think Mr. Danby has got wrong with the world," said Lady Grace, "and cannot see it quite fairly.   I told him the other day that he was growing like the old Calvinist, who at last persuaded himself that the people had become so bad that even the elect had gone over to the side of the Evil One."

"Yes, it is quite terrible to live with him," said Angus.   "It is like living, as I once had to do, under a great black limestone rock, which never allowed the sun to reach us.   He accepts the whole thing as utterly bad, and just goes on with it as a state of things fixed by unalterable forces.   I cannot do that.   If what we are doing as a party is bad, let us say it out, and try to make an end of it and put something else in its place. Why are we to accept as a necessity that we are to do things in politics which we would not do in any other part of life?   Ought not every one who sees and feels our position to be a false one to declare open war upon it?"

"I think you are right," said Lady Grace, "in attacking a wrong, however large it may be, when you once see clearly that it is a wrong, and feel yourself called on to act. It all seems to me to depend upon that inner voice that is within us and speaks so differently to each of us. I see, like you, the harm that party of every kind is always doing us. I see how narrow, intolerant, and stupid it makes us all; how we are constantly mistaking our motives and thinking we are doing some great thing for its own sake, when the mere excitement of rivalry, when dislike of the other side, and recklessness about the means of getting a triumph over them, have most to do with it. I see the evil, just as I see it in London society, but, like thousands of others involved in a bad system, I do not pretend to see clearly any way of fighting the system itself, or even of escaping from it. All that seems possible to me is to try and keep my own direction right, and not to be swept away by the awfully strong current that is round me. That fills up my humble ambition. If ever I am to be of any help to others, it will be because I have just succeeded myself in walking without slipping, and not because I have joined the party of those who declare open war. _ I have too strong an inner feeling that each person must judge what is right for himself. I don't say that war would not be right. I only say war is not right for me. I leave war and forlorn hopes to you and to Maude, who, with her love of fighting, is eminently fitted for them. I wish for

K

both of you great wisdom in attacking the strong places that are in front of you, and great success in capturing them; but I don't see my own way to make one in your invading army."

"Ah! that is the very point," said Angus, "where so often I feel puzzled. Your part at times seems to me so much better than mine. You enter on no crusade, but you go quietly on your own way, and simply aim at increasing whatever good there is already in existence. If everybody did that, I cannot help feeling how quickly our mistakes would correct themselves. There would be such an intention of good that the world must get better, even if all the brilliant crusades were left out of it. But when any one sets himself to attack a whole system and all those engaged in it, is he not simply doing what the world has always done,—and only too often, when it was spurred by its ambitions or stung by its vanities,—denouncing and upsetting one system to put another in its place, that soon reproduces all the old faults? I feel in common with many others that the whole of our political life is full of moral recklessness, but shall I or they do much good by saying it? Does Danby do good by sweeping us all up in one universal condemnation? Should not both he and I do more by accepting, as you do, all the good that is mixed up in it and trying to increase it?"

"I don't think you ought to distrust yourself," said Lady Grace. "Your work is as much wanted as any

other. Mine, after all, is a very tame protest against
what is wrong. The world wants, and always has wanted,
has it not, that some men who see clearly should speak
out and attack without flinching, even though the system
they attack would seem to pull all things up by their
roots when it falls? We should very soon fall into
the sleep of death if everybody began to make a duty of
accepting things. It is only as the result of vigorous
and unhesitating attacks that the humble and practical
work of the rest of us ever gets into a sufficiently right
direction to do any good at all. You scarcely know
what very humble idols women, and I suppose some
men, would be content to worship all their lives if you
left them undisturbed in their idolatry. If writers like
Dr. Colenso and Mr. Greg and Matthew Arnold had
flinched from speaking out, how much more helpless
and hopeless would be the mental condition of thousands of men and women at the present moment. Were
it not for them we should be spending our lives in trying
miserably to stop holes in walls that were falling to
pieces, and kept falling as we continually patched them.
No! our work is divided. Both kinds of life are good.
It would not be right for me to join you and Maude
in your knight-errant excursions against great systems,
which I am content to let alter themselves, under the
silent influence of what we can each do, as individuals ;
it would not be right for you to sit down under a system
which you feel covers untruths and pretence. Your

own feeling dictates your work and you must follow it."

"But am I fitted," said Angus, "to attack a great system just because I see the hollowness of it?   What have I got to put in its place?   To-day as I came through the streets after I left Danby at Stanhope Gate, and met all the good people flocking to church,—man, woman, and child,—the thought of the unreality in which we are living came upon me with bewildering force. Here is one of these enormous systems, accepted by all sorts and conditions of people, of every class and every mind : churches in every street, machinery everywhere for carrying on the work of the churches—zeal, devotion, money, life-service spent upon them, and yet the whole thing hollow, eaten away in the inside, founded on beliefs which—I am not speaking with the least shadow of intolerance, I got rid of all my intolerance five years ago—"

"No, not five, dear Angus, three," interrupted Lady Grace smiling, and remembering that five years would take him back to his college days.

"Well, three then," said Angus with just a trace of vexation ; but looking up and catching the last ripple of a smile (and nobody could smile like Lady Grace) still lingering round those fine mobile lips—so fine, and yet in their fineness losing nothing of the softness that belonged to their perfect texture of flesh and blood— he recovered his good temper at once and went on.

"You are right to laugh at me.   I will not talk such nonsense again.   Who gets rid of his intolerance as long as he lives ?   Perhaps what I am going to say now is full of intellectual intolerance ; object at once if it is."

"I will, sir," said Lady Grace, with some counterfeit meekness.

"Well," went on Angus, "I watch this great system round me ; and speaking as men must speak to whom the new world seen in the new light is the reality, and the old world seen in the old light is the unreality, I know that it rests on beliefs whose rational and whose historical foundations go to powder as you touch them. I see beliefs no longer living, beliefs palpably, demonstrably untrue—"

"I think I object," said Lady Grace, "but go on."

"Well then, at best, with the half-life of old ghosts left in possession," went on Angus ; "and yet here is the bewildering fact.   I see people on all sides of me, of every habit and form of mind, some of them of the most practised intelligence, successful business men, successful lawyers, men distinguished in science, accepting these things thoroughly and sincerely, and making them into the larger part of their life.   And yet as I see them doing it to-day, I know that thirty years hence they won't do it.   What then does it mean ? That to accept the system that exists around us is a necessity under which we all live ?   That we are so under the influence of surrounding circumstances, so gregarious-minded, so exposed to the contagion of opinion, that in real fact we no more choose our beliefs than we do the card that some conjurer offers us, but we go on believing as others believe, until the predestined day is reached in which some moral dynamite explodes, and then after being scattered, all of us, a hundred feet in the air, we fall back into some new form of belief, not because it is necessarily much truer than the old, but because it happens to emerge out of the new circumstances? Can you say of the men round you, can you say of one man in five hundred, that he really owns his opinions? If he does, what is the meaning of this stupendous fact—a Sunday in London, and hundreds of thousands of persons who may be just as keen-minded and truthful and honest as the rest of us, crowding together to uphold a system of mediæval religion which, with all the true and all the good things that can be pleaded for it, yet in its main outlines could not stand half-a-dozen questions plainly asked and plainly answered in this nineteenth century; that would not outlive an hour's real attack, if a man were determined to cast behind him every prepossession and every attachment that he has rather than palter with what is true? Did you hear Aliston the other night describing how he arrived at a city in South America which had been deserted by its inhabitants? A shock of earthquake had shaken all the buildings, but still left walls and roofs standing. Here and there were great rents and

gaps ; but unless you looked closely you might have
believed that a living, work-a-day town existed round
you.   Yet it all stood, just balanced by its own weight,
and at every minute Aliston expected that some breath
of air or some sound would break the charm and bring
house after house thundering down to the ground. Well,
I had the same sense of impending crash in my head
to-day as I walked through the streams of church-goers,
and asked myself, ' Do we also live surrounded by systems that are only waiting for a breath of wind before
they fall upon us ?   Does some fatal charm bind us and
them together in a mock existence ; and are we simply
paying honour and service to the living dead, just as a
nation caps its emperor up to the very hour in which it
rises up and drives him out of the country. Why is it ?
Why do we believe what we only half believe, what we
have no right to believe, what is only in the air round
us, and is in no true sense a real part of ourselves ? '
Now object, and tell me if I am wrong."

"I can only make old and commonplace objections,"
said Lady Grace.   " Underneath the system lies some
true thing to which we all instinctively cling. You
want people in a moment of candour to throw up their
religious system because you feel vividly and painfully
that its external facts and histories cannot be defended.
But who has yet separated in any great human matter
the reality from the mere changing garment ? Surely
time is working, and has already worked with a hand

sufficiently unsparing to please you. How infinitely small and trivial were the old religious questions, which vexed the hearts of our fathers and mothers in the last generation, compared with those in the midst of which we ourselves are thrown. One smiles to think what baptism and prophecies and faith and works meant to them, when we are asking ourselves with aching hearts, ' Is prayer a reality ? is any relation possible with God ? is it given to men to seize and hold a great purpose anywhere ? does the churchyard end it all ?' Well, have not these great changes come quickly enough, and can you not afford to wait and see what are the great truths that will remain as the new knowledge becomes clearer to us ? Would not the impulse of rushing out of the old habitations at the first alarm, because the wind was blowing and the trees were rocking, lead men as much wrong as the impulse of staying in them till the roof falls on their heads ? I don't ask that any one should forbear striking at any point. Let all strike who see where to strike. But the end of the great discussion is hardly yet ; and I doubt if we yet see clearly how much is to be saved and how much is to be lost. I doubt if any person yet guesses how real may be the foundations of religion when all the special religions have melted out of existence."

"Don't be reactionary, Grace, out of the mere desire to be just," said Angus. "All you say is true, and yet you must see that there is some strange enchantment by virtue of which men live on under systems from which one real honest effort of mental free-will would save them. We talk as if we had free-will, a power to choose between all that lies around us; but have we this power ? Are we not simply owned and acted upon by the systems that happen to exist in our own time ?"

"I think you yourself have partly answered that question," said Lady Grace. "I think you are right when you say that we lean so much upon one another that what is thought and felt by others we also think and feel. We are born into a world very strictly moulded and fashioned after its sort, and then, like the coral creatures of the reef, we devote ourself by a sort of instinct to adding our own little fragment of the same pattern to the mass that our coral relations have built up before us. What better example of our limited freedom can you have than fashion amongst women ? Every sensible woman laughs at it, and then probably goes and obeys it. It suits our dressmakers that fashion should change every year, so that we may not be under any temptation to wear our old dresses, and we all obey as meekly as if our dressmakers were an order of deity for whose benefit and at whose commands we existed. We all accept the system, carry it out, and slightly persecute anybody who disregards it. Why ? Just because it is a system, and because it is so easy to accept, and so difficult to rebel against what others are doing. May it not be just the same in far larger matters? Probably both in politics and religion there is somebody in the position of our dressmakers, and you accept their tyranny as long as it continues to be fairly mild. Of course, as regards trouble and worry on one's own account, the dressmaker is an economical arrangement, but just because it saves us from thinking we occasionally find ourselves led into doing very absurd and stupid things. However, as everybody else round us is doing the same absurd and stupid thing, there are few persons left to find it out or to be much shocked at it. That is the reason, I suppose, why women make it slightly unpleasant to the woman who does not conform, and why men get rid of the man who acts independently of party; and it is the very reason why after my own small fashion I lay such store upon each man and woman leading their own life. Every day I see how quiet but how sure is the influence of any one person persisting in his own way in the midst of a world which goes another way. The one life seems at last to have a power of magnetic disturbance about it, whilst the ten thousand people get a feeling of uneasiness in presence of the speck of difference."

"I can understand that it should be so," said Angus. "Those people who formed themselves into a society for the purpose of wearing no clothes were wise when they made it an absolute condition that there should be no exceptions in the party. They held firmly to the rule that everybody should be equally under

the system, and nobody left outside as an impartial
observer."

"And they were right," said Lady Grace, "if they
wished to feel comfortable.   Now, you must excuse me
for a little, as I have a small piece of secretary's work to
finish for my father.   You may be interested in a letter
which I got yesterday from Mr. Graham, enclosing the
address from Mr. Markham.   Put both in your pocket
and send them back when you have read them.   Please
mark the pamphlet everywhere in your usual fashion,
and write me any explanation or notes that will help
me to understand it."

When Lady Grace was gone Angus read Graham's
letter, which ran as follows : " I think you will like the
small political tract which I enclose.   It is an address
given by Markham, about whom I was speaking to you.
I wish you could know him personally.   He is one of
the few men who sees clearly that all our improved
machinery, on which we are setting such store, is only
increasing our present confusion.   I often laughed as I
read your friend Gladstone's letters last year, sown broad-
cast over the country, appealing to constituencies and
committees for opportunity to patch his creaking old
machine, and to remain in possession as head grinder.
' Only give me a little oil, only burn a few more coals,
only let me get a few new wheels fitted in, and we shall
do so much for you all.   We will grind you out any
number of new measures that you order.   Where we

ground you but one measure in old times we will grind you three in the future, and make you as happy—as a millennium of measures can make you.' I remember Chamberlain in the same vein grew quite piteous last year. They found fault with his principle of a Bankruptcy Bill. 'Is it not time to do something?' he asked in a tone that should have disarmed criticism. Exactly, to do something. It doesn't much matter, so long as it is something, whether it is right or wrong. Only keep the machinery going Think of the loss,—ten per cent. at least,—of letting such a vast capital as we have invested in our machinery remain idle! What does it matter if we don't hit off exactly the right principle? Nobody ever has yet, and our work will be quite as good as theirs. It will last half-a-dozen years or so, and probably look well, till it goes to pieces. Thank heaven! there is no inspection of official work, for the only person to inspect us is ourselves; and a generous public doesn't think much of our failures, as long as we grind on and always give them something new to look at. Only silence the talkers, the doubters, the fault-finders. They are an accursed race, who are meant to baffle the Liberal Government and all other benefactors of mankind in their glorious work. But I did not sit down to write to you about Gladstone and Chamberlain. Our age is given up to the grinders, and they may as well grind for us as anybody else. Some day the world will grow sick of grinding, and discover that legislative sawdust feeds neither body nor mind. Meanwhile I wanted to tell you that Markham will be again in London presently, and I want your permission to introduce him to you. I am sure you will like him. For myself, I cannot tell you how much I have learnt from him. You will find him a well-educated—entirely self-educated—and most thoughtful man. He is now well off, but still often works at his old trade. He travels for a short time generally every year, but when at home works for three days a week in a weaving-shed, sharing the looms he looks after with a partner, who arranges to take his place when he is absent. It is the same mill that he has always worked in, he and his father before him. He is a capitalist in a small way, owns shares in and helps to direct other mills, but will not altogether give up work in the old mill."

Angus read the letter, let the pamphlet lie unopened on his knees, and, sitting by the open window, gave himself up to the luxury of wandering thoughts.

"What sort of a man would Markham really prove to be?" he said to himself. "Was he likely to help him? or would he be just one more of the many who had so often disappointed him; who had, indeed, a view, but a view which possessed them far more than they possessed it? It might well be that Markham's system would have some fragmentary truth in it, fitted to claim the adherence of a small section of ardent disciples, but was it likely to be what he was looking for, a truth embracing all other truths, taking all man's nature and the whole world in its compass, so wide in its scope, so sure in its foundation, that a man might henceforth turn and serve it with all that he possessed? Alas! the confused and perplexed world that he saw round him seemed little likely to yield up truth of such a kind at the bidding of any man. And yet somewhere—nothing should quite destroy that faith in him—there must be a clue which could lead safely through all this horrid confusion." So he sat and wondered, looking into the large horse-chestnut tree that faced the window. It was a splendid tree, great in its girth and its limbs and the burdens of foliage that they carried. As some grand señor would stand proudly before all men, so it stood there before him, its masses of light and shade alternating with each other, battlement of light rising above cavern of shadow,—a proud and beautiful alternation, giving him pleasure, like a pageant, or the story of a great life, or a march of music which changes in its meanings, and calls up happy passions that come and go painlessly, as each yields its place to the other. The tree, he could not doubt, belonged to the old days of a freer and purer air. Before London had been doubled and redoubled, sucking town and village into its huge self, and wrapping its deformities in a cloud of carbonic acid and half-consumed coal, it must have grown to be what he saw it to-day. It was a pleasure to sit and watch its generous outline as the May sunlight was poured over it. It would not live probably much longer as he then saw it. Another generation would only know it in decay. How much it represented ; how many pictures it called up before his mind ; not only because as it died, and its fellows in London died with it, an old bit of the past would be gone, but just simply because of its stateliness and beauty, as one of its own tribe of trees, as one horse-chestnut tree out of the many others in the world. As he sat watching it, the long, mysterious struggle of life, out of which this tree itself, and the race to which it belonged, had come victorious, rose up before his mind. How this very race of trees must have striven in the far-distant and unknown days to gain and keep their place in nature ! How many failures of rivals—other trees that might have been as beautiful as this tree to his eye—could they have survived ; how many skilful adaptations and readaptations' must have taken place before that place was fairly won ! What eye could follow the struggle as it must have gone on with all the numberless winnings and losings in the lost centuries of time ? Why, was there a mark in the chestnut's bulging and heavy-headed leaf or a curve in its erect flower that had not been carved, into what he saw there before him, by the ceaseless action and interaction of all those forces which, like servile gnomes, had been ever busy mingling and separating, destroying and creating, shaping and reshaping, during the life of this world, and it might even be, of world upon world, before this last-born world came into form and existence ?　And what was he himself but what the tree was, the result, only a thousand times more complicated, of the same forces, and yet others added to them, until at last there resulted he—such as he was,—and Lady Grace—such as she was,—and, for matter of that, all that seething multitude of men and women who filled the great wilderness of houses and streets for miles round him,—such as they were,—and who lived and slept and died, with their cares and their hopes, their crimes and their virtues, their something of the animal and their something of the god ?　Was there a thought or a feeling, a system or a belief, a habit or a ceremony amongst them all, that, like the tracings on the chestnut-leaf, had not been formed in its smallest detail by the infinite succession of touchings and retouchings, too many and too delicate to be imagined, which had fallen upon them from that marvellous and eternal surrounding of matter wedded to force,—of which indeed all these things were the creatures, and yet of which, when once called into existence, they themselves became a living and reacting part ?　And as he thought of the never-ceasing conflict between life and life, of the destroying and escaping, of the untiring elements combined and liberated and recombined, of the new forms built up from the dust of the old, of the ever-revolving machinery, of the endless chain beginning where no eye could trace it, and stretching away where

no eye could follow it, his brain turned sick, and thinking itself became a weariness to him, until he broke
into the same complaint that so many others had done
before him. "What can a man do, except merely to
creep through it all as he best may? It is all too
terrible and too large. It is best not to think. Who
dreams that he can alter or shape the great forces as
they carry him along their unknown path?"

CHAPTER V.

It was not long before Lady Grace came back, but they did not again take up the thread of their past conversation. They talked on other subjects till the luncheon-bell rang, and then went downstairs to find that the others had arrived. Lady Maude, however, was lunching out, and Lord Mannaley rarely appeared till near the end of lunch, a biscuit and a glass of sherry contenting his frugal appetite.

" Well, Danby," said Holmshill, when they were all seated at luncheon, "have you been in a better humour with the Government since Gladstone rejected Parnell's overtures for a new Land Bill, and the Government refused to grant exceptional relief in Ireland ? Hartington evidently has been very decided in the matter from the first."

"I always begin to feel uncomfortable when Hartington is very decided in the matter. Hartington has more clear sense than most of us, and seems to know what he wants ; but I suppose he discovers what inconvenient things opinions are in politics. He has lived for many years in an excellent school under the Prime Minister for learning how to do without them."

"I should have thought," said Holmshill, "that you would have found some words of encouragement for the Government just now. You are hard to please. They are at last trying to resist the pressure put upon them."

"They give me a good deal of amusement," said Danby. "They seem to live and enjoy themselves like the Antinomians under a free dispensation of their own. When they are in the humour to be virtuous, then all the rest of the world is to be virtuous; and it is shocking to think that there are any persons anywhere who are not so. When they are not in the humour, who shall suppose that virtue has any obligations for these saints? Hartington, Henry James, Forster, and even Gladstone, in a much more guarded manner, have all seemed anxious to tell us lately that at last poor Ireland wants rest; that more excitement would be bad for her; that she should be saved for a little time from the hands of her doctors, and spared even allusions to her land laws. There is an irrepressible tone of apology in what they say, though, like a dentist who has pulled out the wrong tooth, they all take care to add with effusion, 'It was quite necessary,—you know.' We are now given gently to understand that even Land Acts and Arrears Acts are painful incidents, and, like wild oats, not to be sown often in your career, and then never by dissolute Tories, but only by persons of irreproachable character like ourselves. For the future, therefore, no more adventurous exceptions, only stern economics. We have now all forgotten with one accord, and with that artlessness that specially belongs to us, how great and inspiring was the remedial course on which we had entered ; how generous were the measures which we were passing ; how our office was to heal the injuries of centuries, to make Irishmen love Englishmen, and to prevent the cement falling out of the empire. Yesterday we fell into the arms of the Irish as if we had all been French citizens of '89 ; to-day we stand off with cold and prudent manners, and have suddenly remembered that even in politics we cannot always escape from saying that unpleasant word ' No.' "

"I think Trevelyan has come forward," said Pennell, " in a fearless and ·straightforward manner. He has sternly refused all quarter to Irish heresies."

" Yes. He has shown courage and conscience," answered Danby, " though he owed us something for sacrificing the valuers who represented the first attempt made to work the Act honestly. But lately he has played his part well, and spoken out as honest men speak. I notice that Gladstone discreetly effaces himself on these occasions. To tell people to help themselves and not to climb on to the back of the State is scarcely such a favourable opportunity for eloquence, as uttering ' gracious messages ' to Ireland, with a reduction of twenty-five per cent. of rent in them."

" But still you ought to encourage the Government,"

said Holmshill, " if they are doing right now.   You are like the Tories, who are almost more vexed when our Government does a right thing than when it does a wrong one.   Have you never a word of congratulation for the repentant sinners ? "

" They are singing low now," said Danby, " because times are bad for them. Tides of political feeling seldom run long or deep in this country, and healing the woes of Ireland is a phrase that just now falls flat on the public ear.   But don't you think that when the auspicious moment returns, when we are less sick of Parnell and his leagues, when dynamite is a little less in fashion, when the Guards are off sentry duty at Westminster, when Harcourt no longer composes epistles to 'my dear Shiel,' which the schoolboys of the next generation will not be asked to translate into Latin, don't you think that they will tune up once more in the old fashion ? Chamberlain, like the robin who hides his sweet little head in the cold wind, is mute for the moment, and finds occupation for his progressive soul in protecting the minority of a man's creditors—I thought all minorities were new-fangled inventions, only created by philosophers to trouble the unity of the Liberal party —but the cloud will pass by like all other clouds, and presently he will be in full song again, inviting us to purchase a united empire as long as anything that can be called a landlord continues to furnish the wherewithal, or there are public funds to be devoted to brilliant Irish enterprises. Do you really think that when public opinion goes through its next change, the business of the session won't let Gladstone find time for another amended edition of the Land Act, or that justice and generosity cannot as easily make short work of the large grazing farmer as of the landlord, and defend as well as denounce prairie-rents?"

"Please remember, Mr. Danby," said Lady Grace, "that you are not easy to satisfy. Prime Ministers may come and go, but the one finds as little favour with you as the other. You did not love Dizzy. You don't love Lord Salisbury. You always found as much to say against the Tories in office as you do against the present Ministers; and I feel quite sure, whatever happens, you will not find less to say in the future against Lord Hartington, or whoever is Mr. Gladstone's successor. Are all Prime Ministers worse than the rest of the world? I believe that if the Archangel Michael became head of the Government, you would find some objections to him."

"Perhaps I should," said Danby. "But there is a considerable interval between the Archangel Michael and our present men. I had hoped better and straighter things from Hartington. But when a man once begins to discover 'methods of living,' either between landlords and tenants, or between himself and his own opinions, I look upon him as getting into a very bad way. We shall now probably see Hartington as universal in his employment of this new political formula as Gladstone has been in the employment of that paint-ruddled and street-bedraggled Venus of his that goes by the name of Justice.   I am quite of your opinion, that no leader we are likely to have will get my blessing."

"But whose fault is that?" said Lady Grace.   "Is it impossible to believe in some good intentions?   I think Lord Hartington showed too much public spirit and disinterestedness when Mr. Gladstone returned to office not to make us inclined to trust him.   Here are six of us in the room, and five of us, at all events, cannot persuade ourselves that either this Government or any other Government do not sometimes try to do their duty.   But of course, Mr. Danby, we are all quite wrong and you are quite right; only I don't see as a matter of justice why you spend all your blame upon the leaders and reserve none for the followers."

"Leaders or followers," said Danby, "they are all tarred with the same brush; I have no saving clause for any of them.   You are a sensible young woman, Lady Grace, and if any of us can, you ought to be able to see that from the highest to the lowest we all belong to a system that is rotten through and-through.   If lies can make a thing rotten, you will hardly find a sound patch amongst us on either side of the House.   Hartington is no worse than the rest of us. I have sometimes been weak enough to think him a little better, but of course he shares the common plague-spot with everybody else.   Are you really going to believe in us Liberals because of our stale eloquence and our superfluity of moral discourses ? Do you not see that we are by profession the party of moral pretensions, and that it is upon our moral pretensions that we depend for our daily bread ? It is true that you will find us occasionally in the court of moral bankruptcy; but then, fortunately for us, Chamberlain has forgotten as yet to appoint an official receiver in our line of business, so that we can start again as often as we like, with scarcely a scratch to show for it. Have you never watched the Liberal party engaged in its special occupation of extracting a profit from any motive or emotion that has a plausible look or a virtuous ring belonging to it ? Justice, generosity, sympathy with the weak, equality, progress, liberty, faith in the people, democratic aspirations—these are the wares we sell; and as in our trade you cannot distinguish the forgeries from the genuine article, there is a most prosperous business to be carried on, with both the smallest outlay and the smallest risk for ourselves. If any of you were interested in such dull things as figures, I could easily make you out a list of the profits to be made on our leading commodities. A generous sympathy with the independence of other nations,—that is worth at least three per cent. of the votes of any constituency ; a generous indignation against the oppression of an Irish landlord,—that is, or was, worth from three to five per cent., though rather flat at present ; an active determination that whatever is done for the tenant, no bill shall be sent in to the nation on his account, always remains worth seven per cent. ; a generous view of tenants' improvements, two and a half per cent. ; a generous view of public works, five per cent.—"

"What do you say," asked Pennell, "about Labouchere's proposal to take one-half of all incomes ? "

"Something shaky about the offer" said Danby. "Smells a little of the *People's Banner* office and Mr. Quintus Slide, with a glass of brandy-and-water on the table. You should never make a bid that has a look of setting up in trade about it, like the ferryman in America who sticks up a placard offering five cents a head for all who cross in his boat. It is not artistic. Say a quarter per cent. ; may be worth more, if it ever gets a better brand upon it."

"There is, however, a happy touch about it," said Wolleston. "The abstraction of the fifty per cent. is only to begin after you have satisfied all your real and acquired wants ; and this leaves a very comfortable margin for cigars and champagne, and any other little necessaries of life. I think there is some neatness in handing over the great mammoths to the democracy, and leaving all the rest of us smaller men as comfortable as we were before. Labouchere believes in lightening the sledge if he himself can stay in it."

"Ah ! but will the workman say 'thank you' ?" replied Danby. " I suspect that he will prefer the

French workman's proposal of a progressive income-tax on incomes over £120. That's a good deal more definite and businesslike. There are no hidden traps for him about real and acquired wants, and no margin for champagne and cigars. On second thoughts I withdraw that quarter per cent. It was only a splash in literary waters ; but, come, I will allow you in return ten per cent. for an intelligent perception that force is no remedy and that wholesale bribery is. That was a master-stroke. Then there is a heroic determination to preserve the unity of the British Empire,—that's generally worth two per cent. Is that enough, or do you want some more figures ? I could soon compile a complete guide for a young politician. If he would only study my percentages carefully, I could promise him success in a session. Come, Angus, give up your impossible philosophy and devote yourself to this new and practical branch of political science. I could point you out some excellent investments for feelings and opinions, that would bring you in the best of returns."

" Thank you," said Angus ; " but I should prefer watching Standish or Bastian for the present to setting up on my own account. In my country a young farmer always looks over the hedge to see what his neighbour is doing before he sows his own corn."

" I see you are improving in wickedness," said Danby, nodding his head in approval, " but you should train yourself on the best models, not the second-rate men.

Study the past masters at the top of the tree. And remember, whenever you lay in your stock of moral convictions, that they are not intended to keep long. You must clear out one stock as quickiy as possible to make room for the next. That's the reason why the present Government are always in such a buoyant condition. They never let themselves be encumbered with what is out of fashion. They always have something new on hand, and are never, like the old style of traders, filled up with stale lots. When it suits us to pour our troops into Egypt, we don't encumber ourselves with the Midlothian eloquence on the subject of national independence—that old lot has had its day and has gone as a clearance—or cry 'hands off' to our own fleets and armies. Business is business, and when the hour comes—if it should come—in which it will suit us to leave Egypt, whose little finger will be bound by the old declarations that it was England's task to save Egypt from anarchy and military pretenders? Do you think that anybody will then stop to explain to you why it was our duty to crumple up one military adventurer, and not to trouble ourselves about the next and the next and all who come after? That little lot, like the other, was useful just in its own time, but the dead must bury their dead, and an enterprising Liberal party that, like John Brown's soul, is marching on, must hold itself equally prepared,—according to the circumstances,—to declare that it is their highest duty to let Egypt stew in her own juice, or to establish the

Pax Britannica on the banks of the Nile. If you want progress you must be practical and adapt yourself to circumstances. I do not know if the dukes and the manufacturers have yet settled the question between them about toiling and spinning—I see a French workman remarks that they are both *canaille*, and both live on the sweat of his own much-perspiring brow—but I know that the Liberal party itself has giving up toiling and spinning, and, like the flowers of the field, no longer needs to take thought about the day after to-morrow. Sufficient for the day is the Caucus thereof, as Graham once told them. A happy instinct as regards their own preservation will, under all circumstances, tell our managers what to do when the moment comes. Joe Cowen says we worship the immediate. He is right. That is the religion which Mr. Gladstone, after a life of immeasurable oratory, as immeasurable as Falstaff's sack, has lived to establish and endow. It is true that we don't often like calling the god who presides over us by his own name. Mr. Gladstone has generally a number of grand names for him, as an Eastern people calls the brute, who flogs and flays them, by every high-sounding title in their language. But underneath it all our god is always true to himself—the god of our necessities, our interests, our love of power, our unsatisfied vanities, our self-deceptions about ourselves and our motives. They say there were not five righteous men in the plain. Are there five righteous men at Westminster who speak the truth either to themselves or others ?   Five men, who would even know how to set about speaking it ? Are there five men who could use plain English and tell you that our moral law is made from day to day by our daily wants ?   When Mr. Gladstone wishes for the support of any class in the country, does he hesitate to promise what is necessary to get it ?   What is the unavowed history of two out of every three measures that the Government passes, and of the changes which that delicate instrument, the Government conscience, goes through in the course of a session ? Is not convenience the only inspiring principle that directs all that we do ?   It was convenient in old days to get the support of the middle-class by promising to remove the income-tax ; it is convenient now to rest on the support of the workmen, and to throw aside that old idea, as an inventor does, when he finds one which promises to be more fruitful.   It was convenient in 1880 and in 1881 not to enforce order in Ireland—simply because order was right—without syruping the dose by a reduction of rent ; it was convenient to flaunt the Land Act before popular constituencies, as the true Liberal anodyne for grievances, but convenient since then to drop silently back into Tory methods ; convenient to smooth the way by giving cheerful assurances to the landlords, but convenient afterwards to ignore the fact that landlords cannot get a bidding for their land ; convenient to tolerate the Land League as long as it helped the passing of the Land Act in the House of Commons, but convenient to smash it as soon as it stood in the way of its acceptance in Ireland ; convenient to wear Mr. Parnell like a glove on and off the hand ; to treat him at one moment with civility and deference, but at the next to cut his spurs and claws without hesitation ; convenient to use his party one session, but convenient to let them clamour like unheeded children the next ; convenient to let Bradlaugh shift for himself as long as the mere abstract justice was only on his side, but convenient now that elections are being lost to think of opening a door for him, or at least of going through the form of taking hold of the handle ; convenient to make proclamation of the Queen's authority in South Africa, but convenient to let the Boers put both feet through it ; convenient to-day to publish a convention for the protection of the natives, but convenient to-morrow to explain that it conferred rights, not obligations; convenient to win an election on the "unspeakableness" of the Turk, but convenient to invite him to restore order for us in Egypt ; convenient to appeal to Europe for her sanction, but convenient to act without the remotest reference to it ; convenient to go on a filibustering expedition and pick up a little martial renown, but convenient to say that what those unhappy Tories did in the year ' one ' obliged us to pitch shells into Alexandria ; convenient to make war for *status quo*, but convenient to end by edging France out of

Egypt ; convenient to have a score or two of reasons for making war, but convenient that none of them should be the real one ; convenient to let Arabi have English counsel, but convenient to let Mr. Blunt pay the bill ; convenient to declare that between the English and Irish land questions there is no resemblance, but convenient to satisfy English farmers and to lay the foundation of an English tenant-right ; convenient not to have convenient measures too much discussed, and therefore convenient to reform procedure and establish clôture ; convenient to have a sliding scale of conscience that depends on the votes given, and to agree with Stansfeld and Lawson as soon as they can win divisions ; convenient to do anything and everything that helps the politician to keep his head above the water.   Great is our god, the Convenient One.   Let us all fall down and worship him ; and whoever does not fall down and worship, when he hears the ministerial cornet, flute, harp, sackbut, and psaltery, shall be cast, not into a burning fiery furnace, but out into the cold, amongst the miserable damned, who shiver on the outside of the Liberal party.   However I am glad to say that all of you, including Lady Grace, are good and orthodox worshippers, and you have only to pray your god that he will continue to inspire King Nebuchadnezzar's Government with the special moral convictions that shall suit the occasion.   Without moral convictions nothing is to be done.   If you have not got them, you must invent them, borrow them, steal them, as you can. The more the better. Should fresh complications arise in South Africa, it is greatly to be hoped that King Nebuchadnezzar and his Government will still be in office. I have much faith in their well-practised moral convictions extricating us from our difficulties. Practice in these matters is everything."

"You are just like Lord Salisbury in his attacks on the Government," interrupted Holmshill; "you know quite well, as regards South Africa, how hopeless a campaign after the Boer filibusters would be. You neither of you think that we ought really to entangle ourselves in an affair of the sort, but that does not prevent you both being very virtuous at the expense of the Government."

"It is very good of you calling me virtuous," said Danby, "but you lessen the compliment when you join me with Lord Salisbury. His pretensions in that direction are, I presume, even smaller than my own, and my own are of a very humble description. If Mr. Gladstone and the Liberal party would only make the same frank confession, all my disinterested criticisms would fall to the ground. But what they love to do is to play the saint and live the sinner. They want to enjoy the best of both worlds. They use the same breath for speaking *in Gottes und Teufels Namen.* They want to do what suits them at any particular moment, to please the electors and enjoy office, and yet at the same time to carry on a splendid trade in moral convictions. The income-tax payer, the British workman, the British sailor, the British farmer, the Irish tenant, the Bulgarian patriot, the Greek patriot, the Armenian, the Transvaal Boer, the African native, Jumbo of the Zoo—I forget whether Mr. Gladstone wrote a pamphlet on Jumbo—the oppressed Egyptian, the historic Nile, have all had their turn in supplying opportunities for moral convictions, and moral convictions that instinctively knew on which side to range themselves. Whatever goes with the stream is right; whatever goes against the stream is wrong. There you have in a nutshell our political philosophy. ' Put her head down stream ' is our captain's order for every emergency that arises. I offer to my party as their motto, ' With wind and tide.' Let them inscribe it in solid golden letters over the door of their new temple in Trafalgar Square. Most of the party will believe it is a text taken from one of St. Paul's boating expeditions, and will read it with a religious emotion. It is my best though humble contribution to the cause of progress. I wish I could do more for them, but they are sure to get on if they faithfully observe this sacred principle."

" I think you fire a great deal of unnecessary powder and shot at our leaders," said Wolleston. " As Manley is not here, take it for granted, if you like, that our only principles are winning elections and slipping out of difficulties; but is it the fault of any leader, is it Gladstone's fault, that he is what he is ? Whatever Gladstone is, depend upon it, that we also are in the House ; and what we are in the House, that also the country is. We are each of us causes and products of the other. We are all partners in what you call this trade of moral convictions. It is simply impossible that any of us can be much better than the others."

"I shall ask Mr. Gladstone," said Lady Grace, "the next time that I meet him, whether it is true that he always says, 'Put her head down stream.' I have never yet heard him say it. But please, Mr. Wolleston, not to be so unkind to Mr. Danby. You are taking the very bread out of his mouth. If you could once persuade him that Mr. Gladstone and Lord Salisbury, and every other member of Parliament, had not made some frightful compact about their souls, you would take away his occupation for the rest of the session. Besides, it is such a dry and commonplace way of putting the thing to say we are all as bad as each other. To begin with, I am sure I am not so bad as Mr. Danby—nothing shall persuade me that I am—and then it is much more interesting to a poor woman like myself to believe in these depths of wickedness that he has revealed about you all. The next time I am taken in to dinner by some member of the House, I shall think of the awful secret he is trying to hide from me under his pleasant conversation. It will be almost like a scene out of *Der Freischütz*. And I must pay you all the compliment of saying that you disguise your real selves under a very nice outside. I never should have found out the real truth but for Mr. Danby."

" You need not fear my making a convert of Danby Lady Grace," said Wolleston. " He is about as impressible as a bit of millstone-grit. But what I suppose he means is that we all live, as Bright said the other day about the people who build churches and make campaigns—he did not say in Egypt, but that was in his mind—'in a state ' of vast and unconscious hypocrisy.' I had an uncomfortable feeling, as I read Bright's speech, that his word covered more ground and more people than he intended, as so often happens with him. He sees very clearly, but likes to arrest his own thought at certain favourite points of his own—which, by-the-bye, is what most of us do. But justify yourself, Danby. Here is Lady Grace pleading for the many agreeable men she has been sitting by at dinner, and upon whom you have passed such sweeping sentence. Will you make no exception for Lady Grace's friends ? Please to think of the many interesting and accomplished men there are in the House of Commons, who, if they are politicians, are what they are first, and only politicians afterwards."

" Interesting and accomplished ! " growled Danby in a rage ; " you talk like the proprietor of a girls' school when he is writing a circular. Of course they are interesting and accomplished. A man can be all that, and yet take the price paid for him. Don't you remember the passage in Macaulay about Charles I.'s virtues? I could say the whole page by heart. 'We charge him with having broken his coronation oath, and we are told that he kept his marriage vow. We accuse him of having given up his people to the merciless inflictions of the most hard-headed and hard-hearted of prelates, and the defence is that he took his little son on his knee and kissed him. We censure him for having violated the articles of the Petition of Right, and we are informed that he was accustomed to hear prayers at six o'clock in the morning.' Well, we may say pretty much the same kind of thing about Lady Grace's House of Commons. Including the present company, they are amiable, they are cultivated; they have been to the Mediterranean in their yachts, and shot wild geese on the Nile; they are devoted to the political party that gives them what they want; they have all the social and domestic virtues; they are pleasant enough when you meet them in society, especially pleasant when they sit by Lady Grace at dinner, and quite touching when you see them riding with their little daughters in the park; but I fear none of these virtues stand in the way of their selling themselves and their opinions for that seat at Westminster in which their soul delights. Of course it is more comfortable with you all, or even with Bright, not to see too much—to see only an outlying part of this 'vast and unconscious hypocrisy' in which we all live, but if you don't wish

to walk through the world with closed eyes, it is not a
great discovery to make that there is about as much
reality in us all as there is in the dolls of a marionette
show.   From our great master-doll, Gladstone, down to
little Angus here, we strut and throw our limbs about,
and declaim with souls and bodies that, perhaps in a
sort of a way belong to the electors, but certainly don't
belong to us.   You may not like confessing it, Lady
Grace, with your amiable views of society, and those of
us who live by it may not like confessing it, but the
plain truth is, that we and our opinions are as much an
affair of the market as the cakes and dried fruit on
your luncheon-table.   Of course there are a hundred
ways of doing the thing decently.   Of course it is a
pleasant social convention to suppose that all the cultivated members of Parliament you meet are men of
free and independent souls, who do not hire out their
own feelings and opinions like hack-carriages.   Why
should I disturb any of your comfortable prejudices on
the subject ?   You heard that travelling fellow's story
the other night.   He came to a village amongst the
hills where everybody had goitre, but it was the common
understanding that everybody should affect not to know
it.   Let us do the same by all means.   Why should
any of us five acknowledge to you, whilst we discuss the
social problems of the day and show a profound interest
in their moral bearings, that we have all sold our freedom to think as we will.   I could count on my fingers,

and have some fingers to spare, the number of men in the House who have ever given free play to their own minds, who have anything that you can really call convictions, or would hold to them if that particular tide of public feeling, with which they generally move, were once fairly set in opposition to them. From the best to the worst of us we are only corks on the water, waiting for the next ebb and flow ; we are only shadows of that shadowy thing that we call public opinion. Everybody says the American representatives are corrupt; they are not one whit more corrupt than we are. ·The price in each country may be different. They generally want money ; we want success in the game, either position in the party, or influence in the country,—something to add to our feeling of self-importance. We are of the same virtuous fibre as the lady who could not, like the others, be bought for gold, but could for diamonds. How I wish to Heaven that a fit of delirious candour would one day send the party sufficiently out of its mind to make them all walk down to Westminster in a row, each penitential sandwich-man carrying a placard ' for public hire,' like that honest young woman, who went to the ball with ' for £5,000 a year' pinned on her dress ! If we could only be stung by some virtuous gad-fly, so as to be inspired to speak the truth about ourselves for just five minutes ;—think what a lovely vision it would be,—the soul of the Liberal party draped only in truth, seen once

for those few fleeting moments, and then no more for
ever!   Alas! unfortunately the Liberal party is a prude
jade, and is not to be coaxed out of the multitude of her
garments. Still all the same, I place myself, as you
know I always do, unreservedly at the disposal of my
party. Should it ever please Heaven to touch their
minds and lead them to accept me as their spokesman,
I could draw up an election address that would state
the case for them with beautiful simplicity. 'Dear
Fellow-Countrymen, —We hereby place ourselves at
your disposal. We pledge ourselves to see with your
eyes and speak with your lips. What you praise, that
we will praise also, and what you condemn, that we will
condemn also. Should it happen on any occasion that
you do not quite know your own minds, we will wait
patiently until you do, and shall then be proud to think
in agreement with you. In return we would only ask
you to remember that we can both be useful to each
other. On your side there are many little services
which it will be in our power so happily and pleasantly to
perform for you ; and on our side you can so easily and
simply gratify our one innocent ambition of possessing
a seat in Parliament. We only ask for that, and are
willing to do much in return. Are we to be reproached
because we take a little humble pleasure in ourselves,
and our speeches, and our party divisions, and our
beautiful sentiments, and our patriotic work of educating and improving and protecting you ? Oh ! my

friends, let us be a little more intelligent in our perceptions and generous in our emotions! We both have our wants. Shall we not believe in, shall we not practise the Christian precept, and do good to one another?' Don't you think such a frank interchange of views would be more to the point than the maundering stuff of which election addresses are usually made up? Perhaps the party would renew some of its rather faded plumage, and come back from the country with restored youth and vigour. But Lady Grace need have no misgivings. None of her pleasant and cultivated friends will take my advice. They will all declare positively that whoever else has goitre, they have not got it. Here is Angus, who thinks that Bastian and Standish may possibly have it, but is quite sure he has not got it himself."

"He is so extreme," exclaimed Angus, "that he never helps one. Say what you like about those of us who sit in the House,—and perhaps we are corrupt enough,—but what do you say about that great body of men whom you find in every constituency ready to work hard for their party, and to make sacrifices for it, with little, if anything, to gain for themselves; if they are bribed, who bribes them, and what do they get?"

"I admit," said Danby, "that there are everywhere, probably in every town in England, simple-minded men who just do their share of work without asking for wages—who don't want to be on committees, who don't want to move resolutions, who don't want to be known as having a finger in the pie, who don't dream about the day when a little daring ambition may lead them to higher places.   With but a feeble light of their own, and the need of worshipping strong upon them, they simply fall down before the first god whom they find set up in front of them, and give their confidence unreservedly to those who have learnt the way of asking for it.   These are the men for whom I could feel real pity. In the midst of the general scramble there is something pathetic about them.   If you wish to swell the good side of the account, I will make you a free present of scores of such men.   I am dealing only with those who reap the power, influence, or position, the men to whom politics mean the things they want ; whether it is the young Whig who is too well brought up to be on the turf, and wants some safer and more intellectual form of excitement ; or the society man, who finds society more enjoyable with a seat in the House attached to it ; or the successful business man, who, having made his money, wishes to return to his old neighbours clad in the new honours; or the philanthropist who indulges in his philanthropy at the expense of the nation, and gets all the incense that comes to him for nothing ; or the trading orator who lives upon the passions that are easiest to excite, as flies live on the refuse of the streets ; or the adventurer, who floats in all waters by the law of his own specific gravity ; or the minister, to whom the admiration of a nation has become as the breath of his own life ; or the sucking official, who lives in the happy sunshine of his official pay and his growing importance ; and all those smaller tribes behind him who have the same wants in their own still smaller fashion ;—it is about the salaried knaves alone, whatever their salary is —position, influence, daily bread, or mere gambling excitement—that I have anything to say."

"And are we to leave no room for any better or nobler feelings by the side of these personal ambitions, Mr. Danby ?" asked Lady Grace. " Do you not sometimes see noir, as a Frenchman in a fit sees rouge, and rushes on his neighbour with a knife ? To you, as to Schopenhauer, the world seems wrapped in one great envelope of evil. But then how much of it is the reflection of your own two brains ? Remember that each man makes his picture as well as sees it. Take office, Mr. Danby, and then tell us if the work done in a day that fills sixteen hours out of the twenty-four is all done for selfish purposes."

" The knaves get interested in their work, just as I do in trying salmon-flies, and then they work hard," said Danby. " There is sharp competition amongst them. Each is close at the heels of the other and makes him gallop. But see with your own eyes and not with mine, Lady Grace. Look at the world in which you yourself move, and which you yourself know. Is that clear as crystal and pure as snow? Or is it true what those who live in it say? Is it true that everywhere and every day you may see the meanness, the pushing, the jostling of each other, the pride on the part of the few who hold the inner circle, the abject efforts on the part of those who wish to be inside? Is it true that a trade goes on night by night in your London drawing-rooms almost as admirable as our trade at Westminster—a trade in which you women are as ready as we are to throw honour and self-respect at the feet of the great prizes which are to be won—a trade of which the daintiness on the outside can hardly disguise the ugly facts that are within? Do you not think that, if Dante were alive with us to-day, he could paint a picture of what you women are in your modern London life,—a picture, not so dark perhaps in its shadows, but as terrible in its inner meanings, as any picture of the old world? Come, Lady Grace, be frank with us. Do you think, when women live to sell their daughters openly for the best price going, that men, with their stronger ambitions and fiercer passions, are likely to be pure and scrupulous in their struggle to seize and to hold what they want? Do you choose to think so, because you see us given up to serious occupations, turning over the pages of blue-books, studying social questions, and filling our speeches with the moral sentiments that the world likes to listen to? If you think so, it is because you like to be cheated, as those men also like to be cheated, who think that a fair, tender, and religious woman cannot tread other women under foot in her effort to win the best social place for herself and those who belong to her."

"Nothing you can say shall sting me into defending London society," said Lady Grace, getting roused. "But I say here, as in the case of your own political life, that you see all that is bad, and nothing of that which mitigates and half redeems the bad. Granted that mothers plunge into a very unworthy struggle on behalf of their daughters, and degrade themselves and all who are concerned in doing it, yet to many of these women, such as they are, that struggle represents the best side of their nature. In your own words, they are worshipping the god that they find set up before them, and that worship of theirs, miserable as it is, often represents an unselfishness and affection that are quite unknown,—at least in practice,—to those who look on and moralise. You don't know—how should you ?—all the devotion that is mixed up with what is bad in the system. There are jealousy, intrigue, and meanness, it is true, but the great mass of women believe that they are discharging a duty, and have never even supposed that there can be a question about it. It is this belief which makes us all not half so bad in reality as you believe us to be. You have never yet learnt that men and women may not be wholly infamous—may do many good and unselfish things—though they live under bad systems; and just as you misjudge us, so also it may be that you misjudge your own political world and the men who sit on the same benches with yourself."

"Yes," said Danby, " perhaps it is all right both in your ball-rooms and in our House of Commons. Perhaps in this excellent world telling lies is a special implement devised by Providence for our good. Perhaps the final purpose of provident mothers is to sell their daughters to those who can give the best price, and of intelligent politicians to talk about justice and generosity, sympathy with the weak, and devotion to the people, with such persuasive eloquence that they shall keep themselves in office and other people out. I don't profess to know, Lady Grace. I didn't make or help to make the world, so that I don't presume to offer an opinion. I only wish to *prendre acte*, as the diplomatists say, of the fact that telling lies forms the substantial basis both of your world of fashion and of our world of politics."

" Upon my word I think Lady Grace is right in protesting against these universal condemnations," said Pennell. "If you are right, we ought all of us to be quarrying stone at Portland instead of lunching here. I am not a great admirer of your party, but I could find better things to say of them than you do. You have always had some men who will not let party drag them to all lengths."

" I shall be delighted," said Danby, "to except the five righteous men of Westminster if only I can be more successful than Abraham in finding them. Fawcett has been swallowed by the Government whale, and I fear that gallant and sturdy independence of his has only gone to make another official. Peter Taylor and Joe Cowen are amongst the few who do not always shiver in front of their constituents, or make galvanic movements by way of protest to the public that they lead those who prick them on. Lawson goes straight, but I should like to see him do a really unpopular thing, — something outside his own rôle, of water and peace. Bright speaks more truth to the world than all his old friends put together, but the dose wants strengthening. The Liberal party is in that state of health just now that it requires the drenches that a veterinary surgeon gives to a sick cow, instead of the delicate globules and tinctures of homœopathy. Then there's Goschen serves his conscience; Forster has glimmerings that you must choose between being a man or a politician; George Campbell seems occasionally inclined to resist pressure; John Walter, I believe, stood to his guns on the Eastern question down in Berkshire in 1880. There used to be stuff in Dilke, and Courtney, and Trevelyan before they took office. But as soon as a man has taken that devil's shilling, neither you nor he nor anybody else knows anything more about him, as to what he'll be or won't be. Well, I dare say there are some more who help to keep Sodom and Gomorrah going, but looking for them is like looking for needles in a stack of hay. And all the others who make up the party? What of them? You yourself know more about the Whigs than I do. I remember you once did them full justice with Hartington as their king. They will doubtless continue to beg their bread as successfully in the future as they have done in the past. I think you told us that sweeping the streets would be a better occupation for them, but I leave it to you to decide, as an authority in the matter. Then there is the ruck and the mass of the party ; well, they are the ruck and the mass, and that says almost enough about them. We have all heard them tell us in a loud whisper, ' My dear fellow, my people won't let me ; my dear fellow, my people are excited about it. I shall have to vote for the Bill.' They are little more than catchword men. Their principal office is to take up the party phrases that somebody makes and to distribute them over the country. An enterprising member of a large telegraph agency told me earlier in the session that he could wire a summary of the speeches of two hundred and fourteen of the Liberal party before they spoke; and offered to do it for the speech of any member that I might choose to name out of the lot. They all recognised the paramount duty of England to prevent anarchy on the banks of the Nile (twenty-seven or twenty-eight per cent. of them, however, at that time regretted the necessity) ; they were all equally determined to pursue the noble task of doing justice to Ireland with one hand,

and with the other of grinding to powder the gang of hired assassins (my enterprising telegraphist is obliged to be a little careful just now, as, I am grieved to say, that since Gladstone kicked out Parnell's Bill, we are growing a little hotter against the assassins and a little cooler in our love of justice); and they all demanded that the scandal of obstruction, from whatever quarter it came, should cease, and no further delay should stand in the way of those legislative blessings which an earnest Liberal Government, inspired only by the purest love of its fellow-creatures, is straining. every nerve to provide for an expectant nation. I need not say any more about the two hundred and fourteen. Each session has its own mould—the warlike, the peaceful, the educational, the extravagant, the economical, the teetotal —and the mass of the party never fails to fit the mould. They are not usually a very distinguished, but they are a long-lived set of men. There is an invincible instinct of life about them. They are almost as careful in the matter of their own persons, as those soldiers of Napoleon, who wrung from him the exclamation, 'Do the scoundrels wish to live for ever?' when he saw them bolting in all directions. And our heroes have the same little weakness for wishing to live and vote for ever. Next to them come the half-minded Radicals, who are very anxious to get on in life, but are always being balked for some five minutes by an inconvenient scruple. They haven't nerve either to stand to their

book nor yet to hedge effectually.   I am afraid that
they will succeed neither in this world nor in the next.
Five minutes of conscience is more than enough to lose the
race in politics, but I suppose hardly enough to square
accounts with the Higher Powers.   So they are always
starting, and stopping and starting again, with a general
look of unsuccessful toil about them.   If they were open to
advice, I should recommend them to get rid once for all
of such conscience as they have, which is a mere encum-
brance to them, like a hussar's hanging jacket, and then
start fair with the others.   Lady Grace's friend, the
Spectator, if I may venture——"

"Please venture, Mr. Danby," said Lady Grace.   "I
consign it and everybody else to you.   My father used
to say that it took more than a hundredweight of lead
to kill every soldier, so I have hopes that some of my
own friends may still survive."

"There is no reason for anxiety," said Danby, "a ton
would not destroy the modern politician.   He is as
bullet-proof as a rhinoceros or a crocodile.   How can
you hurt a man who got rid of his soul when he was
dipped into the Styx of politics, heels and all ?   He
believes in the divine right of his party to fatten on
their fellow-men, and there is no point about him,
morally or intellectually, inside or out, that can even be
scratched. But you are right to love the *Spectator*, Lady
Grace.   I have no doubt it sometimes offers you a
refuge on Sunday mornings, when Angus gets a little

prosy over the troubles of his soul.   But could you not persuade your friend to accept the logic of the situation, and be a little bolder either in its vices or its moralities ? At present it is too much like the parson who would go hunting in his Sunday's frock-coat, and was left in the bullfinch owing to the quantity of broadcloth in that valuable garment.   Why should it moan helplessly after every Radical who takes too great a stride for its own shorter legs ?   It asked quite plaintively the other day, when some adventurous young politician, like Labouchere, threw overboard a gilt spoon for anything that could be caught on a summer day's sailing, ' Are we not as good democrats as he, though we do not make these wicked proposals ? '   A little more courage in sinning would add much to its own peace of mind in this hot weather."

"The *Spectator* is only like a host of others," said Pennell.   "It has loved not wisely, but too well.   It is one of the many Marguerites that Faust has beguiled. Its injured ghost will knock some night amongst the other ghosts at sweet William's door, as they all do in the ballad, and ask, ' What have you done with that conscience and intelligence with which I so fondly trusted you ? ' "

"I am sorry enough for all political Marguerites," said Danby. "But if those who have brains as disorderly as Lady Grace's work-basket was the other morning when the kittens had taken up their night's lodging in it, and emotions that go off, like Birmingham cheap guns, at all wrong times and in all wrong places, will follow those whose brains and emotions are in the same condition, there is every chance of bedraggled drapery. A little Socialism to-day, a little political economy to-morrow ; fragments of science and specks of Rationalism compounded with masses of interminable theology ; gorgeous dreams that come no whence and go no whither ; idols worshipped in the morning, and used for household consumption in the evening ; a magnificent scheme for the reconstruction of society, followed by a protest against stealing from the richer classes ; a pennyworth of liberty and then five pounds' worth of paternal government ; a brilliant scheme for annexing a continent, tempered by a sermon in favour of peace ; miraculous bolts launched out of blue skies——"

"That will do," said Pennell. "You are like the friend of an omnivorous gourmand who tried to effect his cure by throwing into a pail beside him a part of every dish from which he had helped himself, and then showing him the mixture afterwards. But it was not a nice process ; and I'll undertake to say you won't cure the *Spectator* or any other would-be eclectic Radical by it."

"Danby would be wretched," said Holmshill, "if he thought there was the least chance of curing the *Spectator*, or anybody else. The world will be a very dull place for him when we all get a little nearer perfection. He would cut his throat long before it came about. But I think you all magnify the crimes of the *Spectator*.

Its little weakness is that, like a good child, it finds goodness rather dull, and likes the occasional relief of playing at being naughty."

" Arrange it as you like," said Danby, " I don't care. It chiefly concerns Lady Grace and some aspiring country parsons. What amuses me is to watch the great race of the lame, and that is not likely to come to an end just yet. The Radical apes the Socialist, the half-hearted Radical apes the Radical, the Whig the half-hearted Radical, and so on *ad infinitum.* Each toils after some one who is in front of him, in whose company he dares not travel, but by whom he is afraid of being left behind. Not one man out of the whole set is content to be his own self, and for better or worse to stand by his own opinions, but, like Lady Grace's friends of the fashionable world, all live in daily terror of losing their place. So the short-legged man toils after the long-legged man, and throws away enough conscience and self-respect,—not to catch him, for the other understands the art of throwing away better than he does—but just enough to keep him in sight."

" Please keep a little breath for the Radicals," said Pennell, " if, indeed, there are any Radicals left nowadays. Most of your men at present are so afraid of being caught and whipped on the spot by Gladstone, that whenever they do anything naughty they say in the next breath, ' Please, sir, I did not mean it.' "

" I have not much to say about our modern Radicals,"

replied Danby. "They are not a very striking or suggestive study. I can only piously wish on their behalf, as I do also in the case of their imitators, that some day Heaven in its pity may be pleased to arrange their ideas for them and teach them what they want. An old Radical, if he had not the largest mental horizon in the world, yet kept his ideas in an orderly condition ; he knew what he was looking for, and asked plainly and straightly for it. But his feckless descendants of the present day go wandering about in the happy-go-lucky fashion of bone-and-ragmen who pick up anything that lies in their way and may possibly turn into a prize. They have accepted Mr. Gladstone's happy idea that to live open-mouthed and catch flies, voting everything for everybody,—provided he is not a land-owner,—is popular government, and then to let the everything and the everybody settle it between themselves as best they can. That settlement is no affair of theirs. With them, sufficient for the day is the voting thereof. They are generally to be found in a state of feeble protest against something, and feeble demand for some other thing ; but it makes them the smallest difference in the world whether they get what they want or what they don't want. All that they have to do is, like flies in winter, just to keep moving enough to show that they are still alive. Some enterprising person may happen to propose a little more education or a little less payment for it, or some new sanitary arrangement and some new health officers, or another Factory Act and some new inspectors, or a bath, or a washhouse, or a picture-gallery, or a bit of land for the people, or a lodging-house, or a little less rent for the tenant, or a Government clause in the contract, or a new minister and a new department, or failing all things else, a catalogue of new penalties for some newly invented crime, and then they can at once make a speech about it, and work up all the old phrases again, and vote for it; but if nobody proposes anything, it clearly is not their fault that they were dumb dogs that did not bark. With their faded personalities they grow very like the Cavaliere Giacosa, 'out of whom the soul had leaked away.' They neither inspire me, nor amuse me, nor terrify me. It is such a fall in life to leave off upsetting thrones and live by filching from landlords. But perhaps we ought to be a little charitable about the present generation. It has been their fate to live under a dispensation of universal sloppiness in talk and thought. Many years of Gladstone, the penny emotional, and the chapels combined don't harden the mental fibre. Definite views, the deliberate attempt to foresee the future, and consistency in action, are things of which no man at present dreams in politics. The Radical of our day may be a worshipper of the powers that be, or he may be in half-hearted opposition, or he may be one of the party-manipulators with views about organization ; but there is nothing to grasp or to hold in the man's self or in his opinions. There is no hard pan anywhere in the semi-fluidity. Such force as he has is not in himself, but in the facts outside him.   He does not try to form or direct or even understand these facts, but simply places himself at their service. I do not know if the facts are great and admirable,—they are beyond my philosophy,—but I can see that the men are small. Goldwin Smith says you must not take Labouchere very seriously, and I say the same of Bastian. In spite of all their heroic efforts to drive a team, they are born to be gigmen, and gigmen they will remain till the end of their days. How can you be anything else but a gigman, when you have not got convictions; and convictions are the one thing in modern politics which these men have not got, do not know how to get, and do not desire to get! The modern politician is so unreal a person that you will probably see him collapse altogether, whenever the great forces are in motion. Unreality is at the heart and core of all he says or even thinks. I suppose it has partly come from the abject haste with which, not being democrats at heart, we have all, from Gladstone to Angus, hastened to worship and conciliate and serve the new-democracy. How can you be more than an imitation-democrat, you, who have merely followed the political fashions of the day all your life? Anyway, I declare that I positively look forward with pleasure to the day when Lewin's Socialists will increase in numbers and power. It will be refreshing to escape, even by their help, from this atmosphere of perfumed lying. The real Socialists—I don't mean any of the half-breeds, the Tory democrats, or the Gladstonites, or the Christian *sans-culottes*, or whatever they call themselves—have convictions, even if they are of the 'blood and iron' kind. I should feel it a true pleasure to be shot by a genuine Socialist,—or to shoot him, as the matter might turn out,—if only in return we might be quit of the modern politician, who smirks and bows like the draper's assistant, while he cheats us out of an inch in every yard. Only may it please the Lord to shorten the time and deliver us from this universal sloppiness. If 'justice as our guide,' generosity, and 'gracious messages' may be consigned once for all to the rhetorical dusthole, I shall breathe freely again, and feel grateful to the men who say in a straightforward dialect, ' You are the few, we are the many ; we have the force, and we intend to have the enjoyment. Do you keep, if you can ; and we will take, if we can.'"

" Why on earth don't you become a Tory, Danby, as there is nothing to satisfy you on our side," said Holms-hill?   " It is time he should, is it not, Lady Grace ? He is getting more foul-mouthed every day, and he'll die some day, like a toad in its hole, of his own venom."

"I think you'll be more at home with us than where you are now," said Pennell.   " We rather cultivate and like a little open disreputability on our side."

" If I wanted to become a Tory," answered Danby,

" I should remain where I am.   Our men are rapidly becoming Tories—not your modern ones, with the stuff left out, but good old Tories, slow to hear and swift to smite, who hate discussion, who think their way the only way in the world, and are ready to apply very summary methods when other men think differently from themselves.   There is no occasion, as far as I can see, for any Liberal to take the trouble to change sides. He can do better, if he likes that sort of thing, by remaining where he is.   But even if your men, Pennell, were better Tories than we are becoming, I would as soon take my berth in one of Plimsoll's coffins as join myself to what by courtesy we call your party.   It is a matter of mere conjecture, from one session to another, whether either you or the French Legitimists will be in existence or not.   You are only walking about, like other economical people of whom we have heard, ' to save your funeral expenses.'   And why should you continue to exist ?   What good are you to yourselves or to anybody else ?   You are the last, the hopelessly last, in the race of the lame.   There is no man living who could handicap you so as to give you a chance of getting a place.   The Radicals, the would-be Radicals, and the Whigs are all anywhere in front of you.   If some chance wave throws you to the top for a moment, the next wave washes you out of sight again.   I can see no claim or right that you have to live.   You are both stupid and cunning at the same time ; you have no

patriotism inside your selfish hides, much and loud as
you boast of it.   You would join with the Irish party
to-morrow, if you felt quite sure you could beat the
Government ; you would trip Gladstone up for carrying
out your own policy, if you could be said to have one,
in Ireland or anywhere else.   You have no opinions.
You not only surrender your old positions, but you
betray them ; you are always waiting to play again the
old tricks you played about Catholic emancipation and
the corn-laws and reform.   Just as you opposed compulsory education and then yourselves brought in a
Bill to extend it, just as you denounced the trades'
unions and then did their legislation for them, so you
are ready to-morrow to take up any measure that doesn't
belong to you, from giving household suffrage to the
counties down to making English farmers part-owners
of their farms, if by doing it you can steal a ten-minutes'
march upon your rivals.   Trickery has eaten into your
very heart and marrow.   All things are the same to
you.   Any bedfellow is good enough company for you
in your present low estate.   You are ready to lie down
with fair-traders, free-traders, protectionists, or whomsoever else the night's lodging offers you as companion.
You are ready to be on anybody's side for any cause in
any quarter of the world—on Arabi's side or against
him, on the side of the African tribes or against them,
on the side of France or the side of Germany, on the
side of annexation or the side of independence, just as

you seem to have the best opportunity of taking your opponent at a disadvantage, and getting what ?—five minutes of office ! But it all does you no good. Your changes and shifts and " sharp curves " only leave you farther behind when all is done. You are scarcely thanked by the people, even after you have thrown away the last shred of self-respect in trying to serve them. You lie down in the road and ask them to walk over you, but you get less gratitude than your cleverer rival, who only takes off his cloak for the purpose. The people know well enough why you serve them, and what is more to the point, they know that there are others who will serve them better. What is the good of giving in handfuls when others are ready to give in cartloads ? You dream that a Tory democracy can keep its head above water. So it might possibly have done, if the Manchester school of free-traders would have obliged you by remaining for ever in existence, and if Socialism had not become the largest fact in the world, and altered all other values. What is the profit, at this time of day, of Salisbury's gentle insinuations that the Workmen's Dwellings Act is the principle of Tory Government, and the unexpressed promise that more of such principles will come into existence, when he returns to power ? Or that fair-trade is an open question to all parties having the advantage of the empire at heart, when men like Lewin are ready to tell the workmen plainly that their skill and their industry have made every valuable thing they see around them, and that they are the true heirs of what they made ; whilst Bastian's tribe is in waiting to take up the burden of the new song, as soon as the workmen's votes get sufficiently consolidated to make it safe to do so ? If Socialism, like Pharaoh's lean kine, were not swallowing up all other political parties, why there might be a place for you ; but as it is, the world is settling all its questions, as if you did not exist. At your best and bravest, you are only a feeble adumbration of the Radical, as the Radical in his turn is of the Socialist. What chance is there for you ? Even Bismarck's hand cannot make a Tory democracy keep its head above water. The water flows in faster than he pushes it away. And then what you do, you do clumsily, and with half a heart. Why, Gladstone's manner of giving makes a shilling go farther than Salisbury's pound. When Salisbury tells the farmers that legislation will bring them no appreciable blessing, but he thinks it may restore courage to their hearts, they only growl under their breath, 'He wouldn't give it if he could help it.' You are but copyists and clumsy copyists. You don't see that sloppy legislation must be served with the sloppy sauce ; that when you take from one man to give to another, your gift loses all its gilding if you do not know how to tell him with convincing eloquence that eternal justice demands the transfer."

"But what on earth would you have us do ?" said

Pennell. "Are we to rally round a white flag, whilst the world laughs and goes on ?"

"You are not worthy of a white flag," said Danby. "I wronged the Legitimists by comparing them to you. Your flag should be a rainbow flag, dipped once a year in all the colours that exist."

"Well, but what do you want us to do ?" persisted Pennell.

"Do !" said Danby ; "do the one thing which you have made impossible to yourselves. Believe in your own opinions, instead of for ever retreating from them and disowning them ; throw your trash overboard— every party has its own heirlooms of trash—then stand firmly on what you really believe. The world will perhaps listen to you, and respect you when you begin to respect yourselves ; and if the world won't listen to you and won't have anything to do with you, you can at all events die with the dignity of the untamed red man who sees the palefaces taking his place. It is better to die with your spear in your hand and your war-paint on, and fighting for something you believe in, than to become the camp-followers of the stronger race, and die slowly of his and your vices compounded together. As it is, you are a pitiable object for gods and men. You are ready to sell your mother's last garment in order to live another day, and yet your sacrifices of decency profit you nothing. You keep yourselves in existence from year to year by a series of petty pilferings from your rivals which you think very clever and the rest of the world thinks very mean ; you live like a vagrant in a succession of states of bluster and apology about yourselves ; and the only result of all your tricks and your disguises and the false uniform you are always putting on will be that, instead of being shot in fair fight, you will live to be hung by the provost-marshal when the day comes in which at last he lays his hands upon you."

"Well, Mr. Danby," said Lady Grace, "so be it. Every party is equally sunk in infamy, and we shall now look to you to hold up the torch of honour and good faith in the midst of our universal darkness. Please remember how much we are all depending on you, and take great care that your torch doesn't go out."

" Forgive me, Lady Grace, I am no guide for others ; I am only playing the part of an 'approver.' I am just as corrupt as everybody else, and the only difference between us is that I am at no pains to hide it. I know of no lie I have not told, of no mean and villainous thing that I have not done. When I wanted a seat in Parliament, I bought just as many men at £1 a head as were wanted to get me my seat, neither more nor less. If I wanted a man I bought him ; if I did not, I was virtuous, as all the world is virtuous, and left him alone. Some of your friends, Lady Grace, would be very much shocked by such exact details. They satisfy their conscience by not knowing too much of what is done. I knew everything. I picked out the most trustworthy and efficient man I could find ; I gave him precise instructions where I thought I knew better than he did, and left him with full liberty of action where I thought he would judge best for himself. There is my confession : and now do you call me worse than the others ? Am I worse than the men who are careful to keep just within the law, whatever the law is, and who lift up their hands in pious horror if any ugly word like bribery is mentioned ? Am I worse than the men who don't pay in coin but pay by blank cheque, promising whatever is wanted, and drawing for the amount upon what by no intelligible theory can belong to them—the land or the property of others ? Am I worse than Gladstone, who tried to buy the middle-class by promises of doing away with the income-tax, who tried to buy the Irish tenant, who will try to buy the English farmer this year, and the labourer next year, and who gave and will give, as I did, neither more nor less, but just what is wanted ? Of course the world has one verdict for him and another for me. The lords of wholesale business enjoy privileges which are not conceded to their humbler imitators in the retail trade. It is shocking for me to buy an individual, and quite right for Mr. Gladstone to buy half a nation, who, unless he buys them, are likely to transfer their votes to the other side. Perhaps also you are amongst those who prefer Mr. Gladstone's eloquence in such matters to my own unvarnished story. It is a matter of taste. We may agree to differ; you like your vices white-washed and painted, I like mine in their natural state. But I have done worse things than merely buying votes. It suits our modern sickly conscience to suppose that a workman who votes for £1 placed in his hand is worse than the workman who fills himself to bursting with Bastian's windy pledges, who refuses my pound in gold to take a hundred in Labouchere's paper currency, who is promised so much education for nothing or such a share of the land, with museums, libraries, baths, washhouses, dwelling-houses, and all that sort of thing, *quantum suff.*, as the doctors say of water in their prescriptions. All this in your party jargon you are pleased to call social legislation, and of all this it is quite moral for the workman to take as much as he can get, without asking any questions as to who pays for it, or who has the right to give it him; and it is not only honest for him to take it, but there is so much merit and intelligence in the mere act of taking it, that he becomes in consequence an earnest Liberal, a model citizen, and a friend of progress; whilst the man who took my pound is a pariah, to be hunted down by your Acts of Parliament, and driven out as unfit for the society of his virtuous brother, who takes his bribes in the more discerning and remunerative manner. After all, the pound was my own, which is more than Mr.

Gladstone can say of what he so generously gives away. Well, do you honestly find this party-work lovely and sweet-smelling?   Do you think by any possible effort our Prime Minister can separate his virtuous person from my sinful one?   Believe me, we are flesh and blood and something more to each other.   No amount of rhetoric can establish any true difference between us. We both have our objects to gain; he wants power, I want a seat in the House; we both appeal to interested motives; we both use the selfishness of men; we both pay the price which is necessary.   Mr. Gladstone does not include the leaseholders in his Land Act, and I don't pay 30s. instead of £1, unless it is necessary.   If it is necessary, we both rise to the occasion.   Pah! in politics we all stink alike, though I don't try to disguise it by essence of oratorical millefleurs.   All politics are bribery!   The whole of party government rests upon it and could not go on a day without it; and the only difference is that the bribes which politicians use in public are varnished over with lies, till they shine like the faces of modern saints, and those that they use in the dark are publicly damned in Acts of Parliament. But I told you there were worse things than bribing a man.   What do you say, Lady Grace, to men who lost their vote and their speech against their own sense of right?   I have told lies on lies; I have joined myself with men who I knew were in the wrong, and have helped to silence men who were upholding what I believed to be true. I voted for reform whilst I did not wish the workmen to have power; I voted for the ballot though I looked on it as a patent incubator of lies; I voted with Plimsoll whilst I laughed at an impulsive, ill-considered movement that I knew would come and go like a scud of wind across the surface of water; I helped to clamour for the liberty of Bulgarians, and Roumelians, Montenegrins, Abyssinians—no, I mean Armenians—and Heaven knows whom besides, though to this day I have never looked in my map to see which is Bulgaria and which is Roumelia, and know that if I had looked, I should have forgotten it within the six months, as all the rest of England has forgotten; I approved of invading Egypt, though I knew there was no shadow of justification for having a battue of those poor devils, who scuttled like rabbits before our men; I have voted for all Gladstone's gifts as if he were a little god to give or to withhold as he pleased; and I have never scrupled to call him 'that heroic champion of the people,' that 'soul of courage and generosity,' whenever I wanted a cheer during a speech, or wished to satisfy my electors about the soundness of my principles. Well, you can all see for yourselves the sort of liar that I am, and the only difference I can find between myself and the other politicians whom Lady Grace loves so much, is that I don't mind your seeing or knowing what I am, whilst they would raise their eyes to Heaven and thank God that they do not eat out of the same dish with me.   I have done these things not because I care much for what is to be gained by doing them—I scarcely care a brass farthing for any part of it—but because I saw everywhere that lies are told, that every-where either the force of the strongest or the lie of the cleverest rules the world ; that everywhere some men prey on others, whether it is the richer who rob the poor, or the poorer who rob the rich ; whether it is the Churchman who hunts down the Dissenter, or the Dissenter who hunts down the Atheist, or the Atheist who hunts down both the others.   And then it amuses me to do my devil-worship at noonday, in the sight of all men, and not creep into my master's temple after night-fall with a mask on, as all these other men love to do. I don't say I am better, I don't say I am worse, than they are.   It is all a matter of taste.   Only if Lady Grace is particular about the morals of her company, I should not advise her to sit down to lunch either with me or with any of Her Majesty's Ministers."

There was a moment's pause.   Then Pennell exclaimed, " Great heavens, Danby, what an awfully perverted mind you have ! I call it disgusting.   Why cannot you eat your lunch quietly without undressing yourself and inviting us all to look at a skeleton inside ? Do button up your coat again like a good fellow, and try to be decent.   What earthly pleasure can there be in turning up the seamy side of everything ?   We are none of us saints, and raking up the political sewage that has settled to the bottom is hardly a savoury business."

"I wish to heaven," said Angus, "you could be serious for a quarter of an hour. How is it possible to tell what you mean or don't mean ? Why do you stay another hour in the House if you really think it is what you say ?"

"I think you are too hard on us all," said Wolleston. "I don't think that we are quite as bad as you yourself are. I expect that men have always told lies, without exactly knowing that they were telling them, whenever anything was to be gained by the process. I have little doubt the practice began in the earliest times with our four-handed ancestor, who probably doctored his first beginnings of a conscience, and persuaded himself that he ate the best nuts to save his wives from indigestion. In politics we tell our lies almost unconsciously, or only in part consciously, and that takes half the harm out of them at once. Why, all the best men have been im- postors on one side of their character ! The real and the unreal are so mixed up in our natures that it is impossible to separate them. You cannot tear the dead from the living flesh without doing more harm than good. Who shall say where self-persuasion ends and where telling lies begins ?"

"You are easily pleased," said Danby, "and must enjoy this glorious moment in your age of progress. We are all busy telling lies, but for the life of us we cannot make out whether we know or we don't know that we tell them. What a noble and interesting question for the race to solve about itself! We sell our opinions, abandon our pledges, throw over the weakest, side with the strongest, and flatter and serve all who are of advantage to us; and then we look complacently on ourselves and say, 'Yes, our faculty of self-persuasion about what we wish to believe is perhaps a little more developed than it ought to be.'"

"I can believe, Mr. Danby," said Lady Grace, with a rather grave voice that had lost all trace of vexation, "that we are none of us worse than you are; I can believe that we all cheat ourselves about what we really are; but if the life is to you what you have told us, then, as Angus says, why do you continue it? Surely that must be wrong."

"I have at last done with it," said Danby quietly. "You see my conscience is not a very tender one, and has stood a great deal for a great many years. But at last, like gout to a *bon-viveur*, the twinge has come. I shall make a clean sweep of this business of telling lies. I have had enough of it. I have done my share of harm as successfully as if I had been a Prime Minister. So I applied for the Chiltern Hundreds yesterday."

"What on earth," exclaimed Pennell, "are you going to do?"

"I shall clear out and try to lead some kind of a useful life where lies are not a necessary part of the

day's work.   Perhaps I shall go to Australia, or to
Canada, and see if I cannot get the plough into a bit of
forest-land.   That's an old dream of mine, to see the
good corn grow amongst the stumps for the first time.
It has broken many a man's heart, but my muscles are
better than yours, and I have used an axe all my life.
Perhaps I shall try the prairies."

"Oh! how sorry I am, how sorry I am!" said
Angus, in as real grief as a small schoolboy who loses
his older comrade.   Then turning to Lady Grace he
added, "You don't know how honest and true-hearted
he is, notwithstanding all he says about himself and
everybody else."

"Yes, I think I do," said Lady Grace in a voice not
quite free from emotion.

Then Lord Mannaley came in and sat down and ate
his biscuit; and the conversation dropped out of the
region of politics, and they quietly discussed the acting
of Mr. Irving and Miss Terry.

CHAPTER VI.

In a small but cheerful lodging overlooking the Thames, Angus found Markham. After a few words he began to pour out his old troubles. Was it possible to act honestly with one's party? Did it not lead to a constant sacrifice of convictions, or, indeed, to learning to live without them? And then was any party itself, morally speaking, better off; would not convictions, if simply and straightforwardly followed, place the party that so acted at a fatal disadvantage in its struggles with its rival? Were not politics an art in which a clever manipulation of the electors, and a nice opportunism in selecting measures that satisfied one portion of the people without too much offending another portion, took the first place, while the high motives and great causes to which all politicians loved to appeal were but bits of broken mosaic that the Jew dealer throws in as a make-weight to complete the bargain?

"What course is open to a man," he asked, "who wishes, above all, to be honest and to speak the truth; who wishes neither himself to be corrupted nor to corrupt the people; who has no desire to preserve any privileges for the richer classes, but yet will not go one step beyond what he believes to be just in gaining the favour of the masses ?   The common theory of modern government seems to be that we have given power to the people, and therefore, whatever may be our own opinions, we must acquiesce in their wishes. We may dexterously pare a little off here and a little off there, at this point or at that point, but, having placed power in their hands, we must accept and act upon their views. Should it happen that we can add a little semi-spontaneous enthusiasm on our own account, why, so much the better. Now, with this theory I cannot come to terms.   I always stick at the same difficulty. Shall a man look first and foremost to his own sense of what is right and follow that as his guide, or shall he follow his party ? "

" Does not the question answer itself when once fairly stated in words?" replied Markham. " If the world is to make any real improvement, does it not depend more upon the individual resolution to see what is true, and to do it, than upon any possible combination into which men may enter ? Is not the great thing that we have to hope for that a man should cherish and respect his own opinions beyond every other thing in life, so that it should be impossible for him to act in disregard of them ?   What form of slavery can be more debasing than that which a man undergoes when he allows either a political party or a Church to lead him to and fro when he is in no real agreement with it ?   Truth to your own self or faithful service to your party? Can you hesitate about the choice?"

"But might not a man say," urged Angus, "'the highest truth to me personally is to follow faithfully my own party?' Might he not say, 'I feel that I am doing the best of which I am capable when I act under and obey a man in whose capacity and devotion to great ends I believe. I prefer his judgment to my own. I do not trust my own views as regards all these complicated questions of the day; but I have faith in those who lead us, and wish to strengthen their hands in all ways possible.'"

"Yes, a man might speak in that sense who accepts the Catholic theory; who is ready to hand himself over to authority, and believes that he need not solve great questions himself, but may leave others to do it for him. If he slavishly give up the attempt to bring this world and that higher part of himself, his own intelligence, into harmony with each other; if he be content to act without seeing the just and the true and the reasonable in all that he does, then he may use this language, and plead an easy faith and easy devotion in excuse for effacing his own reason and making default, as far as he is concerned, in the great plan of the world. Your words are well chosen to snare a man's soul, but they cannot alter the fact that you are born a reasonable being and that there is no rightful deliverance from the use of your own reason."

"But is not party a necessity?" replied Angus. "Here are two great parties in existence, and is it not a 'counsel of perfection' to say that a man must follow his sense of right, and act in complete independence of party? Suppose all the clearer-sighted and nobler-minded men did this, and retired from party, would it improve matters?"

"Have a little faith, Mr. Bramston, in right for right's sake. More good will come from the best men being true to themselves than from any co-operation of theirs with others. Unless the good man keeps true to himself, you will get but little profit from his goodness, which is sacrificed in order that he may work with others."

"But is not party," again urged Angus, "a reasonable thing in itself? Is not co-operation a natural and right means by which men unite their strength to obtain certain results?"

"Yes," replied Markham, "as an instrument, as a means towards a distinct end. A party organised for some common purpose in which men distinctly and definitely agree, in which each unit preserves his own consciousness and volition, is a natural and right instrument for men to use. But you politicians, Mr. Bramston, make party an end and not a means. You do not strive to live in real harmony with your own opinions; you have not even discovered that this is your first and greatest duty, and after one or two faint struggles you generally end by leaving your opinions in the rear with the baggage, whilst you are marching forward with the party. What you care for is not to cultivate the true self within you which is to dictate all thoughts and actions, but to be one of a party—to shout with it, fight with it, win with it."

"Ah! I know quite well what you mean," said Angus. "That is a very old trouble and distraction of mine. I could see in 1881 that many men acquiesced in the Land Act just because it was a party measure, and because they had not the courage to stand alone and oppose what was noisily declared to be in the interests of the people. But suppose for a moment that my sense of right went entirely with the most popular measures of the party; suppose that I sincerely approved of every gift which it was possible to take from the richer and give to the poorer people. Suppose that I were Bastian—you probably know Bastian—with only this difference, that I believed heart and soul in what I promised, and so long as these services were done for the people, I cared little or nothing what was the exact form that they took?"

"And suppose the party were divided by three or four rival schemes for thus endowing the people?"

"I probably should be guided by the wishes of the people," said Angus hesitatingly.

"Yes; that is pretty nearly the only answer which is left you," replied Markham. "As you have dismissed your own intelligence as your guide, what else can you do but follow the wishes of the people? And now please to say, Mr. Bramston, however good may be your intentions, is this a true position for any man to hold? Has he the right as regards himself to give to others the keeping of his intelligence, to become in consciousness as a polype that leads but a semi-detached life in the polype group? Can he really help his fellow-men by such mental subservience and denial of his own reason? Do you think that progress lies before us, if we simply exchange holy mother Church for holy mother Party, and efface our own individuality?"

"And yet," said Angus again hesitating, "granted that men ought not to accept a party programme any more than they accept a Thirty-nine Articles, granted that no man who has once freed his mind can take either his theology or his politics in a lump from others, still practically if any Government is to do great services for the people, if it is to educate them, if it is to give them decent dwellings, to improve their sanitary condition, and on all sides to soften and improve the circumstances of life, I cannot disguise from myself that I can do more towards this end by simply supporting the Government of my party than by insisting on my own opinions."

"Ah, Mr. Bramston, you are introducing a large ' if.' You ask me, *if* a body we call Government—which please to remember is the creature of a successful competition that has existed between two parties in the not very noble art of momentarily pleasing the people—has for its true object, in all the greatest matters that affect human life, to proclaim a certain number of universal schemes, be it for education, for regulating labour, for providing against distress, or for adding to the comforts of existence, whether in such a case we must not dismiss our separate intelligences to the second place, and simply support our own party against the rival that waits to dislodge it.   To which question I at once answer 'yes;' as I should if you asked me whether the men who make up an army, that is sent to conquer a neighbouring country, had not better give up their own judgment in all things and be moved at the will and by the hands of their general.   Defeating an enemy and defeating a political rival have only too many points in common ; and in either case separate intelligences would be a great hindrance to success.   It would be best in both cases—to use the mildest phrase—that they should be disciplined."

"Is it a fair comparison between what men do in war and what they do in politics ?" asked Angus, forgetting how often he himself had compared the two parties to two armies.   "We almost all condemn war and its violence ; you cannot compare these with the peaceful methods of discussing and voting."

"Are you sure," replied Markham, "that the two systems are so far apart ?   In war you use force, in politics you only imply force, but it is still there. What reason can you find why twelve millions of men should accept the views of sixteen millions after they have voted, except that it is taken for granted that the sixteen millions could smash up the twelve millions, or as many of them as was necessary, were it a trial of strength between them? You take numbers, because they represent force, as conclusive of the verdict in what we call a constitutional country; but can you give me any moral reason that will bear five minutes' examination why you should do so, or why three men should compel two men to accept their views of life? Of course you cannot. Any moral scheme built upon numbers must break to pieces under its own inconsistencies and absurdities. There is only the one reason to be given, as I think Sir F. Stephen has seen, that a superior number of voting papers implies superior force. The sixteen millions are presumably stronger than the twelve, and therefore the twelve submit without having recourse on each occasion to practical tests. But don't suppose that the opinion of the sixteen millions has any more moral validity about it than the opinion of the twelve or eight or two millions. How in the name of reason can it? Once free your mind from the stupid idolatry that exists at present about the sovereignty of a majority—a doctrine as stupid and as idolatrous in its own way as the worship of a king or a high priest—and you will both laugh and blush at yourself for ever having bowed down before that shrine."

"But is it impossible," said Angus, "to defend the authority of numbers ? May it not be right that if five men differ, the two should give way to the three ? It would be absurd to ask the three to submit to the two."

" Why should either two men live at the discretion of three, or three at the discretion of two," replied Markham? "Both propositions are absurd from a reasonable point of view. If being a slave and owning a slave are both wrong relations, what difference does it make whether there are a million slave-owners and one slave, or one slave-owner and a million slaves ? Do robbery and murder cease to be what they are, if done by ninety-nine per cent. of the population ? Clear your ideas on the subject, Mr. Bramston, and .see that numbers cannot possibly affect the question of what is right and wrong. Suppose some man with the cunning brain of a Napoleon were to train and organise the Chinamen, and should then lead them to annex such parts of the West as they desired ; on your theory of numbers, if they exceeded the population of the country that they appropriated it would be all right, I presume."

"I do not say that it is a satisfactory answer ; but might not a majority inside a country afford a right method of decision, without extending the rule to the case of one country against another ?"

"On what ground ?" said Markham. "From where are the rights to come which you have so suddenly discovered ? Do you think that the moral laws, that govern men, are made of such convenient fibre that they will appear and disappear at our convenience ? Forget that you are a politician, Mr. Bramston, and admit that if you can plead any moral law as against the numbers of a stronger race, you must be able to plead it equally against the numbers of the larger half of a nation; you must be able to plead it whether on behalf of two men against three, or of one man against a million. Either there are or there are not moral conditions limiting force ; but if there are, they cannot conceivably depend upon numbers. That would be too queer an arrangement for us to believe in, unless we believed at the same time that the world had been shaped and ordered by the · capricious intelligence of some all-powerful dwarf, such as you meet with in the fairy stories. Think for a moment, Mr. Bramston. A certain thing is wrong to-day, because I can only get twelve millions to say 'yes' to it, and right to-morrow, because there are sixteen millions on its side."

"Then you would condemn the Birmingham doctrine of the sovereign rights of a majority, and refuse to treat it as the foundation-stone of democratic government," said Angus. "Bright preaches the doctrine eloquently, but I am continually doubting the easy-going philosophy which assumes that the majority will always be on the right side and will only ask for what is just."

"I share the common respect which England has for Mr. Bright," said Markham.   "We all instinctively feel

that he is more of a man with living beliefs, and less of
a politician, than the rest. But can anything be less
defensible than his position? He declares force to be
no remedy; he declares war, which is force in its
most naked form, to be wrong; but he looks on the
outcome of the ballot-box, which however is just as
much force, pure and simple, as the orders issued by a
Prussian field-marshal, and is only obeyed because it
implies the breaking of heads—if it is not obeyed—
almost as a divine and inspired thing. What is the difference between force, openly calling itself by its own name,
and force wrapped up in platform phrases? Has it not
the same self and the same cloven foot? What does
it matter about the mere garment in which it is
clothed? If in the one case it is to be dreaded
and resisted, so also is it in the other. You can read
plainly enough in past history the curse that force
has been in the hands of men over their fellow-men.
I do not say it could have been otherwise. We were
obliged to pass through the period of force, not only
because man was what he was, but because only so
could we learn to make the moral renouncement of
it. Still the great truth remains that in the history
of force almost all the crimes and sufferings of men
are written. One long track of misery follows the
steps of those who have held power; and can you
not see that what the curse has been in the past that
it remains, and must remain, in the present? All

beliefs and systems founded on force, whatever may be the machinery which they employ, are simply a renewal in disguised form of that old division of the human race into slaves and slave-drivers, those who have no real self belonging to them, and those who desire to possess more than their own self."

"Then you separate yourself altogether from the usual theory of democratic government?"

"I believe myself more democratic than your politicians," said Markham, "but I reject utterly their view of what democracy is. They have not the courage to bid the people accept the universal and therefore truly democratic conditions which perfect liberty offers, but wish, in imitation of departed kings and emperors, to build anew every sort of artificial privilege, as if such privileges,—for whomsoever they are created, the few or the many,—ever had lasted, or could last in defiance of moral law. Well, Mr. Bramston, the world has lived through many lies ; it has lived through the priestly lie, the kingly lie, the oligarchical lie, the ten-pound-house-holder lie, and it has now to live through the majority lie. These other lies are gone to their own place, and this last lie will follow after them. The law of universal freedom and universal justice condemns them all alike."

"But you do not mean to condemn the use of force for all purposes," asked Angus?

"Will you undertake to define for me the purposes for which I am and for which I am not to use force?

For myself I fail to be able to do it.   I cannot suppose that three men have power to compel two men in some matters without finding myself presently obliged to conclude that the three men must decide what these matters are, and therefore that they have power to apply force in all matters.   Between the some purposes and the all purposes I can find no settled boundary.   You cannot draw, and no man living can draw, a force-line.   If you sat down with Mr. Gladstone to-day to do it, to-morrow his party exigencies would have eaten out the line, and its authority would be gone—at all events for our planet.   Do not let us play with these things, and build up pleasant fictions that have no real substance in them.   Either a state of liberty—that is, a state where no physical force is applied by man to man—is the moral one, or we must recognise force as rightly applied by those who possess it for all purposes that they think right."

"I still remain puzzled," said Angus.   "Is a majority never to employ force for what we call good as against bad purposes ?"

"Please to define good and bad purposes," replied Markham.   "You will find that your definitions hold as much meaning as a sieve holds water.   If you wish to see how hopeless is the task, read Sir F. Stephen's book, in which he tells us not to employ compulsion, even though calculated to obtain a good object, if it involves 'too great an expense.'   What possible binding power is there in such a rule over the minds of men? Where is the common standard of measurement? Who sees with the same eyes the accompanying expense or the resulting good? It is far better to look the truth in the face and to say that when you sanction force for good purposes, you sanction it for those purposes which the holders of power think good; and as men's power of believing that to be good, which they happen to want, is unlimited, it simply means that when once you recognise force as right, you must leave all the applications of it to be decided by those who possess it. I want you and other politicians to face this truth, and to see that there is no possible escape from it. If anything is wanted to convince you, I say again, read Sir F. Stephen's book, written, as all he writes, with vigour and animation and picturesqueness. Force seems to him the one element of redemption in an almost irredeemable world. But yet, like everybody else who believes in force, of course he wants it applied in his own direction; as if force, when you have once recognised and sanctioned it, would not flow in the direction of the wants and wishes of those who are the most numerous, and therefore the most powerful. And so, I think, the mass of our electors have generally more reason on their side than he has. If force is a right thing in itself, if it is an instrument which men may rightly use, they do well to brush away all refinements and to use it freely to remove the difficulties of life. If Sir F. Stephen is right in his belief in force—tempered, I should say, by the three conditions,* which, as I must own, convey little or no meaning to me—if he is right in his contempt for liberty, and if the ordinary politician is right in his occasional use of force according to his daily necessities, then the Socialist is more right than either of them, since he is thorough, logical, consistent, and practical in the matter, and makes force do all that it can do in the service of men."

"Sir Fitzjames Stephen is rather a pessimist, is he not, in his view of things?" asked Angus.

"Yes," replied Markham, "and that makes his position the more indefensible. The worse you think of men, the less willing should you be to place power in their hands over their fellow-men. If you despise the mass of your fellow-men, it seems a very rash thing to appeal to force as the great social arbiter, considering that, construct what system you choose, in the long run the mass that you so heartily despise will get possession of this power and turn it to their own uses. I should have said that the more you distrust mankind, the more careful you should be to keep power out of their hands."

"Do you trust or distrust the mass of the people, Mr. Markham?" said Angus.

"I heartily like and respect our people," said Mark-

* See page 49 of "Liberty, Fraternity, Equality," 1873. I have not seen Sir Fitzjames Stephen's latest edition.—T. M.

ham. "But I do not trust them or any other people, or even any single man, with power over their fellow-men. One of the greatest truths that we have to learn, however unwilling we may still be to do so, is that no man amongst us, good or bad, is fit to possess power. As soon as he has it in his hands, that very moment he begins to confuse together his sense of what serves his own opinions or his own interests, and what is universally right; he begins to measure the world upon the last of his own foot. To have power placed in your hands,—you, who have not yet conquered your own vices, who are probably not even conscious of them, who are just one of a sect or a party,—to be told to decide not simply what is good for yourself, but good for others, to decree virtue and vice, adversity and prosperity for them, is the most corrupting thing that can befall a man. It must produce a reckless selfishness, for you will suddenly discover that you can push your own interests unchecked by the interests of others. It must produce self-deception and hypocrisy, for you will not say openly to the world that you are only thinking of your own interests, but you will wrap yourself up in expressions about the common good of humanity. To have power over your fellow-men is to become as a god in your own eyes, and then to suffer Herod's penalty, by having the best part of your moral nature destroyed by your secret infirmities And please look carefully at this matter of human selfishness. Selfishness, in one sense, is and always will be an integral part and a necessary part of our nature? I must take care of and provide for myself before I can do so for others. Nothing could be so topsy-turvy, as Mr. Spencer has pointed out, as everybody caring only for somebody else, and nobody for himself. The selfishness that makes a man care for himself is right and necessary for the good of the whole; only, observe, it must be limited and checked everywhere, not only by his own moral feelings, but by the same selfishness in others, if we are to use this word,—which is perhaps not very fit,—to describe the care which everybody has to take of his own interests. But this useful selfishness of each man in caring for himself must not be confounded with the aggressive selfishness of those who possess power, and who would disable all others who stand in their way,—be they the many or the few,—by restrictions and disqualifications in order to better the position of themselves. The one selfishness is the true, right, and proper care of a man's own interests in his own fashion; the other selfishness is the treading under foot of the rights of others because they have succeeded better than we ourselves have, and because their success is inconvenient to us. The one selfishness belongs to the system of liberty, the other to the system of socialism and all its political imitations. See clearly the difference, Mr. Bramston. Men are selfish and must be selfish in first caring for themselves. Restrict that selfishness by the establishment of universal rights, and it then works for the good of the world, each man doing his best for himself in his own way and according to his own faculties. Enlarge that selfishness by giving to a majority power over a minority, and it springs at once into overweening proportions, and becomes the most deadly plague of the human race. And please notice in further connection with this subject, that if ever you could succeed in putting down by social-istic arrangements the natural form of human selfish-ness,—this care of a man for his own interests,—you would also put down all really unselfish actions. For really unselfish actions can only exist where a man, having free scope and liberty to serve himself, prefers to serve others rather than himself. To apply force, there-fore, to correct selfishness, is not only a blundering at-tempt to destroy an integral part of human nature, which cannot be got rid of, but is also a fatal attack on the highest qualities that men possess. Compel us to be Socialists, and you will have no more real and conscious unselfishness amongst us than there is amongst ants and bees."

"Might not a believer in Socialism make the criti-cism," said Angus, " that under the name of liberty you are only destroying the ruder methods of force and leaving in existence all the subtler and more injurious forms? You deny, for example, to a workman the power to protect himself by means of a Parliamentary majority, and meanwhile you leave him to the tender mercies of capital. 'What is the good of liberty to me,' a workman might say, ' when I must accept the terms my employer offers me ? On all sides I am being coerced by my necessities ; why am I not in return to defend myself by coercion ? ' "

" What you want to do, Mr. Bramston, is to justify our direct coercion of each other by the fact of that indirect coercion to which we are all subject in this world. You are mixing up two things which are quite distinct. If you and I are writers of books, we both indirectly coerce each other. If I do not write up to your standard, your books are bought by the reading public and mine are not. This indirect coercion of each other exists everywhere, must exist, is a fixed and un-alterable condition of life ; and life, as far as we know, could not go on without it. But that is no reason why you should come to me and say, ' You write better books than I do. You are starving me. That is not fair. You have coerced me, and therefore I will coerce you by preventing your writing more than so many hours a day, or receiving more than so much for what you write ; or, as you can make more than I can, you shall divide with me your higher gains.' To try to get rid of the indirect coercion of one man by another, as the Socialists do, by substituting direct coercion for it—to replace the natural and inevitable condition of life by the unnatural and the artificial—is only worthy of those who have breathed Irish air all their life. Moreover, as I often tell my brother workmen, it is not true that all the coercion comes from the employer. There is a good deal of unwise coercion on both sides, which will in time disappear, if only the workmen do not allow themselves to be tempted into building up institutions of State-Force, as an escape from their present difficulties. If once they do that, their consciences will be blinded as regards the use of force, and the world will for a dreary season become merely a cock-pit for the brutal struggle between opposed interests and opposed opinions, using any and every instrument to defeat each other."

" And now please to tell me a little more exactly why force is necessarily a bad thing in itself ? " said Angus.

" Do you not see," said Markham, " first, that—as a mental abstract—physical force is directly opposed to all true morality ; and, secondly, that it practically drives out of existence the moral forces ? Contrast force and morality with each other. How can an act, done under compulsion, have any moral element in it, seeing that what is moral is the free act of an intelligent being ? If you tie a man's hands there is nothing moral about his not committing murder. Such an abstaining from murder is a mere mechanical act ; and just the same in kind, thoughless in degree, are all the acts which men are compelled to do under penalties imposed upon them by their fellow-men. Those who would drive their fellow-men into the performance of any good actions do not see that the very elements of morality—the free act following the free choice—that is to say, free as regards external compulsion, not free as regards that inner mental compulsion, which is the true bond—are as much absent in those upon whom they practise their legislation as in a flock of sheep penned in by hurdles. You cannot see too clearly that force and reason—which last is the essence of the moral act—are at the two opposite poles.   When you act by reason you are not acting under the compulsion of other men ; when you act under compulsion you are not acting under the guidance of reason.   The one is a force within you and the other a force without.   Moreover, physical force in a man's hand is an instrument of such a brutal character that its very nature destroys and excludes the kindlier and better qualities of human nature. The man who compels his neighbour is not the man who reasons with and convinces him, who seeks to influence him by example, who rouses him to make exertions to save himself.   He takes upon himself to treat him, not as a being possessed of reason, but as an animal in whom reason is not.   The old saying, that any fool can govern with bayonets, is one of the truest sayings which this generation has inherited and neglected.   Any fool can reform the surface of things, can drive children by the hundreds of thousands into schools, can drive prostitutes out of public sight, can drive dram-drinking into secret cellars, can provide out of public funds pensions for the old, hospitals for the sick, and lodging-houses for the poor, can call into existence a public department and an army of clerks and inspectors, provided that he has the handling of money that does not belong to him, and a certain number of people ready to applaud everything that has somewhere about it a surface-look of philanthropy; but what is the good of it all when he has done it? To be compelled into virtue is only to live in order to die of dry rot."

"I see the conflict between reason and force," said Angus; "still, I hesitate in the matter. It is clear that I cannot use force to make people reasonable? Why may we not compel them to educate their children, to give up public-houses, to only work a certain number of hours in the day, and many other things of the same kind?   May not force be the instrument of reason?"

"It would be false to call such acts reasonable. You may use *your own* reason when you say that compulsory education, or compulsory temperance, is good for certain people, and proceed to carry it out; but in so acting you disallow the existence of reason in those whom you compel. You place them in a lower rank to yourself— you retaining and using your reason, they being disfranchised of it. Now this unequal relation between men, in which the reason of some is replaced by the reason of others, is one that reason acting universally rejects as a denial of itself. Why should your reason be recognised and not that of the man you compel? Moreover, can you not see that the very idea of force necessarily involves a fatal absurdity? If A has

power over B, you must assume that in the first in-
stance he has power over himself; no man can be
master of another man before he is master of himself.
But if so, then B (if you are to assume equal rights
as the basis of the social order) is also master of himself, which entirely destroys any rightful power on the
part of A to be his master and to make him act against
his will."

"I must confess, whether I agree or not with the
abstract condemnation of force," said Angus, "that I
sometimes regret to see the love of force and the belief
in it growing so fast upon us.   All our would-be re-
formers can only suggest compulsion of some kind.
The word is always in their mouth."

"Yes, the mood is on us," said Markham, "and
utterly debasing it is.   We are filled with the Celtic
spirit of wishing to govern and be governed; we creep
into one pitiful refuge after another, as if anything could
save us from our appointed heritage of the free reason
and the free act.   But I live in faith, Mr. Bramston.
Exoriare aliquis!   The time will come when some
Englishmen of sturdy common sense, a new *martellus
monachorum*, will arise to rout these good gentlemen
who delight in tying the English people to their apron-
strings, will smash these revivals of a pagan Catholicism,
—for such it is, this blind submission to authority,—will
strip these 'cloisteredvirtues' of their seeming excel-
lence, and bid the peoplelive again in a free world, gaining

their own good, trampling on their own sins, and saving their own souls.   But let me ask you, Mr. Bramston, have you read Mr. Herbert Spencer's writings ? We shall do little good unless you have done so. We owe to him the placing of this great truth—that man must be free if he is to possess happiness—on its deepest and truest foundations.   No discursive talk of ours will really help you until you have felt the marvellous power with which he has read the wider and deeper meanings of the world, and given order to our disorderly conceptions of it."

"I must confess with some shame that I have never read his writings," said Angus.   " I have always believed him to be the great teacher of *laissez-faire*, and everybody to-day supposes that *laissez-faire* lies on the other side of the horizon behind us."

" Ah," said Markham, "I fear that all you political gentlemen live in a greater state of ignorance than most of us. How can it be otherwise? With your committees and debates, and speeches to prepare, you have but little time for watching the graver discussions that are going on.   Like lawyers in busy practice, you have no mental energy left to give to abstract questions ; and yet I do not notice that any of you are wanting in courage when you come to deal with the very foundations of social things.   So the world believes in the failure of *laissez-faire?* Believes that you cannot trust men to act and think for themselves.   Believes that the miserable farce of some thinking and acting for others is to persist for ever? No, Mr. Bramston, it is not *laissez-faire* that has failed. That would be an ill day for all men. What has failed is the courage to see what is true and to speak it to the people, to point towards the true remedies away from the sham remedies. But read Mr. Spencer and judge for yourself. Believe me, you are hardly fit to be exercising power over others until you have done so. You had better leave some of your Blue Books unread than remain in ignorance of his work."

"What is the chief feature of that work as regards politics?" asked Angus.

"He has made the splendid attempt," replied Markham, "to give fixity and order to our moral ideas, and to place the relation of men to each other on settled foundations. The love of disorder is so great in the human mind that probably men will yield but slowly to his teaching, perhaps not yield till they have passed through many troubles. But it is along the track that he has opened out to them, and that track only, that every nation must escape both despotism and anarchy and find its happiness."

"And the drift of his other work?"

"I should say that the result was to make the world, as a whole, reasonable to men," said Markham. "He has connected all human knowledge, establishing interdependence everywhere; he has taught us to see that everything in the world is part of a great growth, each part, like the different structures of a tree, developing to its own perfect form and special use, whilst it remains governed by the whole. He has helped us to rise everywhere from the reason that governs the part, to the reason that governs the whole ; and in tracing back this great growth of the past,—compound form rising out of simple form,—he has shown us the long, slow preparation towards perfection through which the world has travelled and yet has to travel. It is scarcely too much to say that he has given us a past and he has given us a future. In a time of sore need, when the old meanings were splintered to drift-wood, he has seen that the true meaning of the world was to be found, and in finding it he has restored to us the possibilities of a higher religious faith. The influence of modern science has been to make men too easily satisfied with their own separate and fragmentary knowledge. Each man has settled down in his niche in the vineyard, and there laboured industriously and successfully, but with his eyes closed for the wider meanings. To read a learned paper before a learned society, to be the highest authority on some special subject, have been objects which have unduly influenced our generation; and it is only such a work as Mr. Spencer's that recalls us to the truth that the use of knowledge is not simply to annihilate a rival on some particular subject,—that we look on as our private property,—but to lead men to understand the great whole in which they are included, to bring that whole into perfect agreement with human reason. Specialism, however necessary, is not the end of science. The end of science is to teach men to live by reason and by faith—the faith born from reason,—to grasp the great meanings of life, and to see clearly the conditions under which they can give the truest effect to those meanings. At present we are too content to be merely brick-makers; and to make and pile up our scientific bricks almost without a further purpose. But bricks in themselves are not profitable. Their real use begins when we have grasped the idea of the great whole, in which each brick, that every man has made, is to find its place. And hence it is—just because this sense of the whole is still so feeble in our minds—that science fails to take its true place, and to help us in our general concep- tions of life; as we can see, for example, by the quiet ignoring amongst politicians of the vital meaning which Darwin's discoveries have for them. And hence also it is that, great as has been the multiplication of scientific facts, they are still so powerless to reform the mental being and to reshape the conduct of men. Have you never felt, Mr. Bramston, a sense of disappointment at the influence of scientific work and -teaching? It so often fails to strengthen and enlarge. It leaves many men not as ignorant, but as narrow and confined, as they were in the old theologies. And so notwithstanding our num- berless classifications and arrangements, our intellectual life remains disorderly. We have reclaimed an island of order and are surrounded by an ocean of disorder. We are each of us, at our best, merely like a page in an encyclopedia or a separate text-book thrown anywhere on a shelf. And thus it will be until the sense of the whole becomes supreme in our eyes—the sense of the great language in which our many forms of special knowledge are only the separate letters. It is here that Mr. Spencer has helped us so powerfully. With the most faithful appreciation of all scientific work, he has seen that the world belonged neither to the physicist, nor to the chemist, nor to the biologist; but that it was something larger than any world of theirs. He has seen, as Carlyle and Emerson and Ruskin and Walt Whitman have seen, each in his own way, the wonder and the miracle in which we are all enveloped,—the marvel of the knowable world, and the marvel of the unknowable world, lying beyond the enchanted mountains and their impassable barrier; he has looked through the nature that surrounds us to the meaning at the heart of it all; he has used science as the interpreter of the sacred thing, but not stayed in it, as if it were the sacred thing itself. We owe to him more than to any man—unless perhaps it be Emerson—the power to realise the harmony and unity embracing all things, the perfect order and the perfect reason, in the light of which men may walk confidently with sure aims. We owe to him new possibilities of that faith, of which the theologian with his combined pettiness and rashness has almost robbed the world. We owe to him " the beginning of the end" of that intellectual anarchy,—which arises whenever the value of special knowledge is exaggerated,—and the opening of the gates of the new knowledge to those who are outside the learned class. For remember that science can be as aristocratic and exclusive as the Government of Venice. It is always tending to become the technical possession of the few ; and it is not by any system of education at Whitehall or elsewhere, but only by insisting on the universal meanings and the coherence of every part in the great whole that this tendency can ever be resisted and overcome."

"Notwithstanding all my Blue Books," said Angus, "I will promise you to read Mr. Spencer, and to read him very seriously. I have 'First Principles' and 'Social Statics,' though I am afraid that I have never yet cut their pages. But now returning to his political work, please tell me on what foundations he places individual liberty ? " asked Angus.

"He founds it on the right of every man to use the faculties he possesses. It is evident, as he insists, that all sciences rest on certain axioms. You remember Euclid's axioms, such as, 'a whole is greater than its part,' 'two things, which are equal to the same thing, are equal to one another,' and you can easily perceive that any science, however complicated it may be owing to its dependence on other sciences that have preceded it, must rest on its own axioms. Now politics are the science of determining the relations in which men can live together with the greatest happiness, and you will find that the axioms on which they depend are, (1) that happiness consists in the exercise of faculties ; (2) that as men have these faculties there must be freedom for their exercise ; (3) that this freedom must rest on equal and universal conditions, no unequal conditions satisfying our moral sense."

" Why do you insist on my treating these truths, if truths they are, as axioms ? " asked Angus.

" Because you cannot contradict them without involving yourself in what is inconsistent and absurd, without in effect giving up the belief that the world is reasonable, and, therefore, that it is worth our while to try to discover what we ought to do. Place before your mind the opposites of these statements, and try to construct a definite social system out of them. Just try it. Happiness is not the exercise of faculties ; men having faculties ought not to exercise them ; the conditions as regards their exercise should be unequal and varying. Can you seriously maintain any of these statements ? Perhaps you are inclined to challenge the last axiom ? But when you propose unequal conditions of freedom, do you offer a standing ground which men universally can accept, and which they can look upon as the perfect condition of their existence ? "

" Might I not claim greater freedom for the abler and better man, for the more civilised race ? "

" Why should you ? " replied Markham. " What does any man or any race want more than freedom for themselves?   Admit that any one may take more than his share; that is, in other words, that he may restrain by force the exercise of the faculties of others, and in what a sea of moral confusion are you at once plunged. Who is to decide which is the better man or the more civilised race, or how much freedom is to be allowed or disallowed? To settle this question men must act as judges in their own case; and this means that the strongest will declare themselves the most civilised, and will assign such portions of freedom as they choose to the rest of the nation or the rest of the world, as the case may be.   Are you prepared for this?   Do you see in this the foundation for a universal system which men could accept, and under which, having once accepted it, they could live in peace and contentment?"

"I agree in some measure," said Angus; "but how can you persuade the strongest not to use their strength?"

"Only by bringing men to see that the moral system regulating their actions towards each other is as true and fixed as the system of the planets, its parts as orderly, its whole as reasonable; and that force—I mean, by my use of the word, physical compulsion of one man by another—has no possible place in it; that force is the Antichrist of that moral and reasonable state at which we have to arrive."

"But can men see this reasonableness, this orderliness, of which you speak?"

"Surely," replied Markham. " Is it not plain that between the world,—the outcome of the highest reason, —and the human reason as it evolves, harmony is ever necessarily growing? The evolution of the human mind means that its power increases to read order everywhere ; and it is only as it perceives order that it can gain perfect confidence in its own conclusions. You must remember that a science is not a mere mass of separate truths or conclusions which may, so to speak, lie anywhere as regards each other in the same heap. As Mr. Spencer has so well pointed out, men at first begin by learning the detached truths, and then in later stages see that each truth has its own place in an indissoluble and reasonable whole, which whole, as we learn to perceive it, gives certainty to the separate truths. The separate truths are like beads before they are strung on a string, and which do not gain their full meaning until the string is there. Take Mr. Spencer's example of astronomy. By countless observations you learn that the orbits of planets are ellipses of a certain kind, and then presently you learn the great central cause in obedience to which these forms are what they are ; you have gained a master-key which, as you know, will unlock every fact—whether at present within or not within your observation—in the group that belongs to it. Hence it arises that a separate truth only becomes really known when you know the system of which it forms a part. Is it different in moral matters ? Do you

think that there are order and system for the facts that
concern the planets and not for the facts that concern
the human mind,—for mineral and for plant, and not
for the relations in which men are to live towards each
other? Do you think that with order and system in
every other part of the universe, that here—at the
highest point of development yet reached—you suddenly enter a territory sacred to disorder and conflict, a
sort of moral Alsatia, where alone the writ of the Great
Power does not run? Surely you cannot defend such
a belief. Surely you have some faith in the perfect
reasonableness that underlies and over-arches everything. To the politician it may be torture to believe
that social and political questions are parts of a reasonable whole, and can only be rightly dealt with in strict
obedience to that whole. His own course is just so
much easier as he may disregard this reason of the
whole, as he may by turns plead the law or the exception, as he may ignore all fixed moral relations of
men to each other, as he may urge plaintively that all
is so uncertain and subject to change, and therefore may
claim permission to deal with the circumstances that
exist as the light of the moment and the ever-urgent
personal interest direct. The world does not yet see the
impertinence and the danger of such claims. It will do
so as the consequences of existing mental disorder
thicken upon it."

"But do you mean when you say that the moral

relations of men are as fixed as the physical relations of things and that force is excluded from them," asked Angus, "that we can get through the world, such as it is, without the use of force? Why, even in a London street after dark a man may be obliged to fall back upon force to protect himself."

"I have not said that. Six months ago I knocked a scoundrel down who had snatched a lady's watch from her, and handed him over to the police. I do not say we can get through life without using force ; but when we do so, in the simplest and apparently most justifiable case, even to repel force, we are outside the moral relation ; and are simply living again in that force-relation in which man as half animal once lived, and in which the animals now live. Underneath all life lies the great law of self-preservation (a law which we may fulfil either by using force as the animals do, or by universally accepting the reasonable relation which, forbidding force, guarantees equal freedom to all), and those who use force may compel us at any moment to act towards them in the force-relation ; but the important thing is to see that it is only when we are living and acting in the reason-relation that we have distinct moral guidance to tell us what are right and what are wrong actions ; whilst in the force-relation we can only act by guesswork and without any certain guidance. When I am in the force-relation towards my fellow-men, right and wrong become just as uncertain and imperfect in their guidance of my actions as they are when I am dealing with animals, over whom, for the sake of my own convenience, I have assumed powers of life and death. In the case of animals, right and wrong have not disappeared, but in presence of the powers that, lawfully or unlawfully, I have assumed, they necessarily have become indistinct and imperfect guides. Please notice therefore that, morally speaking, I can only imperfectly defend the act of knocking the thief down. Clearly, in doing it I am outside the moral relation which essentially consists in my acting upon the mind of my fellow-man and not upon his body. I can only say that the thief had put himself outside the reason-relation, and had established the force-relation between us, and therefore I fell back upon the law of self-preservation and certain other imperfect moral considerations, as I should have done, if a wild and savage beast had attacked the lady or myself."

"Do you then hold that the law of self-preservation is paramount?" asked Angus.

"No, certainly not," answered Markham. "I look upon the law of the reason-relation as modifying the law of self-preservation. The two acting together are the law guiding and determining the relations of reasonable beings. But as by the thief's own conduct the reason-relation was no longer existent between us, I fell back on the law of self-preservation, and acted accordingly."

"What did you mean by saying, 'other imperfect moral considerations'? I still think as you were helping a woman that had been attacked, your act must have been a moral one," said Angus.

"It was only moral in an imperfect sense. It was so, as far as I was doing for my neighbour what I should have done for myself. In the moral confusion that necessarily ensued from the thief's conduct, I did what was right as far as I could judge, by helping the lady at the thief's expense; and also what was right from a public point of view, by way of preventing similar aggressions of one person upon another. But as I was outside the reason-relation, on which all morality as a system depends, I was deprived of that certainty which belongs to the system of morality as it does to every fixed system or science. Every science is a science only in virtue of its certainty, a certainty which may not be within our grasp, but which nevertheless is there. And being outside the moral system I was like a man trying to make a calculation, when the multiplication table had ceased to exist for him, or to solve a physical problem when the principle of gravitation had disappeared out of his perception. There were still certain detached parts of the moral system—as there would be certain detached physical truths, even after gravitation had been lost to me—which might help as a guide, but all that certainty which belongs to system, and to system alone, was hopelessly lost. It may be the best plan for all the social interests concerned, when you see a thief snatching an honest man's watch, to knock him down, and afterwards to put him into prison, but to hold such a belief is simply to do so in virtue of a certain amount of imperfect and limited experience as regards thieves ; and the belief in itself can possess no guarantee of moral certainty. It is in such cases as these that the real difficulties of life, as regards conduct, present themselves, and are sometimes almost insoluble. A wrong action done by one person may involve all subsequent conduct in confusion, may compel an action on the part of others that is *absolutely* wrong in itself, though *relatively* right under the circumstances. Mr. Herbert Spencer has stated the matter with his usual admirable force. ' Ethics, or the principles of right conduct, ignore all crime and wrong-doing. It simply says such and such are the principles on which men should act, and when these are broken, it can do nothing but say they *are* broken.' And that was my position. The thief and I were outside ethics. The wrong of the thief compelled me to an action wrong in itself, though as far as I could judge relatively right."

"I still hardly see," said Angus, "why you hesitate about calling your action right. I still instinctively cling to the feeling that it was right."

" Let me put before you another case that partly resembles this one," said Markham. "A friend of yours is brought into serious difficulty through a lie that has been told about him by some unworthy person. You could free him from this difficulty at once by telling another lie ; but would you be right to do so ? You would say, ' I must not use the wrong weapon, although I use it to defeat a weapon of its own kind, and although my motive of defending my friend is a right one ; ' and you would know that if you told the lie that would save him, you would probably still further confuse the right and the wrong of the world. You can probably see for yourself where the two cases are not exactly similar, and therefore I need not now go into the differences. If they were the same, one would be morally forbidden to use force even to repel force, which I hold not to be true. The true law, I conceive to be, that you may use force to defend yourself against those who themselves assume the force-relation towards you, but only against them. On no other ground whatsoever may I use force towards my fellow-man, if that force is applied against his own individual consent. I add these last words, because men may voluntarily place themselves under a force system."

" Are you referring in these last words," said Angus, " to the case of popular government."

" No," replied Markham, " certainly not. In popular government there is no individual consent given to the use of force by the majority. The majority assumes the right to do as they choose, and all others not included in that majority are asked to obey. Mill long ago pointed out how wrong we had gone in our use of the word self-government. We can only describe modern popular government correctly as the government of some by others, or government by the majority."

" But a majority must decide certain things for us," said Angus.

" Yes," replied Markham. " But for all that, as a majority, they can possess no real moral authority, as you will all learn to see some day when a large number of men begin to deny their authority. What will you then do ? Will you once more assert the divine nature of your authority by imprisoning and massacring those who deny it ? "

" And now returning to the subject of the law of self-preservation," said Angus, who thought he might safely leave this last question unanswered until a larger number of men were of Mr. Markham's way of thinking, " Do I understand you rightly that we are only justified in falling back upon this law as against those who by their own act place themselves outside the reason-relation ? "

" Yes," replied Markham, " that is so. You must remark that the original law of self-preservation always persists, though it is being perpetually modified by other laws, as evolution goes on. Nature's first and earliest command to us, as animals, is, ʻPreserve yourself.' In that state the animal preys on his own kind and every other kind. Her second and later command is, ' Preserve yourself by preserving others who help to preserve you.' In that state you have communities of animals and of men whose members respect the rights of each other because the common life preserves the individual life. Her next command in presence of reasonable beings is, 'Preserve yourself by accepting equal and universal conditions affecting yourself and all others alike.' This is the state of liberty, where each man preserves his own life in the best way he can, but does not infringe on the equal liberty of his neighbour to do the same. And the latest command is, 'Preserve yourself in the highest way by learning voluntarily and of your own free will to make your happiness and the happiness of others inter-dependent on each other.' These four commandments represent the four great periods of mental evolution. Of course, like the stone and the bronze and the iron periods, they overlap and interlace with each other, though the later ones have been a development from the earlier ones. At present, as you can see, we are living in a state of great mental confusion in the matter. I can give you no better example of this mental confusion than the existence of State or Force Socialism. Many of its adherents are animated, or believe themselves to be animated, by the spirit of the last or fourth command, but are in reality act-ing in obedience to the second command, that strictly only applies to communities of animals and half-savage men. They propose to use force, as the half-savage community uses force, for the preservation of the community and the furtherance of all common interests. We may there-fore say of them that they are stone men living on in the age of bronze, and fashioning their stone weapons somewhat after the bronze pattern. Of the selfish and reckless part of the State-Socialists, who are chiefly influenced by a desire to increase their material welfare by the use of force, we may say that they wholly belong to the stone age. They properly belong to the communities of bees and ants, where whatever benefits the community is done without any regard to the rights of the individual. In these socialistic communities you will find many excellent qualities, industry, bravery, devotion ; but the qualities appear rather to be the result of physical than mental evolution, and to be of a low mechanical order as compared with all that higher group of feelings that are only developed when the individual is no longer sacrificed to the community. And notice, that wonderful as are the actions performed by bees and ants, yet, following Sir John Lubbock's observations, the individual intelligence seems but feeble. The all-powerful social life has rendered it unnecessary, and has therefore limited it. But the consideration of this side of the question would take us too far from our immediate subject. It is only worth remarking that State-Socialism is a retrogression ; a descent to a form of life which some animals have carried to the very highest perfection without developing great individual intelligence."

"Let me ask you a question about the Socialists," said Angus. "Might they not claim on their side that their attempt was to preserve life on equal and universal conditions for all ? "

"They might," replied Markham, "if they understood neither their own words nor their own intentions. State-Socialism (and the same thing applies to all its political imitations) is the attempt to prevent the growth of natural inequalities by recourse to artificial inequalities. It is the attempt to prevent the shadow of injustice by the infliction of actual injustice itself. It is the suppression and disqualification of the minority, wherever it is convenient to suppress and disqualify them. How can there be equal and universal conditions when the system essentially consists of restraints devised at every hour of the day and in every matter of life by A and B for C? And how large and integral and necessary a part of the system are these disqualifications and restraints is shown by the very nature of Socialism itself; for State-Socialism is founded on the theory that men cannot find happiness except they are all forcibly placed under an elaborate series of restraints and disqualifications, which series must of course be invented by those in power."

"But the restraints are so far equal and universal, that they apply to all alike," said Angus.

"Yes," replied Markham, "they are. But they are unequal and partial in their creation; just because they rest on no natural rights, but on the denial of natural rights. They are the arbitrary creation of a majority having the power to enforce them; and it merely depends upon the fancy of that majority what form they take ;—whether for example a man is allowed to have a limited amount of private property, or no property at all ; whether he may have a limited number of children, or no children at all.   You are simply in the region of arbitrariness.   All depends upon the fancies of your majority in power.   You are outside rights, you are outside morality.   The majority in power is your god, and its statute-book is your revealed religion.   In it you live and breathe and have your being."

"And what do you understand by equal and universal rights?" asked Angus.

"There are only two forms, I think, which equal and universal rights can take," answered Markham.   "One consists of the rights of free action, under which a man gains and acquires what he can for himself, or for those who act in voluntary association with him ; and the other is absolutely common property in all things.   But this last is impossible, since no man would have the right to use any material in the world, or to apply his labour to it, without first getting the consent of the whole human race.   And as it is the whole human race that we suppose to be seised with the world's property, no majority can give a true authority to any one for its use, for it is not they who are seised, but the whole human race. And please to notice here that whether you look to the individual as the possessor of rights, or to the whole human race as the joint possessor of them, there is no standing ground in the one case or the other for the rights of a majority. They are simply a usurpation. And now let us return to our subject in hand, if we can find it again after this digression into Socialism."

"Our subject was, I think," said Angus, "the thief whom you unceremoniously interrupted in his employment, and the question of your moral right in doing so, in view of the four commandments. May I ask you to explain a little more exactly what is the relation of the four commandments to each other?"

"No command of Nature can repeal another," said Markham. "Each persists in moral science and has its action modified by the other exactly as happens in any natural science. Gravitation is not repealed because, should the earth take to revolving at a considerably greater speed on its axis, we should all be whirled away into space. Nature still says to us to-day, as she said some millions of years ago, ' Preserve yourself; ' and she does not repeal that first command because she has added to it another which tells us that we are to do it by accepting equal and universal conditions. We are to preserve ourselves,—not by the use of force and the physical repression of each other,—but we are to do it by taking as our basis the universal rights of free action."

"And now, how can I distinguish," asked Angus, "between the different binding power that there is in these commands of Nature? Why am I to accept them in the order in which you have chosen to state them?"

"By this marvellous power of reason that unlocks the whole world to us," answered Markham, "we can read the necessary—that is the reasonable—course that both physical and moral evolution have followed; and just as it would be impossible to believe that physically the sense of touch was developed from the sense of sight, so also it is impossible to believe that the socialistic system of forcibly preserving some at the expense of others can be a true development from universal rights. We can see that it is, as I said before, a mere retrogression.   In a certain fixed and reasonable order morality is developed just as life itself was developed, and each great moral command builds itself on those that have preceded it, making a harmonious whole.   Your conduct therefore must contradict none of the parts, else harmony becomes impossible.   You must preserve your own life, you must preserve the life of those who most nearly affect you, you must accept universal conditions for the preservation of your life and the lives of others, you must identify your life and its happiness with the life and happiness of others ; and you must do all these things and leave none undone if you wish to live at one with Nature."

"And why may I not simply obey the last command and disregard the other commands?" asked Angus. "Why should I not simply think of the happiness of others without troubling myself about rights?"

"Because Nature asks more of you," replied Markham. "She asks your obedience to the whole of the moral system as she asks your obedience to the whole of the physical system. If you were simply to think of the happiness of a certain number of men, and in doing it disregarded the rights of some others, you would destroy the reasonableness and the harmony of the system of right doing, and become the mere creature of such impulses as might happen to move you. All right doing must be just as much vouched for in its order and in its system by reason as are the movements of matter. If you found a movement of matter that at first sight seemed to be unreasonable, you would feel sure that it was only so in appearance. You would feel this because of your faith in the perfect reasonableness of all things. You would know that either you had observed the fact wrongly, or that some law as yet undiscovered would presently restore to your perception the harmony that had seemed to be interrupted. You would not doubt about the persistence of gravitation if for the first time in your life you saw a balloon ascend. And you must have the same faith in moral matters. There are no contradictions except those of your own making."

"What sort of contradictions do you mean?" asked Angus.

"I mean such a moral contradiction as that implied by your own question," said Markham, " when you talk of simply regarding your neighbours' happiness as the

law of life. To think of the happiness of your neighbour whilst you disregard the rights of other men is
unreasonable, and therefore—if you believe in the reasonableness of all things, as I do—untrue."

"And why is it unreasonable?" asked Angus. "Please
forgive my persisting in my questions," he added. "It
is my desire to catch the whole of your meaning that
makes me press you in this manner. I shall presently
see my way more clearly."

"It is unreasonable," said Markham, "because, speaking from the point of view of reason, justice must
necessarily precede generosity? Am I to benefit one
man by compelling another? To compel a man is to
deprive him of what he rightly possesses, the freedom
to use his faculties, and therefore is an act which I am
bound not to do. To assist him for purely unselfish
reasons by any gift or service of mine is an act which
I am also bound to do as a moral being, but only in
obedience to the preceding command of respecting
rights. Without now discussing such conflicts as may
arise, when I have to choose between preserving my own
life and that of others, my life must be in obedience to all
the commands as a whole, not to one of them detached
from the rest."

"And yet might not some persons," said Angus,
"urge that the happiness of our neighbour was a more
imperative law than the law of regarding the equal
rights of all?"

"Yes," replied Markham, "if they had no fear of plunging into Serbonian bogs. Which neighbour am I to help, and in what fashion? Am I to help one at the expense of another? Am I, like Robin Hood of old, to take the purse of the rich man and give it to the poor? Try to construct a definite and certain system that is really to guide men in their dealings with each other on such a foundation. You may amuse yourself some day for half an hour, Mr. Bramston, by trying to do it, but you can hardly hope, I presume, to obtain a result that will possess such certainty and precision that it will imperatively guide the consciences of men."

"I see the difficulty," replied Angus slowly. "To say we must do good to others means nothing unless there is some fixed system which tells me the conditions under which I am to do good. As you say, I may help a poor man out of my own purse or out of another man's purse. Are both actions good?"

"Exactly ; there must be a fixed system, and that system must spring from rights. Without rights, no system ; without system, no guidance. If you wish to realise the moral confusion that results where rights are neglected, glance at the world of to-day, and observe the good intentions which impede rather than assist the general cause of good. Do we not see Nihilists and Invincibles devoting themselves, often in the spirit of self-sacrifice, in order to obey an order of assassination; slave-owners showing kindness to their slaves; politicians carrying out what they believe to be useful measures for the people by appealing to selfish passions and infringing upon the rights of others; Socialists hoping to regenerate the world by deciding in what way and to what extent men shall exercise their faculties. These and a thousand other examples show us that actions springing from good intentions, but done in disregard of preceding moral commands, may increase the sum total of unhappiness instead of happiness. Order in the moral world, order in our moral ideas, is as absolutely necessary as order in a physical science and in our ideas respecting it."

" Then I am to accept as a ground-truth, if I may use such a German expression," said Angus, " that all my desires and efforts to do good must be founded on the unalterable recognition of universal rights ; and that it is vain to attempt to obey the fourth commandment unless I obey the third commandment at the same time."

" Yes, you are right," said Markham. " Remember that you must think of the moral world as ever evolving like the physical world ; and in watching evolution you can see that at all times there is an antagonism between the old forms which are being modified, and the new forms which are arising. At the beginning of social life men act upon the law of self-preservation applied to their own community ; but innumerable small forces are at work to modify this law, until presently a stage is reached at which reason asserts its claims to regulate conduct, and then, as men begin to see dimly, it requires of them to respect each other's rights. But this, though the necessary condition of all happiness, is not sufficient for the perfecting of it. A further development of this command is morally evolved, and bids us not only respect rights but also feelings, so far at least as such feelings do not tend to restrict rights. There are many actions which we may,—as far as the command to observe rights is concerned,—lawfully do, but which, as they cause unnecessary pain to others, we ought to abstain from doing. To these actions Mr. Spencer gives the name of negative beneficence. Again, succeeding to these acts of abstention are the acts of positive beneficence, the direct acts which men do for the pure sake of increasing the happiness of others ; acts which, as human nature evolves, will become more and more a necessary and integral part of the happiness of each man. But you must steadily learn to see that to add to the happiness of our neighbour, or even to avoid giving him unnecessary pain, excellent as such acts are, are of no moral value unless you begin by respecting his rights. Except on such a foundation they cannot lead to the settled happiness of men ; they can only lead to such confusion between good and evil as we see around us at present. And now observe a further development. From respecting rights we learn to recognise the self in each man as the true governing centre of all his thoughts and actions. We learn to see the false side of those great systems which lower and debase a man by offering him comfort—whether it be intellectual or material comfort—at the price of interfering with his own free choice and his own free action, of weakening his self-guidance and his self-responsibility, and making him but a semi-conscious unit in Churches and parties. We learn to see that all social as well as political systems must be framed to make him in every-day life the intelligent director of his own energies, as well as in higher matters the possessor of his own soul. Do you perceive how fruitful, how far-reaching, will be the influence of this recognition of the self in each man? Our every act towards others will be shaped and determined by it. Is it a matter of helping some fellow-man in distress, we shall ask, ‘Am I merely lifting the man by an external machinery out of a momentary trouble at the cost of depressing rather than increasing his own self-helping energies?’ Is it a matter of assisting masses of men to better their position, we shall ask, ‘Can I rightly lighten the burdens of one man by increasing the burdens of another, to however small an extent, and however easily the latter may be able to bear it? Can I do so without weakening in all minds the sense of the universal agreement, and in the minds of those who are helped, that self-respect which cannot rightly claim more than free-play for the energies of each?' Is it a matter of spreading opinion and bringing others within a Church or party, we shall ask, 'Have I joined these men to myself by the true and pure conviction of each soul, or have I treated them as a mere crowd, to be moved by some cunningly arranged machinery, to be bribed, cajoled, and driven towards the ends that I desired?' Is it a matter of education, we shall ask, ' Am I mechanically impressing the self of my own opinions on another mind ? Am I merely gaining the ends on which the world of the day sets store, and am I content, for the sake of these, to follow such lifeless and mechanical methods as promise the readiest success? Am I willing to make my own task easier by employing systems of bribes and threats, or is my one effort to develop another equal being that shall be strong in its own self-confidence and able by dependence on its own reason to make a life for itself?' There is no part of human life, no question of morality, that will not be illumined by the light thrown from that intense respect for each human self which in due time will succeed to the perfect recognition of each other's rights. The creed of rights leads as certainly to the elevation of the human race as the creeds of Socialism, founded on force, lead to the degradation of it."

"And now could you without trouble summarise for me what you said?" asked Angus.

"Using the fewest words," replied Markham, "I should say all truths belong to their own system. There is not such a thing as a stray or independent truth in existence ; and it is only as you know the system to which the truths belong that you know with certainty the truths themselves. Moral truths, then, like physical truths, are united in a system, and as this system must rest on certain assured foundations, the question is on what foundations does it rest? The answer is, in Mr. Spencer's words, on the freedom of men to exercise their faculties. From this foundation arises a coherent and harmonious moral system, governing our political and social systems, and illuminating the most complex questions of human conduct. Apart from this foundation, morality is a mass of indistinct and contradictory commands, men often obeying a generous emotion whilst they disobey fixed commands."

"In all you have said you have only used a deductive argument," said Angus ; "will you not now sacrifice to the gods of the present time by speaking inductively?"

"Ah! that greatest of all inductions!" replied Markham. "Some younger man with fuller stores of knowledge must give that induction to the world. It will be for him to follow the history of liberty as he would follow a great river in the East, whose banks are covered with rejoicing crops, whilst away from it all remains desert. You can see for yourself how vast is the material that is waiting to be used. Has any race of men ever fairly tried even the humblest experiment of freedom and found it fail? Have not the human faculties grown in every field just as freedom has been given to them? Have men ever clung to protection and restraint and officialism without entangling themselves deeper and deeper into evils from which there was no outlet? But to-night we cannot enter upon these wide fields of history. There is only one group of facts, those that belong to the development of plant and animal, at which we can glance. See how clearly under Darwin's revelations comes out the saving meaning that there is in competition, the destructive meaning that there is in protection. Protect the plant and animal by some mere external protection, as that of an island or an impassable barrier, and you reserve it for certain destruction, when the day comes, in which at last the life that has ranged over wider spaces and become better adapted to the conditions of existence enters into competition with it. The very conditions that seemed to protect it have ensured its destruction. Had it not been protected, it had passed through the same gradual adaptations that other life elsewhere has passed through. It was separation from the mainland that preserved the Australian marsupials, that has made islands such as Madagascar the curious relic-houses of a life that had not been competent to survive unless so protected. So also has it been, to use nearly the words of Mr. Darwin, that the

European plants, which by ranging over wider tracts have more thoroughly undergone selection, have beaten the native plants of La Plata, New Zealand, and, in a lesser degree, of Australia, whilst speaking generally the plants of these countries cannot obtain a footing in Europe ; so also it was that the intertropical mountains lost their true vegetation, and accepted those hardier forms which in the Glacial period were able to reach them ; that the wingless and therefore defenceless birds, such as those of Mauritius, and Bourbon, and Rodriguez, have only been found where beasts of prey were absent. But why multiply examples ?   The history of the world and the bettering of it turn upon the fact of the hardier forms, perfected by a wider and sharper competition, inevitably replacing the weaker forms.   And do you not also see how the lower kinds of self-protection die out before the higher kinds ?   The huge armour-plates and spikes that once protected animal life are replaced by higher organisations, better adaptations of bone, and muscle, and therefore quicker movements, by improved special organs, by increased size of brain.   It is the same with men.   The clumsy restrictions and defences which parliaments provide must give place to those higher forms of self-protection which depend upon mental qualities.   Is it not plainly one and the same sentence which Nature speaks to plants, to animals, and to men, ' Improve in the true way or be eventually destroyed ? '   She affixes everywhere her two great conditions of improvement, variety (or difference), that both in the physical and in the intellectual world brings into existence the beginnings of a more highly developed life, and competition, that selects for survival these all-precious beginnings out of the midst of the lower forms; whilst outside these conditions she reserves no way of salvation. It is wrong and unfaithful to disguise or evade these truths. Whatever it costs, you must say plainly to all men that variety and competition are the only conditions of their advance, and that these conditions can only exist under a system of perfect liberty. All infringements of liberty sin in a twofold way. They tend to uniformity by excluding natural variety, and they give external protection at the cost of preventing the development of self-protection. They save the pain of the present at the expense of doubling and quadrupling it in the future. Does such a law of competition seem hard to you? If so, remember that it is no longer a competition like that of animals and savages, to be decided merely by physical force or cunning, but one in which the more powerful brain, the truer perception, the more temperate habit, the more upright conduct, the greater devotion to truth, and even the more loving nature shall prevail in the end ; and that thus the better type shall be always evolving, until moral and mental pain shall become almost as rare for us as physical pain is for the wild animal, with its perfect physical development. Our present pain is but the necessity that clings to our passage from the fit to the unfit."

"And now," said Angus, "leaving further consideration of the principles themselves, let me ask you for their application. How would you give practical effect to such views?"

"The Government, as pointed out by Mr. Spencer, must confine itself simply to the defence of life and property, whether as regards internal or external defence. You can defend neither of these defensive systems, both of which involve the use of force, on true moral grounds; they can only be imperfectly defended under the law of self-preservation. But in the world as it is, those who use force must be repelled—and effectively repelled— by force. By their own act they place themselves in the force-relation, and, barbarous as is the relation, we must accept it, just so far as they thrust it on us. Farther the Government must not go. Just because it is an organisation resting upon force, it must not attempt any service of any kind for the people, from the mere mechanism of carrying their letters to that most arrogant and ill-conceived of all universal schemes, the education of their children. All services which the people require must be done by themselves, grouped according to their wants and their affinities in their own natural groups, and acting by means of voluntary association. The system would be one of free-trade carried out logically and consistently in every direction.

We should then be quit both of the politician, with that enormous bribing power which he possesses by offering services to one part of the people at the cost of another part, and of that fatal compression of ideas, energies, and experimental efforts which results whenever universal systems are imposed upon a nation. Those people who wish to make their fellow-men wise, or temperate, or virtuous, or comfortable, or happy, by some rapid exercise of power, little dream of the sterility that belongs to the universal systems which they inflict with so light a heart upon them. Some day they will open their eyes and see that there never yet has been a great system sustained by force under which all the best faculties of men have not slowly withered."

" As regards property, what would be the system which a Government ought to maintain ? " said Angus.

" There is no choice except between an open market in all things—that is, free acquisition and complete ownership—or a more or less socialistic Government. If Government undertakes in any way the task of arranging and distributing property, it at once enters on the force-relation. It presumes to set itself above the fixed moral relations of men, and to create for them out of its own imagination certain new and fanciful conditions under which they are to stand to each other. Mr. Gladstone inventing land bills is but a type of such moral and intellectual conceit. And notice that free-trade and free acquisition of all property stand and fall together. Either a man may do the best for himself with his faculties, or he and his faculties may be sacrificed for the advantage of others. It is here that lies the great choice of principle that the people have to make to-day. For those of us who wish to build up the idea of a complete and perfect liberty, the great effort at this moment should be to reconcile our people heartily to private property, whether in land or in any other thing (Mr. Spencer draws a line between the two, but I am unable to follow him), and to lead them to see that no nation can in any true sense be free, which allows the Government of the day to model and remodel that which touches a man's life so closely as his property. That English land is not largely held by the small owners is a great public calamity, but it is not to be repaired by the greater one of either petty or vast confiscations. Remove at once—as you would have done years ago, had the Liberal party remained true to its traditions, and not gone popularity and sensation hunting under Mr. Gladstone's leadership—all legal impediments that yet exist to free sale. Insist that the living owner shall be the complete owner as against the dead owner, in the sight of the law courts; avoid all ridiculous and time-serving measures for patching up the present landlord and tenant system, and the land will soon naturally and healthily find its way into the hands of the people. Any way, it is better to bear the evils of delay, such as they are, than to demoralise a whole nation in their spirit and their aims by accepting the bribes of the politician to take from the few to give to the many."

" Let me ask you how Mr. Spencer would deal with the land ? "

" He would, as I understand, recognise it as national property, and then let it by public auction. Every one in possession of land would be a tenant holding by lease from the State."

" And why do you object ? " asked Angus.

"I cannot follow Mr. Spencer either in theory or practice. If there is no private property in land, how can there be private property in all other matters of production, seeing that they are simply derived from the land. I may extract minerals, dig stone and gravel, cut timber, grow corn, wool, and cotton, and thus take into my private possession one part of the soil—or one part of what is beneath it—but not of another part. How can you justify this abrupt beginning and ending of rights ? Not I think by the plea of 'the landless man.' For if 'the landless man' has an equal inherent right with all others to the soil, I feel obliged to say that he also has an inherent right in all these other things that were once part of the soil, though now separated from it. Then if the land really belongs to society as a whole, how can a mere majority assign it away to any persons whatever at their will and pleasure? Moreover, if it is denied that there is sufficient authority anywhere to allow individuals to buy and to own, neither is there authority anywhere to allow individuals to possess it for a term of years. If a thing is not yours, and you are not competent to give me possession of it, neither are you competent to lend it to me. Lending a thing implies rights of ownership, as well as giving or transferring. Again, if you demur to the present ownership of land, because it was originally founded on force, you must let me ask you if there is any other title at all for the whole of our present race being here to-day ? In what way, except by force, did Celts, Romans, Saxons, and Normans obtain possession of this island ; and if to-day you were by an act of violence to turn the present holders of land out of possession, do you think that you would have atoned for the use of force many hundreds of years ago by employing it anew at the present moment ? But whilst it can hardly be said that the public have suffered injury because the possessions of the land-owners came to them by force, since the presence here of each race in succession is marked by the common taint of force, it should be clearly seen that a very real injury has been done to the nation, so far as we ourselves in modern times have prevented a system of free-trade in land from existing, and have by various laws favoured the large land-holders. And please to notice, Mr. Bramston, that your Liberal party are most gravely to blame for having slumbered in this matter year after year, until, as a natural penalty of their extraordinary negligence, and of their want both of clear sight and of faith in their own principles, they have called into existence such light-hearted proposals as those of Mr. George for a general scramble."

"And what are your practical objections to State ownership, Mr. Markham?" asked Angus.

"As a practical matter I think the real free-trade system—buying and selling without let or hindrance of any kind whatsoever—will always express a nation's real wants far more truly for it than any other system. If the labourers strongly desire land, and the law removes all old impediments and creates no new ones, I am confident that they will soon become possessors of it. But if they are to do so, you must not throw over them the mischievous shadow of coming legislation, which holds out hopes of the land dropping into their hands apart from their own efforts. Nor must you depart from your free-trade principles, and interfere in such a matter as the contract between landlords and tenants. It is often difficult to measure the amount of harm you may do by these haphazard interferences. By attaching a sort of tenant right to each farm, you tend to keep farms fixed at their present size, and make the process of cutting up a more difficult one. If you want great changes to take place easily and without strain, in obedience to new desires, you must always resolutely preserve the free-trade system intact at every point. A stiff and mechanical piece of legislation barbarously introduced into a system that by its very nature is fitted to yield and accommodate itself at any point to new forces, will produce mischief and derangement of many kinds that are quite impossible to foresee. And please remember, whilst we are talking of free-trade, that the feelings of a people and the systems under which they live will always tend to be in unison with each other. The highest advantages of free-trade are the qualities, which it helps a people to acquire, of providing for their new wants as they arise. Politicians don't choose to remember, when they tamper with any part of the free-trade system, that they are tampering with the strong and progressive qualities that are nursed by this system of health, just as when they adopt any form of protection they are thereby fostering the faint-hearted qualities that grow up under that system of weakness."

"Have you other practical reasons against the State ownership of land?" asked Angus.

"Yes, there are others," replied Markham. "If you make Government the owner and disposer of the soil, you bring us back into all the troubles and annoyances that belong to the system of interfering Governments. Under a complete system of individual liberty you minimise the politician, you make the life of the individual almost independent of the Government, you make the market, as it should be in all things, the impartial distributor of wealth, you prevent the Government from being a fountain of gifts, and therefore you prevent the curse of two powerful parties each trying to obtain possession for themselves of this fountain. But once make any Government either an owner of the soil, or an educator of the people, or a director of labour, and you at once split the nation into halves, each of which wants to get the direction of so great a function into its own hands. Accept as one of the most certain laws of life, that wherever you build up power, men will strive for it between themselves with unceasing bitterness. We want to get rid of that, just as we want to get rid of great departments and crowds of officials and the innumerable forms of official leech that, without fault of its own, lives by official suction. State ownership of the soil would simply perpetuate all these curses. Moreover, think of the other disadvantages. A man, his wife, and family live for, say, thirty years on a place. They build and fashion just according to their own fancies. Are they suddenly to break with their old existence and become nomads in the last years of their declining life because their lease has run out? Surely you want to give as great not as little fixity as you can to the lives of men. And is the State to be an English or an Irish landlord? Is it to make the improvements itself, or to let them be made by the tenant? If the former, then you will have officialism and jobbery rampant everywhere in the country. If the latter, how great becomes the hardship of turning the tenant out after the lapse of a certain number of years, and how difficult the question of compensation for his improvements. No. I differ with Mr. Spencer very strongly on this point, and believe that a system of State-ownership of the soil could not survive with individualism. It would either destroy individualism and develop into State ownership of many other things, or it would be itself destroyed as out of harmony with all the ideas and habits that belong to individualism."

" And you don't mind differing from Mr. Spencer's system ? " asked Angus.

" I should be a disciple very unworthy of his creed and his method if I did," answered Markham.

" And how would you deal with Factory Acts and measures intended to protect labour ? " asked Angus.

"They are utterly wrong in principle and utterly wrong in practice," replied Markham. "We must all learn, whatever it costs us, to protect ourselves, and in doing it we shall make more real advance in good and true sense in ten years than we should in a hundred years, or even a thousand years, under a protective system. Please bear steadily in mind the one and only way in which men make progress. They do it, not by evading or forcibly repressing difficulties—that never yet made any man stronger—but by developing under the pressure of the difficulties new resources in themselves. Remember, as we have already said, that this internal development is Nature's fixed plan and intention, and that all external protection ends in death. Those who labour for weekly wages must learn to protect themselves unless they wish to become a stunted and incapable class; and they must do it, as I always tell them, without using compulsion even amongst themselves in their trade-unions."

"Do you approve of trade-unions?" asked Angus.

"Yes, distinctly," replied Markham, "though they must and will undergo great alterations. Like all other institutions, if they are to take a higher place, they must lose much of their fighting character and increase largely in their respect for individual rights."

"But must they not be always liable to have great fights with capital?" said Angus.

"I doubt it," said Markham. "I think a trade-union that simply laid itself out to publish facts, to collect and give full information about its own labour in all parts of the country and in other countries, that published its information so fully and faithfully that men in the trade would really learn when they ought to seek other employment rather than continue in their trade, and that helped its members, as it might be required, to shift their quarters, and also attempted some work, which I cannot describe now, in periods of depression, would do more than a fighting trade-union. The more a trade-union thinks about fighting—it is just like a nation in this respect—the less will it think about the real individual intelligence and self-helping qualities of its members, and on this depends far more than on any amount of fighting discipline the alleviation of labour difficulties. Then consider the enormous advantage of friendly relations with capital. A trade that set itself heartily to work with and not against capital would reap a great reward in return for its good sense. Of course capital is shy, and flies the possibilities of the great struggles. Is it not in the natural order of things?"

"And how would you wish to see trade-unions pay greater respect to individual rights?" asked Angus.

"With them, I think, as with the State, no man should be compulsorily carried on the back of another. It is not fair. If they fight the wages question, there should be classes with different rates of pay, in which the better and the worse workman should place themselves as they chose."

"Would not the inferior workman always place himself in the higher class?" asked Angus.

"No," replied Markham, "because if he did he would be the last to be employed, whereas, if he placed himself in a lower class, at a lower wage, he would have the same chance of employment as any other. And in case of a strike I would let those fight who wished to fight, those work who wished to work,—if it were possible, as regards the employer, which of course it might not be."

"And now for that great subject of State Education," asked Angus. "Why do you oppose it, as I gather you do from what you said? Simply on the ground that you must not take money from A to pay for B?"

"That of course is the greatest of all reasons, seeing that it is the foundation of all just dealing between man and man," answered Markham. "The world can by no possibility go right until you have established that great principle, which is of course the death-blow to State Socialism. You are not by force to sacrifice A—be he the richest or the poorest man in the country—in the smallest matter of person or property to B. What A does for B he must do voluntarily, of his own good-will and his own free choice. What right have you—you, the Emperor, or the voting majority—to compel him to a good action? But the other reasons are almost innumerable. Real intelligence will come to a nation by the process of educating itself, not by being educated by an external machinery set up by an enterprising minister. It is the process of carrying out education by every kind of voluntary association, under every kind of difficulty, and at the cost of many sacrifices, that really teaches and influences the people of a country. Your State pot of educational whitewash with which all the children of the country are daubed, whilst you contract to pay so much per thousand for the daubing, will never do more than touch the outside of the nation, morally or even intellectually. A State system of education must be, by the necessity of things, showy, superficial, and vulgar, without soul or truth in it. The American people, like ourselves, will never rise to their true proportions as long as they are cursed by it. It is in

reality a gigantic enforced charity that is without any
of the healing virtues of charity, and is always pre-
tentiously denying the vices of its origin. The real
living and quickening effects of education can only exist
as the parents in every village undertake the thing with
their own hands and with their own resources. Then
education, however deficient in the outside grandeur of
a political system, will become a real thing, a flame
touching the hearts of the children just because it
touches the hearts of the parents. There is a great
sympathy in these matters. But as things are, how can
it be a real thing now that the politicians have got hold
of it; that the rich pay for it; that the Dissenters
have made it their established church; that a conceited
central office undertakes to think for a whole nation;
that, as in some organism of low type, the same parts are
mechanically repeated again and again, each the mere
copy of the other; that the localities quarrel over the
mere externals of the question; that the parents are
cheated into supposing that by voting for a board
they have some real power of direction over the teaching
of their children ? The whole thing is a standing disgrace to our intelligence as a nation; the biggest example perhaps of that hocus-pocus which our people
allow themselves to accept because it comes to them
accompanied with an unworthy bribe of money. I am
always saying to our people in the plainest way, 'If you
wish to be the real fathers and mothers of your chil-

dren, and to mould their education according to your own sense of right and your own intelligence, you must be completely independent, and neither take on the one hand assistance, nor on the other hand submit to direction from the State.   You must choose between your birthright, as true men and women, and the mess of pottage that is offered you.'   But the subject is so large, we might spend all to-night and to-morrow discussing it.   What is your next point, Mr. Bramston ? "

" What about taxes, Mr. Markham ? " asked Angus.

" All taxes must be voluntary," said Markham.

" Voluntary ! " said Angus, drawing the longest of breaths.

" There is no moral foundation for taking taxes by force.   Those who pay taxes have not put themselves outside the reasonable relation, and therefore you cannot justly compel payment at their hands.   The Dissenters were on the right track when they refused to pay Church-rates, and every measure to which a man objects is a church-rate, if you have the courage and the logic to see it.   Your present plan, Mr. Bramston, is to create a powerful machine, that you call Government, and then to tread men's objections as mere soil under your feet. It won't do.   No plan by which one man treads another man's freedom of action under foot will do.   Besides, Mr. Bramston, can you not see what lies before you in the near future ?   This unjustifiable power of taking money from others, even from those unborn, has led to such extravagance, such waste, and such heavy burdens, that the people everywhere, improving upon the honest methods of the politicians, are beginning to ask the question, 'Granted that, as you teach us, our wishes are the only law of right, why should we pay debts we have never incurred?' I am convinced that if you leave in the hands of governments this power of extracting what they like from the people, and of burdening succeeding generations, you will have repudiation at no very distant date. One injustice is sure in time to provoke as its answer another injustice."

"And what about the debt itself?" asked Angus.

"An upright people, not trained to the juggling metaphysics of the present day about the right and the convenient, will redeem, and ought to redeem, every penny of it. But they must do so voluntarily. The question has its difficulties, but I can find no right to force payment from those who did not contract it, great as I think would be the wrong towards the holders if it were not paid. I should, however, give the holders a mortgage on all existing national property."

"I cannot yet," said Angus, "get over your startling proposal to make taxes voluntary. Surely we have a right to take taxes for preserving life and property, if you consider this the true function of government?"

"You must remember," replied Markham, "that you cannot, as we have seen, justify what the law does to repress attacks on person and property by the pure ethical law. It rests only on the same ground as my knocking the thief down; and must be justified on the plea of self-preservation, and on certain imperfect moral reasons, as against those who by their own act have deprived themselves of their rights. But it is only against these persons that the law of self-preservation holds. To extend it to those who have not forfeited their rights would be to make the State, as indeed it so often is, the wrong-doer and the aggressor upon others. But now please to look a little further into this matter. You call it a startling proposal to make taxes voluntary. It would be much truer—if you once freed your own mind from its existing associations and looked at the simple justice of the thing—to call it a startling proposal to collect taxes by force. Suppose six men are working on an island. Would you consider it just or right that four of these men should use their superior physical strength to compel the other two to give as much, as the four dictated, of what they produced to a common fund; that the two men should be obliged, under fear of physical penalties, to accept in all things the views of the four and to act against their own will and judgment? Would not your sense of justice say at once, ' Let each man labour for himself, except so far as he chooses to enter into union with the others and to contribute towards a common object?' And where is the difference between us and men so placed? The difference is that your mind is so accustomed to see

power exercised by governments, you are so accustomed
to take by the machinery, either of emperors, or ruling
councils, or voting majorities, from your fellow-man
what he has got, and to treat him as without rights,
that you have lost all sense of what is just in every-day
matters, though you can still see it where a simple and
fresh case is put before you. The real question is, Mr.
Bramston, do you or do you not believe in the enslav-
ing of some men by others ? There is no other question
in the matter. Please remember what a tax is. It is as
if you said to every man in the country, 'For every
twenty sacks of wheat you produce, you shall give us, the
slave-owning majority, one. For every twenty hours
you labour, you shall labour one more and give us the
value of it.' It is as if you said, 'You shall no longer
labour with wholly free hands and free limbs. We—the
emperor or the voting majority—ordain that henceforth
your one finger, your two fingers, your one hand, your
one hand and a foot, shall be tied up as we may direct.
You shall no more be a free man wholly labouring for
yourself. One-quarter, or one-third, or one-half of you
shall be enslaved to a power that is outside you and
claims possession of your person.' Do you think that
such a modified form of slavery can last or ought to last ?
Do you not think that men's eyes will be opened some
day to see that just as long as you assert power over a
man's property, so long you are asserting power over his
limbs or his mind, according to the instrument with

which he works. A tax taken compulsorily is nothing but a modified form of slavery, and must go to the same outermost limbo as all other slavery is going."

"But would the necessary things get done?" asked Angus. "Would not the generous people pay for everything, whilst the stingy people kept their pence in their pocket?"

"Keep your pecker up, Mr. Bramston," replied Markham. "If really necessary things are not done, there are plenty of penalties in store to make us reconsider ourselves. But of this be assured, that a good many unnecessary things would not be done, things which are only done now because philanthropy is so amusing when carried out with other people's money. As regards the generous and the stingy people, you are still, I see, in the region of the old superstition, that you can by external pressure turn the stingy man into the generous one. If you want to alter the stingy man you may do it in time by the example of the generous man, and the moral appeals that will be always acting upon him as a free man; you will never do it by catching him by the collar and turning his pockets inside out."

"But without caring about the character of the stingy man," said Angus, "or any attempt at reforming him, ought I not as a matter of justice to take the money of the stingy man, as well as that of the generous man?"

"Yes," replied Markham, "if you are God Almighty, and hold a commission to deal with your fellow-men as you may happen to think right. But who has made you a judge over your fellow-man as to whether he is generous or stingy, and who has armed you with penalties to enforce your judgments ?   Where are the titles for your superhuman authority ? "

" Well, then, I fall back upon the enormous practical inconvenience," said Angus.   " Do you think, Mr. Markham, that men will ever listen to the claims of individual liberty as a possible creed and system, at the cost of such a revolution of all their ideas and habits."

" Mr. Bramston, you are talking and thinking as a politician," replied Markham.   " The question is, Is the thing true or untrue ?   That is all that need concern us.   If it is true that a compulsory tax levied by one man upon another is a survival of slavery in a modified form, then men will have to arrange themselves and their affairs in accordance with that truth, or to meet the unpleasant risks which lay in the way of Stephenson's cow.   But, if I may make a shrewd guess in the matter, I do not think the proposal to make all taxes voluntary is going to bring down much popular disfavour upon the cause of liberty.   You have exerted your power of extracting taxes in so tyrannous and so wasteful a manner, that you will find, as I expect, numbers of men drawing a long breath of relief when their eyes are once opened to the fact that the power of extracting taxes rests on no true foundations, but only

T

on an Old-World custom. Possibly this part of our agitation may act only too powerfully in our favour."

" Why too powerfully ? " asked Angus.

" Because many men may join us without really understanding the moral side of our appeal on behalf of liberty. It is the moral conviction that men have no right to compel each other that will reform the world ; and when men see that if you once establish the principle of voluntary taxation, you have in doing it kicked the principle of State Socialism into the same planet as Gladstone in his hurry to pass a land bill tried to kick political economy, they may be unduly influenced by the mere removal of so pressing a danger to place themselves on the side of liberty. We shall gain but little until men learn to act not from their fears but from their reason."

" And now tell me what franchise you would give," said Angus.

" I would make the franchise depend on the payment of an income-tax for which everybody, down to the poorest workman, would be voluntarily liable. Everybody, man or woman, paying it would have the right to vote ; those who did not pay it would be—as is just—without the franchise. There would be no other tax. All indirect taxation, excise and customs, would be abolished, freeing the trading genius of the country with results that we can scarcely foresee."

" And could you ask the workmen to accept such a tax ? " said Angus.

"If you wish to treat them as equal reasonable beings with yourself and to speak the truth to them; if you wish them to cultivate the highest kind of self-respect, to despise all favours and bribes, and to share power because they share burdens—yes," replied Markham. "If you mean to continue the politician's game, to trade upon the selfishness and the unfairness that are in human nature, to tread the principle of true equality under foot, and buy all those who can be bought for your side by favours—no."

"And municipal government, with its care of the streets?" asked Angus.

"It is too large a subject," replied Markham, "to discuss now except in a very imperfect manner. There should be a second local income-tax, and a second local franchise on exactly the same lines as the imperial tax and franchise. But the subject is complicated, because the local government must probably remain for a long time to come the owner of certain common property; and whoever holds property must do whatever is required for its management. I say probably, because so strong is my belief in the inseparable vices that are attached to property compulsorily held in common, that I think it possible in the future that the community may choose to reduce its common property down to the lowest minimum, even if it does not strip itself altogether of this undesirable burden."

"Let me interrupt you for a moment," said Angus. "What do you mean by the vices of common property?"

" Surely they are self-evident," said Markham. "How can you manage property, compulsorily held in common, except by some form of a majority, and that means the eternal conflict and the eternal trickery of a majority ruling a minority. So long as you have common property in any shape, so long you must have complicated machineries, mechanical parties, wire-pulling elaborated as a science, false patriotism, and continual sacrifice of individual opinions. Common property held by the State is the curse of the world, since it forces every man to be a party man and to believe in the dirty trade of making his party win. There can be no real peace, no thorough devotion of a man to his own work in life, until all forms of common State property are reduced to insignificance. Where it exists we are bound to quarrel and to fight with each other. We are like two otherwise harmless animals whom men have sometimes cruelly tied together so that they must fight. And property compulsorily held in common forces the same necessity upon us. A man's duty is to fight for his opinions, and if two men who are linked together by an indissoluble community of property have different opinions, and each holds strongly to his opinion, as men ought to do, one must crush the other. It is this absolute necessity of fighting each other to the death which makes all forms of State Socialism rotten to the core."

" But does not the same objection apply to all voluntary associations?" asked Angus. " Must not men fight for the direction of any society whatsoever to which they belong?"

"No; the evil in this case," replied Markham, "does not exist, just because the voluntary association is not founded on force, is not indissoluble, and is not of the nature of a monopoly. In the first place, where voluntary association is concerned, a natural sifting takes place, and men more or less adapted to co-operate are drawn together for the same enterprise; but the far greater advantage of voluntary association, which fits it to be the civilising instrument of the future, depends upon the fact that the man of powerful energies, who differs from those with whom he acts, may find scope for himself and his energies in entering or creating another association. He is not bound, as he is in the case of a matter placed under the State, either to become a cipher or to spend his life in internecine quarrels with others; either to destroy his opponents and to triumph at their expense, or to consume strength and existence in vain protests against a ruling faction. In the case of voluntary association he simply departs in peace and shows, if he can do so, by practical example, that there is a better way. Some day men who are now tempted by the surface advantages of Socialism will realise this difference, and turn from Socialism in disgust when they see that it would fasten upon their necks in a very intense form all the evils and the pettinesses that belong to our present political life. It would establish as permanent institutions, parties, wire-pullings, caucuses, trading politicians, and all the rest of that odious machinery which will all gradually disappear, as being no longer necessary, when you contract the interferences of the State and grant to the individual his full rights ; when you cease to compel him to be either the slave or the slaveholder of his fellow-men. But returning to the subject with which we are more immediately concerned, of local government of towns, is there more that I can tell you in a few words ? "

" I think I understand your view," said Angus. " As long as corporations hold common property they must, like all other owners, make such conditions as they think necessary for the management of such property ; but if they are wise, all such property will be minimised."

" Yes," replied Markham, " you have stated it quite correctly. And the first great step we have to take is to prevent the holders of any kind of State property from forcibly annexing private property and from levying taxes compulsorily. If the dragon can live after his teeth have been drawn and his claws cut, we need not greatly object."

" Then you would not allow a municipal body to take possession of a new street unless they acquired it by free purchase?" asked Angus.

" Certainly not," replied Markham. " Once clothe any body of men or any institution with powers of compulsion, and you can no longer judge whether they are sufficiently in the interests of society to survive naturally

and of themselves. It is to all effects like endowing a
religion. If you are wise you will never protect anything from its own natural bankruptcy. It is here that
the employment of force becomes so mischievous. It
interferes with natural selection, keeping alive what
ought to die and preventing the appearance of new
forms that ought to come into existence."

"In the same way you would not have given compulsory power to railways to acquire land?" asked Angus.

"Certainly not," said Markham. "Had you refused
to do so, everybody would gradually have learnt out
of a wise sense of self-interest and wise regard for the
public good to facilitate the making of railways to the
best of his power. You would have had railways
created at a much smaller expense. You would have
had a perfect system of free trade and competition in
the matter. You would have had no difficult questions
at present as regards new lines and old lines, no socialistic attempt on the part of the other trading classes
to force concessions by Act of Parliament from the rail-
way companies, but a people every class of whom would
have gained in good sense and public feeling by having
assisted to carry out voluntarily a great national enterprise. How can a people grow in these necessary qualities of recognising both their own interest and the
public good when every time that there is a need for
their exercise you cut the matter short by external
compulsion?"

"And lastly about our existing institutions—the

Established Church, the House of Lords, the Crown—what would you do ?" asked Angus.

" I fear that I must look upon them all as signposts that point the wrong way and condemn themselves. All privileged and artificial institutions, whether for the few or the many, are destructive and anarchical in their character, as they obscure our perception of the great and simple moral relations on which our dealings with each other must be founded. Our object is to teach the people to look on the equal and universal relations that are created by liberty as the most sacred thing in the world, and we must spare no darling institution of any class tending to perpetuate the idea of privilege."

" So you include in your sentence the Crown, notwithstanding the affection which in a general way the English people have for it, especially for the person of the Queen ?" asked Angus.

" I think it would be a very wrong act to make any change, even if it were possible, during the Queen's life," replied Markham, "as we are bound to her by many ties of gratitude for the part she has played. Moreover, I hope that the change itself will not come about until there has grown up a strong general conviction on reasonable grounds in the English people that it should be made. The wrench will be very great to those who believe in a monarchy, and those of us who are republicans by conviction may surely wait with some patience until the new opinion has so far matured itself as to make the change less painful. Whilst I hold that any head of the nation should be named by a self-conscious act of selection by the nation, not presented to them by chance, and whilst I think that a republic is a simpler, less artificial, and therefore truer form of government than a monarchy, I think that it is mere superstition to suppose that the change from the one to the other is going in itself to transform the nation. If ever it takes place simply as a triumph of some classes over other classes, if it is carried out by violent demagogic appeals, and class hatreds, and threats of force, it will profit us, if at all, exceedingly little. The passions which accomplished its fulfilment will only remain to plague us hereafter. The true good of the change will come to us, if we make it, not in a burst of ill-feeling against kings and princes, who are I think much to be pitied for their difficult position, and who often show great qualities in the hour of their trial, but with due consideration to all concerned, and with a deliberate conviction that the institution of monarchy belongs to the old and not to the new world. It is however asking for a great deal, it is asking the nation to become more reasonable, more tolerant, and more philosophical, than it is at present."

" A change of this kind must, under any circumstances, be made by a majority," said Angus. " Does not that show some flaw in your system ?   You see that you are obliged to fall back upon the use of a majority in certain cases."

"I can quite understand, Mr. Bramston," replied Markham, " that you feel very uncomfortable in being told that what a majority does possesses no true moral authority, but much as I should like to make you feel comfortable I cannot alter that great truth for you. It is infinitely safer and happier for the world that it should be so. Think what a world it would be if the acts of either emperors or ruling majorities had any sanction except that of force! Think of having to worship Lord Beaconsfield, Mr. Gladstone, and Mr. George in turn! Fortunately all these gentlemen have a very imperfect moral basis to stand upon. Remember that it is only the aggressions of men upon each other that drive us into the necessity of having governments. Therefore, accepting that necessity as the result of our own wrongdoing, the simpler the form of government—and republican governments when we have fought out the battle of Socialism will hereafter develop in the direction of the extremest simplicity — the less is the burden which we impose upon the consciences of men, and the less is that which we have to justify. You cannot perfectly justify even a government that is the simplest outcome of self-defence, but still less can you justify it when kings and emperors are tacked on to it. But it is just because of the lack of all true moral authority attaching to any form of government that I should like to see the change from monarchy to republicanism made with great consideration for others."

"And let me ask you what you would do about Ireland?" asked Angus.

"Ireland must decide for herself," said Markham. "Why not grant its freedom for the sake of principle instead of for the sake of convenience, as you will do in a few years? But such of the landowners, as desired it, should be bought out by a loan, which the Irish Government would take over; and if the north-east of Ireland elects to stay with England, let it do so."

"Would Mr. Spencer, do you think, agree to all these applications of his principles?" asked Angus.

"I fear that Mr. Spencer would dissent. You must not regard him as responsible for any corollaries which I have drawn. His criticism would be, if I may judge from what I once heard him say on the subject, that a truly equitable social system can be reached only as fast as men themselves become truly equitable in their sentiments and ideas, and in the meantime we must decide as well as we can on the relatively right, referring continually to the absolutely right, with the view of taking care that we move towards it and not away from it," replied Markham.

"And in what way would you defend your own position?" asked Angus.

"I should reply," said Markham, "that as a good disciple of Mr. Spencer, I am bound to sketch out what seems to me the truest application of his principles, since I believe that only by discussing the applications shall we arrive at a recognition of the truth of the principles. Better and truer applications may be found than those I have offered ; if so, they will certainly take their place. But if my applications are true, however thorough-going they may be, it is best that they should be stated by those who believe in them, even though the mass of the people are not yet prepared to accept them. Their mere statement, if they are true, is a step in the necessary preparation."

" And now for the net result," said Angus. " What would be the effect of carrying out such a policy ? "

" Why, such a lightening of the ship as would give her power to float in any weather. You are sadly weighting and crippling her now. You do not recognise how enormous is the amount of enterprise and energy that is restrained by the constant encroachments of politics ; not simply because whenever the State undertakes a great service even those who possess the most energy cease to think and to combine and to attempt for themselves, but by the sheer misdirection of effort. How many men there are who could give more time and thought to their own work—which is the true way of benefiting others—if they were not obliged to be politicians. You have made this bloated matter of politics of such importance that the busiest workers can neither afford to follow it with any care nor yet to neglect it. To all such men it is a perpetual vexation and distraction. If you wish to economise the best brain-energy and the best working powers of the country, reduce politics to the humble sphere that properly belongs to them, reduce Mr. Gladstone and Lord Salisbury to the smaller proportions for which two such men, highly gifted as they are, are fitted ; disband this frightful standing army of politicians that, like other armies, eats up the people whom it claims to serve, and return it to useful occupations in civil life. Our great object should be not only to bring to an end the wasteful processes of Government work—the overgrown departments, the official mismanagements, the heavy burden of taxation, the innumerable occasions of rivalry, of personal ambition, and corrupt uses of power —but to recall all human effort from a wrong direction and to put it in the one right track. We have to make each man a profitable worker by leaving him with undivided energies for his own work instead of letting him attempt to direct the work of others, and to place him under the one true and natural condition, that his reward shall be all he can get in a free world, selfearned, and not adjusted for him by others. Achieve this great though simple result, and we should bring about a mental regeneration within a nation as great as if, in their external relations, nations were to abandon the idea of war. Of all perverted industries, that of accumulating force, whether in great bodies of soldiers or great bodies of electors, is the most wasteful and disastrous, not only because, as we have just seen, the effort to obtain the possession of force is in itself an immense consumption of energy that should go for other things, but also for the sake of other great reasons. And these reasons are, because, so long as men are intent upon becoming the holders of power, they are blind to the true remedies ; because systems founded on force are fatal to the two conditions of difference and competition, apart from which unfitness can never be changed into fitness ; because all fixed laws of moral right and wrong disappear in the presence of force ; because the world can find no repose or security as long as all the great matters of life are left in suspense, to be shaped and reshaped by those who have climbed to-day or may climb to-morrow to power; and lastly, because, as long as we live under force, compelling and compelled, so long the affections and sympathies of man for man— all that is lovely in human nature—must remain sealed from breaking into universal blossom, like the plants of the earth remain sealed so long as winter is with them.   Man is predestined to find his complete happiness, as Mr. Spencer teaches, only when the happiness of others becomes to him an integral part of his own ; but this development of his nature cannot take place unless he is living under the conditions which belong to a free life.   So long as force is paramount, so long must men stand in hate and fear of each other, and the old saying, ' homo homini lupus ' remain true."

"Then you think that this policy of *laissez-faire* and of survival of the fittest would not be, as is so often said, a hard or cruel one?" asked Angus. "So many men shrink from it on account of its apparent hardness."

"They shrink from it because they do not understand it," replied Markham. "They do not see that unless man is to be free in body and mind he had better die from off this earth. Remember all we have said about the free man being alone the moral being. If I am to be really unselfish you must leave me full power and opportunity to be selfish. There can be no unselfishness where the man cannot choose, but must act in a certain way. I cannot too often repeat that if by some socialistic arrangements you compel me to do unselfish actions, you have destroyed the possibility of the growth of the unselfish feelings in me, for there is no need of them, and no opportunity for their practice and development. Perhaps the deadliest curse of Socialism is, that as you take each new step to perfect the system, you destroy one more necessity and one more occasion for the growth of those human feelings which alone can redeem the world. Remember that nothing in nature grows if you take from it the circumstances which force it into existence. In this respect Socialism is an absolute contradiction of its own intentions and desires. And also remember what we said about those communities, whether of men or of creatures, which are simply possessed by the idea of the common safety. Once enthrone that idea as absolute sovereign and there is no cruel and hard act that will not be done. Just as the queen-bees are incited to destroy each other, and the drones, when their use is over, are massacred ; just as the weak child in Sparta was exposed, and the aged parent in many savage tribes is got rid of—in some cases economically eaten—so would it necessarily be with Socialism. These are but logical and consistent developments of the idea of the common safety, regardless of individual rights. The shifts to which modern Socialism would be driven to meet the difficulties that would arise from the attempt to ignore the conditions imposed by nature, and to guarantee existence to some at the expense of others, would be, I doubt not, more polished in their outward form, but they would necessarily be as barbarous in their real nature. You cannot obey directly both the idea of the common safety and the idea of individual rights. One or other must be supreme, and the question is, will you go back to the scheme of common life that bees have elaborated with a success and perfection of its kind far beyond your attainment, or will you secure the safety of the whole indirectly by the free development of the individual. If you go in for the social life of the bees you must be prepared, as they are, to take life without scruple, when the public convenience is at stake, not giving it up for the public good, remember, with all the advantage that follows voluntary sacrifice, but taking it as a thing that belongs to those of you who possess the power to take it.

That is the important point. We have to see that the idea
of the common safety, when raised above rights, always
has been and always must be cruel and unscrupulous.
And then look at it also from another point of view. The
life of the bee succeeds because each bee is endowed with
such marvellous instincts, and possesses, comparatively
speaking, so feeble an individual intelligence.   But you
have gone too far along the road of individual development to make this possible for yourselves. Your instincts
are grown feeble and uncertain, and your happiness is now
to be found in the development of the individual reason.
Think of the refinement of the cruelty that would be
involved in thousands and thousands of cases, in compelling all persons to accept and live under a system
which a certain number of self-confident organisers had
planned out for the world. And then place before yourself
the further consideration, 'Suppose I fail in this attempt
to support some at the expense of others, suppose I find
that Nature is too strong for me, that I cannot disregard
her conditions, that I cannot safely do away with a man's
self-interest, that I cannot withhold from him the greater
reward that naturally follows from his greater intelligence
and his greater industry, that I cannot for ever keep a
minority in subjection to a majority ; suppose that
presently I wake to the preception that I have been
carefully nursing all the weak and feeble types, and have
allowed them to become the parents of the next generations ; what atonement shall I then hope to make for the

indescribable misery that I have caused in lowering and enfeebling the type of a people, and for the arrogance with which I seized supreme power, and forced all men to submit to my crude fancies as to what was best for them?'   No, Mr. Bramston, the one really cruel thing is to disregard the conditions of nature, and to try and persuade the people that they can be safely disregarded."

"And now, Mr. Markham, granting the force that there is in much that you say, there remains the great question—is it possible to look on the view that you have sketched out as practical?"

"Practical!" said Markham.   "And is what you are doing practical? Year by year you are giving away the old rights and the old virtues of freedom! You are making even your cherished parliamentary government impossible! How in the end can anything but a chain of great departments govern, when all this mass of multifarious work is being thrown on the Government? How can the individual Members of Parliament, even if you multiply their faculties a hundredfold, if you relieve them of all the wants of sleep and rest and change which other men have, how can they find time to understand, to discuss, even to know by name, all the business of every sort and kind that is thrust on them? How is it possible for either the press or the public to have any real control over the great machine you have set in motion? Can you not see that you are giving up what has been called free government, and are simply putting in its place one more of those stupid, lumbering, sleepy official-minded extravagant bureaucratic systems that have so often cumbered the earth, and from time to time crash down beneath their own ineptitude. Practical!" he continued, slowly shaking his head. "And do you think, Mr. Bramston, that you politicians are the practical people?   Under the name of serving your party you press on along an unknown road, no man really taking the responsibility of his own actions, no man knowing, or even trying to know, where he is going.   How would any politician of the day meet my demand if I were to ask him to sketch the future of England as he desired and as he expected to see it? Would he not excuse himself from the task by saying that politics were essentially for the day; or, had he the courage to attempt it, would not his picture necessarily consist—just because his very life prevents him from wishing or trying to see clearly—of a few incongruous conceptions thrown together, some not possible some not probable,—a picture strongly resembling in its want of definite ideas an animal drawn by a child, with the wings of a fowl and the legs of a horse?   And yet in the midst of such mental-incoherence you have the courage to act as if you were assured that the power in your possession were a divine gift, and that some shaping hand that you do not see would kindly interpose in the future to give order and meaning to what you do."

" Yes, I see, I feel the prevailing disorder every day of my life," said Angus.

" Practical, Mr. Bramston," went on Markham, geting warmed to his work, and without stopping to reply to Angus's remark. " Is it practical to have created the relations that exist between you and the people ? You meet them, not to speak the truth, not to confess real difficulties, not to help them to understand the real conditions under which men have to live, not to raise them in their self-respect, not to check the human tendency to selfishness and violence, and to bring out the reasonable self, but you speak to them as holders of power on whom power confers the right to be a law to themselves ; and this you do simply in order that you may extract their votes from them. You are but courtiers of the people, as your fathers before you were courtiers of kings and emperors. If you call this practical, Mr. Bramston, please excuse me from having a share in what is practical. Practical! And do you think that when to-morrow succeeds to this reckless competition of parties, when you are called upon to deal with the greed you have appealed to, the expectations you have raised, the rash beginnings you have made, to-morrow, when the untruth, the weakness, and the personal rivalries of men who lead the people, not by real convictions but by beliefs assumed at the moment, when all these ugly things come home to roost, when that dangerous lust of power which is in all human breasts, and can only be overcome by the sense of the rights of others, has taken its full possession of men, do you think in that day of consequences that you will be satisfied that you were the practical people? Practical! And you do not see the meaning of the very things which you are doing! You call yourselves Tory, and Whig, and Radical,—there is as much meaning in the names of Shiite and Sonnite; there was more in those of Guelph and Ghibelline. Can you not see that there are only two creeds in the world possible for men; that there are only two sides on which a man can place himself? Are you for a free world, or for a world placed under authority? Are you Socialist, a believer in the majority, a believer in force, or do you take your stand on the fixed and inalienable rights of the individual? These mixed and party systems, by which you set so much store, are mere half-way huts in which the race sojourns for a day, and then burns behind it. Because you yourselves are content to be confused, indistinct, and inconsistent in your ideas, do you think that the race, as a race, will stand for ever, like recruits beating the ground in the drill-yard, and march nowhither? Time is a great logician, and succeeding generations will either press steadily on to the system that is the perfection of force,—Socialism,—or to that which is the perfection of liberty,—complete Individualism. If men believe that they may rightly use force to gain any of their objects, they will claim in their supposed interest to use it for all their objects, and simply brush aside, like cobwebs, your distinctions and qualifications and refinements about the use of it; if force is not a right weapon, then will they altogether abandon it. On which side then do you take your stand? I look at the parties of to-day and I can get no answer. Is Mr. Gladstone, with his many regrets and apologies, is Lord Salisbury, with his easy adaptiveness, for or against liberty? The one and the other seem to me equally ready to betray it for their necessities. But whatever be the issue of the present, that the world will remain in Socialism—of that I can have no fear. The system is doomed by the great laws as inexorably as was the Tower of Babel. I do not say it may not descend upon us for a time, like a great pall, blotting out all hopes of progress in our time. It may be that the race must pass through their season of it, as men pass through some delirous illness. After all it is only an old story repeating itself. Socialism is but Catholicism addressing itself not to the soul but to the senses of men. Accept authority, accept the force which it employs, resign yourself to all-powerful managers and infallible schemers, give up the free choice and the free act, the burden of responsibility and the rewards that come to each man according to his own exertions, deny the reason and the self that are in you, place these in the keeping of others, and a world of ease and comfort shall be yours. It is a creed destined to prove as fatal, mentally speaking, as Roman Catholicism, but its patrons are skilful enough to offer in compensation very tangible bribes for its acceptance. It goes to the workman with gold in its hands and corrupt promises on its lips, as every politician has gone before it. Still, Mr. Bramston, we must fight on. As the old darkness and mental cowardice come back upon us, we can only trust that the old courage and faith that protested may come back also. Mr. Spencer has set us a bright example of fearlessness in thought and speech. No man quite knows what that magical weapon, truth, can do when he sets himself resolutely to use it. I would rather choose it for our side than either Mr. Gladstone's eloquence or Mr. Chamberlain's organisation. But the night is creeping on. I shall be glad to meet you again. Meanwhile study Mr. Spencer until his methods of order and reason become an intellectual necessity to you. And now, are you a student of Browning? If so, repay me for my long talk by reading me *Galuppi* whilst I light my evening pipe."

" What a strange evening's work," said Angus to himself as his foot crossed the threshold. " Voluntary taxation, and ministers looking out for employment! How those dear wise fools in the House would shout at the idea ; but then every fish believes in the swim to which he belongs. Ah !" he sighed as he walked along the Embankment, and the blue smoke of his cigar parted the fresh night air, " if this were the disentanglement of the mess,—the perfect creed of liberty, the true acceptance by each man of the rights of the other, and yet———"

THE END.

Note.—Perhaps I should here point out quite distinctly that the proposal made by Mr. Markham, to place taxation on a voluntary basis, whether in itself a right or wrong deduction from Mr. Herbert Spencer's principle, has never received Mr. Herbert Spencer's approval; but, as I have some grounds for believing, would be looked on by him as an unpractical and undesirable arrangement.　　　　A. H.

PRINTED BY J. S. VIRTUE AND CO., LIMITED, CITY ROAD, LONDON.